The House on Sugar Plum Lane

Books by Judy Duarte

MULBERRY PARK

ENTERTAINING ANGELS

THE HOUSE ON SUGAR PLUM LANE

Published by Kensington Publishing Corporation

The House on Sugar Plum Lane

JUDY DUARTE

Doubleday Large Print Home Library Edition

KENSINGTON BOOKS

This Large Print Edition, prepared especially for Doubleday Large Print Home Library, contains the complete, unabridged text of the original Publisher's Edition.

KENSINGTON BOOKS are published by

Kensington Publishing Corp.
119 West 40th Street
New York, NY 10018

ISBN-13: 978-1-61664-005-7

Printed in the United States of America

This Large Print Book carries the Seal of Approval of N.A.V.H.

To the Ellie Ruckers in my life:
Emily Astleford, Emelie Johnston,
Betty Lou Astleford, and Ethel
Dunlop. Your love and prayers
for me over the years have
been a real blessing.

The House on Sugar Plum Lane

Chapter 1

The vintage Victorian house, with its dingy gray walls and faded white shutters, stood as a battered monument to days gone by, to family secrets silenced by the passage of time.

Which meant what? Amy Masterson asked herself as she sat curbside in her idling Honda Civic and studied the three-story structure where her mother's biological family had once lived. That her search began and ended here?

She shut off the ignition, grabbed her purse from the passenger seat, and climbed from the car. Then she headed toward a cracked concrete walkway littered with leaves from a massive old elm that grew in the front yard.

A FOR SALE OR LEASE sign sat by a weathered picket fence, but she couldn't imagine anyone wanting to invest in a home like this. Not unless it was a crew of handymen with more time than they knew what to do with.

She paused long enough to note the neglected structure that loomed before her, its windows shuttered tight from the ravages of wind and rain and sun. She did her best to look beyond the chipped, cracked, and faded gray paint of the shingled exterior, as well as the once-white gingerbread trim now yellowed with age, and tried to imagine what the house had looked like in the fall of 1966, when her mother had been given up for adoption as a newborn.

But Amy had always been more practical than her mom, more realistic, so she wasn't having much luck looking past the neglect. In fact, any imagination she'd been able to conjure gave way to an eerie and inexplicable sense of grief.

Not just for the house, she decided, but

for the family who'd never known the baby girl who'd grown up to be a loving wife and mother, a talented pianist, and an amateur artist who'd died before her time.

Amy continued up the sidewalk, where the smell of dirt and decay mingled with a hint of rain in the autumn air.

Several old newspapers lay water damaged and unopened on the porch, but she stepped over them as she made her way past a well-worn wicker chair to one of the narrow windows that flanked the front door. There she cupped her eyes and peered through the dust- and grime-shrouded glass.

There wasn't much to see on the inside, just an umbrella stand and an antique table with several photographs resting on a crocheted doily.

From what she'd gathered in her research, Eleanor Rucker, who had to be well into her eighties now, still owned the place. But she certainly wasn't living here any longer.

Had she died, taking the secrets of the past with her?

Amy pushed away from the window and straightened. She'd come too far to turn around and go back home to Del Mar without any more answers than she'd had when she started out that afternoon.

But now what?

As she walked across the lawn and along the side of the house, the overgrown blades of grass tickled her ankles. The plants and shrubs that grew along the property line were as shaggy and neglected as the rest of the landscaping.

She rounded the corner to the back of the house, unsure of what she was trying to find. A clue, she supposed, as to why her mother had been given up for adoption. And maybe, in the process, she'd get a feel for the kind of people the Ruckers were—or had been.

Warm and friendly? Cold and withdrawn?

Her gaze fell on an overgrown rose garden at the back of the yard, withered and dying. It must have been pretty in its day, when whoever had lovingly tended it by pruning and fertilizing the plants had taken time to sit upon the wrought-iron bench that rested under the shade of a maple, to feel the warmth of the sun, to inhale the fragrance of the colorful flowers.

On one rather large and unruly bush, a single yellow rose still bloomed, providing a hint of what the garden could produce with a little TLC. Mindful of the thorns, she plucked the flower, its stem scrawny and easily torn away from the branch, to take back to her house and put in water. Something told her the gardener wouldn't mind.

Then she turned her back on the deserted rosebushes and made her way toward what she guessed might be the kitchen window.

At five feet four, she wasn't tall enough to see inside, so she searched the grounds until she found something on which she could stand.

Near a gardening shed, which was even more dilapidated than the house, she spotted an old wooden crate. She carried it back to the window, turned it upside down, then used it as a step so she could peer through the glass.

An olive green refrigerator and a bulky old white stove, the kind June Cleaver might have used, took up one wall, while a small wooden table and four chairs adorned the other.

A teddy bear cookie jar sat on the

counter, and she couldn't help wondering if it had ever been filled. If so, what kind of treats had Mrs. Rucker made to keep in it? Homemade oatmeal or chocolate chip? Maybe she only purchased the packaged kind sold in grocery stores.

Susan, Amy's mother, had what she'd called "an incurable sweet tooth" and had always favored snickerdoodles. For that reason, Amy had surprised her with a homemade batch of the sugar- and cinnamon-covered cookies just a couple of weeks before she died.

"They're wonderful," her mom had said. "Thanks, honey." Yet because of the havoc the cancer and chemo had wreaked on her appetite, she'd only managed to eat a couple of bites.

Odd how that particular memory would cross her mind now, Amy thought, as she returned to the front yard, where she glanced again at the Realtor's sign: FOR SALE OR LEASE.

She owned a townhome in Del Mar, which was part of the pending divorce settlement, so she certainly didn't want to buy or rent another place. But perhaps she could feign interest in order to get a tour of the interior. It was the least she could do for her mom, who'd been determined to uncover her roots and to meet her birth family.

So Amy reached into her purse, pulled out her cell, and dialed the Realtor's number.

When Ronald Paige, the listing agent, answered the phone, she introduced herself and said, "I was driving on Sugar Plum Lane and spotted your sign in front of an old Victorian. Is there any chance that I could take a look at it now?"

"Sure, but I'm clear across town. At this time of day, it could take me a half hour to get there. Do you mind waiting?"

"Not at all." Her mother had waited for years to uncover clues about the woman who'd given her up. What were a few minutes now?

In the meantime, she returned to the front porch and took a seat in the old wicker chair, which creaked in protest of her unexpected weight. She'd no more than stretched out her legs and placed her hands on her knees when a boy riding a bicycle slowed to a stop near the walkway. He wore a green T-shirt with a Star

Wars stormtrooper on the front and a pair of faded black jeans. She guessed him to be about ten or eleven.

"Are you going to move into this house?" he asked.

Oh, no, she wanted to tell him. She owned a nice little two-bedroom townhome with an ocean view, a place where the homeowners association made sure the grounds were parklike and the buildings stayed in good repair.

Instead, she said, "I'm thinking about it."

"You got kids?" he asked.

"A little girl. Her name's Callie, and she's five."

"Oh." His expression sank, as though a girl in kindergarten didn't come close to being the kind of kid he'd been asking about.

Still, she welcomed a human connection to the house, to the neighborhood, and said, "My name's Amy. What's yours?"

"Danny." He nodded toward the blue Victorian next door. While not one of the newly refurbished homes on the street, it was still in much better shape than Mrs. Rucker's. "I live over there."

She nodded, as though he'd imparted some information she'd have to file away.

"Do you know anything about the people who used to live here?" she asked.

"Yeah."

When he didn't elaborate, she prodded a bit. "Were they nice?"

"It was a *she.* And yeah, she was really nice. But she went kind of crazy."

That wasn't a good sign—genetically speaking. "What do you mean?"

"She got old." He shrugged and threw up his hands in a you-know-how-it-is way.

Was he talking about Alzheimer's or dementia or something else?

"It's like her brain wore out and quit working," he added. "One day, she came over to our house at lunchtime, but she was still wearing her nightgown, and it was all dirty and torn. She hadn't combed her hair, and it had stickers and leaves and stuff in it. We think she was down on the Bushman Trail."

Amy didn't question his use of the word "we." Instead, she asked, "The Bushman Trail?"

He nodded to the left again, toward his

house and beyond. "That's what me and my friends call the canyon over there. It runs between our houses and the park."

She imagined he was talking about a common area, a preserve of some kind, and a place where the neighborhood children hung out and played.

"Ellie was all crying and scared. And so my mom called the police."

Amy stiffened. "What happened to her?"

"She said her house was surrounded by hippies. And that they were piping marijuana smoke into her vents, trying to get her hooked on drugs."

"Was someone bothering her?"

The boy—Danny—shook his head. "Nope. The police checked it out, but they didn't find anything wrong. And they didn't think anyone had hurt her. But they took her to the hospital. And that's why she doesn't live in this house anymore. She can't be left alone."

Poor woman.

"Well," the boy said, "I gotta go."

Amy offered him a smile. "It was nice meeting you, Danny."

"Yeah. Same here."

Then he pedaled down the street.

Amy settled back in her seat and waited. About twenty minutes later, a white Ford Explorer drove up and parked behind her Honda. The driver, a tall, slender man in his late forties, climbed out and made his way toward her.

"Ms. Masterson?" he asked, reaching out a spindly hand. "Ron Paige."

"Call me Amy," she said, trying to shed any association with Brandon. Then she placed the rose on the dusty, glass-topped wicker table next to her, stood, and closed the gap between them. "Thanks for making time to show me the house."

"No problem." He led her to the front door, where he fumbled with the lockbox. "I hope you can overlook the yard. I just got this listing last Monday and had planned to hire a landscaping crew to come out and clean it up. But, well, my wife and I had a baby a couple of days later, which set me back at work."

"Congratulations," she said.

"Yeah, well, it's number three for us. So it's not that big a deal."

Her heart tightened at the comment. She knew how hard Grandma Rossi had tried to have a child of her own, how crushed she'd been with each miscarriage, how blessed she'd felt when she'd finally adopted Amy's mom, Susan. Babies had always been considered special in the Rossi family.

In fact, that was one reason it had been difficult for Amy to understand why her mom would be so desperate to find her biological family, when the people who'd raised her had been so kind, so loving.

"I can't explain it," her mom had said when she began the search. "The urge I have to find them—not just my birth mother, but the family—is almost overwhelming."

Amy hadn't understood her mom's quest back then, but she felt compelled to honor it now—as a tribute, she supposed.

"Here we go," Ron said as he opened the door and stood back to let Amy enter first.

When she stepped through the threshold and onto the hardwood flooring, the scent of dust and memories accosted her, as well as the hint of herbs and spice.

For a moment, she took another whiff, trying to detect a scent that could be marijuana, which she'd had more than one occasion to smell in the dorm hallway when she'd attended Cal State. She came up blank, though, and was almost disappointed that she couldn't give Mrs. Rucker's story a little more credibility.

"Are you interested in a purchase?" Ron asked. "If so, I'm sure we can have it emptied for you by the time escrow closes."

Emptied?

Amy scanned the living room, where a brown tweed sofa was flanked by two plants that had died from lack of water. She spotted a fairly new television, an antique piano that took up the east wall, a hand-carved fireplace mantel that bore family photos, and a beige recliner.

A worn leather Bible sat on a lamp table, next to a china cup and saucer. She couldn't help noticing a slight stain in the cup that had once held a brown liquid, and she wondered if it had been coffee or tea. Not that it mattered.

Still, Mrs. Rucker had left some of herself behind, and Amy found herself curious about the woman's preferences, by the things she'd chosen for comfort.

As the Realtor continued to give her a tour of the house, both upstairs and down, Amy felt compelled to spend more time in each of the rooms than was appropriate, even if she'd truly been in the market for a house.

For the strangest reason, she'd been intrigued by the choice of wallpaper, by the plaques and pictures that adorned each room, by the handmade quilt that had been draped over the double bed that appeared to be the one in which Mrs. Rucker had slept.

As they returned downstairs, Ron paused at the bottom landing and placed his hand on the banister. "The owner's grandson was going to fix up the place and pack up his grandma's belongings, but he had a heart attack a week or so ago. I told the family that I'd line up the workers for them, but like I said, I've been playing catch-up ever since the baby was born. But I'll try to make some calls as soon as I get back to the office. Just try to imagine the place after we power wash the outside, mow the lawn, and trim the shrubs."

Ron was being incredibly optimistic. It was going to take more than a couple of days to get this house and yard whipped into shape.

They walked outside, and she waited

as he secured the lock. Again, she glanced at the weathered structure, its shutters closed tight, its story silenced.

"What happened to the lady who used to live here?" Amy asked, hoping for a few more details and an adult version of the story.

"From what I understand, she's living in long-term care."

Amy paused a beat, struggling with an idea that was brewing, a wild thought, actually, yet one that suddenly held a lot of merit. She had an opportunity to spend some time in this house, if she acted quickly. But it would cost both time and money.

Somehow, that didn't seem to matter.

"I'd like to sign a lease," she said. "And it would be great if I could have the house furnished. So you can leave it as it is."

"I'll talk to Mrs. Davila about that. She's the owner's daughter. It was her son who had the heart attack, and so she'll be making the decisions now."

Would Mrs. Davila be Barbara Rucker, the woman who'd given up Amy's mother for adoption? Or was she a sister or another relative?

"You know," Ron added, cocking his head to one side. "The more I think about it, the more I like your offer. It's possible that Mrs. Davila will go for it, too. Otherwise, she'd have to conduct an estate sale or put everything in storage. And from what I understand, she's pretty worried about her son's medical condition, so this house is the least of her problems."

Amy tried to conjure some sympathy for the Ruckers and the Davilas, but she couldn't quite pull it off. She might have biological ties to the people who'd once lived in this house, but unlike her mother, she'd been able to completely embrace the Rossi family as her own.

"When would you want to move in?" Ron asked.

"As soon as possible. In fact, I'd be willing to carefully box up any of Mrs. Rucker's personal belongings so Mrs. Davila won't have to bother with it."

Ron stroked his chin, the wheels clearly turning. "You know, under the circumstances, she might really appreciate that. It's possible that she'd even be willing to give you a discount on the rent. Let me call her and get back to you."

"That's fine." Amy gave the man her telephone number. She probably ought to mention something about having a child and a small, well-behaved cocker mix that was housebroken, but she wasn't really going to move in.

As Amy and the agent returned to their respective vehicles, she paused beside the driver's door of the Honda Civic and took one last look at the tired old house.

If only the walls could talk, people often said.

Maybe, in this case, they would.

The call came in later that evening, while Amy and Callie were having dinner in the kitchen.

Amy blotted her lips with her napkin. "Keep eating, honey. I'll tell them we'll have to talk later." Then she headed for the portable phone that rested on the counter.

When she answered, Ron Paige introduced himself and went on to say, "I have good news, Amy. Mrs. Davila is willing to lease you the house furnished. And she'll either hire someone to come in and box her mother's personal items, or you can do it for a discount on the rent."

After Amy's mom had died, one of the hardest things she'd had to do was to help her dad go through her mother's closet, her drawers, her desk at work. But there was no way she would have hired a stranger to handle a heartrending task like that. And the fact that Mrs. Davila had readily agreed to Amy's offer surprised her.

"So," the agent continued, "if you'd like to come by my office tomorrow morning, we'll run a credit check, which is just a formality. And then I'll make a quick call to your current landlord."

Amy didn't have a landlord. In fact, she and Brandon owned both houses they'd lived in, but she'd deal with any explanations and the resulting questions later. Instead, she agreed to meet Ron at the real estate office at ten.

After dinner, she'd give Stephanie Goldstein a call. Stephanie's husband, Jake, worked in the same law firm as Brandon, which had been reason enough to avoid the woman these days. But Amy and Steph had belonged to the same playgroup since their children were babies, and their daughters got along great. They'd also become friends in spite of their husbands' connection. In fact, Callie had stayed with Stephanie today while Amy had driven to Fairbrook to check out the address she'd had for Barbara Rucker.

She wondered if Steph would mind picking up Callie at preschool tomorrow and watching her in the afternoon. Probably not. But what would she think about what Amy planned to do? It was hard to say.

Should she even tell her?

Snooping in the old Victorian on Sugar Plum Lane had to be one of the wildest things Amy had ever done. Of course, she'd always led a quiet and predictable life. That is, until she'd told Brandon she was moving back into the small townhome that had become a rental after his promotion to partner and their subsequent purchase of the sprawling house in Mar Vista Estates.

Their marital separation had been a first for the Rossi family and something that no one but Amy had fully understood.

"But he's a good provider," Grandma Rossi had said. "And you can be a stay-at-home mom, which is more important than ever these days."

Back in the 1950s, when a man's home was his castle and his wife's job was to make life easier on him, being a good provider had probably been essential. But there was more to life than money and possessions. So when Brandon had repeatedly put his job and his career ahead of his family, Amy had told him she didn't want to be married anymore.

Now she found herself living alone, but at least she didn't have to wonder what time Brandon would be coming home or what mood he'd be in when he arrived.

Nor did she have to worry about whether he was having an affair with one of several young women with whom he'd worked late on cases, a worry that had haunted her on many lonely nights.

He'd always claimed to love her and their daughter, but Amy had gotten tired of trying to convince Callie that her daddy truly felt bad about all the special events he'd been too busy to attend, like the Father's Day picnic at the preschool, not to mention the everyday things he'd missed, like dinner, story time, and tucking Callie into bed on most nights.

Amy had tried to blame it on the law firm, but Jake Goldstein had no trouble leaving the office at the end of the workday or spending weekends at home. So it had seemed only natural to assume another woman might be involved.

Brandon had sworn up and down that he'd never cheat, but in the end, Amy hadn't completely believed him.

"Will that work for you?" Ron asked, drawing her back to the telephone conversation.

"Yes."

"Good. I'll see you at my office tomorrow at ten."

After ending the call, Amy returned to the table, where Callie munched on the grilled chicken breast and pasta they were having for dinner. Cookie, the black-and-white cocker mix, sat on the floor next to the child's chair, wagging its tail and licking its chops.

"Did you give Cookie something to eat?" Amy asked.

"It was an accident. The chicken fell off my fork, and Cookie just cleaned up the floor." Callie looked at Amy with expressive eyes the same summer-sky shade as her father's and bit down on her bottom lip.

Amy, who wasn't convinced that feeding the dog at the table had been accidental, decided not to make an issue out of it and took her seat.

"Mommy, can Rachel come over and play tomorrow?"

The girls had just spent the afternoon together, and while Amy hated to ask Steph to watch Callie two days in a row, she might have to.

"I'll talk to her mommy about the two of you getting together, but it would have to be at Rachel's house."

The doorbell sounded, and Cookie let out a bark before dashing for the door. Callie started to climb from her chair, but Amy reached out and placed her hand on her daughter's shoulder. "You wait here, honey. I'll get it."

Once she got to the entry, she peered out the peephole, which revealed Brandon standing on the stoop. So she reached for Cookie's collar with one hand and opened the door with the other, leaving her to greet him in an awkward position. But impressing Brandon was the least of her concerns these days.

"I thought I'd bring the check by," he said.

Most ex-husbands dropped their alimony and child support payments in the mail, but Brandon insisted upon delivering each check to the house—and always a few days early. She supposed she had to give him credit for that.

She pulled the squirmy, barking dog aside and allowed her soon-to-be-ex-husband into the house. Once the door was shut, she released Cookie, who immediately lay down on the floor and rolled over, awaiting a scratch.

"Hey, little guy," Brandon said, stooping to comply with the pup's request for attention.

Cookie, in his pure delight, peed on the floor, and Amy groaned. "Darn it, Cookie," she uttered, when she really wanted to blame Brandon for showing up in the first place and interrupting dinner.

Ironic, she thought. There'd been a time when she might have dropped to the floor and rolled over herself just to have

Brandon arrive home before the nightly dishes had been done.

"Did I hear Daddy?" Callie asked as she approached the doorway, obviously neglecting to follow Amy's earlier directions to remain at the table.

"You sure did, baby doll." Brandon broke into his trademark grin, the dimpled cheeks, the lively spark in his eyes that had charmed Amy when they'd been in college.

Callie, her platinum blond hair pulled into pigtails, ran to her father and lifted her arms for a hug, clearly happy to see him.

For a moment, guilt sprang forth and clawed at Amy's chest, berating her for insisting upon the divorce Brandon claimed he didn't want. But she tamped it down, instead recalling all the times he'd disappointed her, all the nights she'd spent alone in a king-sized bed with only the television or a stack of books to keep her company.

She'd been able to live with her own loneliness and disappointment, she supposed. But she hadn't been able to stand by and watch her daughter suffer through the same thing, so she'd done what she had to do to make them all face reality.

Brandon Masterson might claim to love them, but he'd never been a real part of their family.

As Amy headed for the guest bathroom for a tissue and one of the disinfectant wipes she kept in the cupboard under the sink, Callie asked her father, "Do you want to see what I made at Rachel's house today?"

"You bet I do." Brandon, with his dark curls in need of a trim—when did he ever find time to schedule a haircut?—smiled at their daughter. Then his gaze sought Amy's, stopping her in mid-stride before she was able to stoop down and clean up the dog's piddle on the floor. Something passed between them, although she refused to consider just what it might be. She'd invested too much in an unfulfilling relationship already.

He didn't say a word, but he didn't have to. She read the questions in his eyes. "How's it going? Do you need anything? Are you sure this is what you really want?"

But nothing was ever going to change. His career was still his life, and his tunnel-vision drive to be the best attorney at the firm had been all consuming.

While Amy would be the first to admit that Brandon was an attractive man and that her heart still strummed when he sketched a gaze over her, she hadn't been willing to share him with anyone, whether it was another woman or a prestigious law firm.

At this point, she realized it really didn't matter who or what her rival was and broke eye contact long enough to clean up after the dog.

Callie led her daddy toward the kitchen.

As soon as Amy had thrown away the tissue and wipes and washed her hands, she joined them next to the refrigerator, where the child's artwork was displayed.

Callie was pointing to her latest masterpiece, a sheet of red construction paper on which she'd glued a hodgepodge of scraps: material, buttons, and yarn.

"It's pretty," Brandon told her. "Did you cut all those pieces by yourself?"

"Uh-huh. And I glued them, too."

"I also like this one." Brandon turned to a sheet of paper on which Callie had drawn a picture of her family.

"This is me and Mommy and Cookie," she said, pointing to the three figures that took up the left side of the paper. "And this one over here is you." She pointed to a rather small, nondescript stick man whose only claim to fame was a big red smiley face.

Amy knew that teachers, therapists, and social workers sometimes analyzed the pictures children drew. She hadn't needed any kind of degree in art psychology to see that the daddy figure in Callie's picture was small, underdeveloped, and clearly separated from the others. But Callie had drawn similar sketches when they'd still lived together in the sprawling house in Mar Vista Estates, and Brandon had been noticeably detached, too.

"Want to see my new shoes?" Callie asked her father.

"Sure." When the little girl dashed off, Brandon returned his focus to the family picture. "She's got me smiling, but that couldn't be further from the truth."

Before Amy could even consider a response, his cell phone rang. He looked at the display, then frowned. "I need to take this call."

Of course he did. He'd never received a phone call that he didn't answer.

Each time Amy felt herself weaken, each time she looked into Brandon's apologetic eyes or listened to him make promises to do better, something like this would happen. And she'd be reminded of the day she'd finally told herself that enough was enough.

She'd had a late hair appointment and her babysitter had canceled. There was a work-related dinner party that evening—a "command performance," he'd called it. So she'd called him at the office. "I'm going to let Callie stay the full day at preschool, and the sitter can be at our house by seven. But will you please pick her up on your way home?"

"Sure."

"I can ask Stephanie to do it if you're going to be too busy. . . ."

"It's okay. I need to get home early so that I have time for a shower."

"You'll need to make sure you get to the school before six," she'd added, "because the afternoon director is going on vacation and has a plane to catch. She'll need to leave on time today."

"That shouldn't be a problem."

Amy had gotten home at a quarter to

seven and found Brandon already dressed and talking on his cell phone. He ended the call, then smiled. "Your hair looks great, honey."

She'd only been able to appreciate the compliment for a second because he glanced behind her and asked, "Where's Callie?"

"No!" she'd shrieked. "Don't tell me you didn't pick her up." She'd rushed to the phone, only to see the red light on the answering machine flashing.

There'd been two calls from Kathy Webber, the director, asking where Amy was, each one getting a little more panicky. Then a third, telling her she'd had to drop off Callie at the home of another teacher who lived near the school, a new hire Amy had never met.

"I can't believe this," Amy had said, her voice a couple of octaves higher. "You forgot to pick her up! What kind of father forgets his own child?"

"I'm sorry, honey. I was busy, and . . . it just slipped my mind."

Had Callie been left in the care of someone she'd known, someone she'd been comfortable with, Amy might have been annoyed with Brandon instead of furious. But by the time she'd arrived at the new teacher's house, her daughter had been sobbing hysterically.

"Mommy!" she'd cried before racing across the room and flinging her arms around Amy in desperation. "I thought you died and went to Heaven, just like Grammy. And I was scared that nobody would find me. And that I would be all alone forever and ever."

"She's been inconsolable ever since Miss Kathy left," the teacher had said. "I'm so glad you finally got here. I didn't know what to do."

Maybe Amy's grief after having just lost her own mother had fired her up. Maybe all the times Brandon had failed to call home or show up at a family event, all the times he'd let her down or disappointed her, came crashing in on her, too. But that no longer mattered.

Amy had scooped her daughter into her arms, held her tight and swayed back and forth, softly shushing her. "I love you, sweetheart. And I promise that I'll never let anything like this happen to you again."

And she wouldn't.

Brandon's final act of abandonment, which might have traumatized his daughter for life, had been the last straw.

Once Amy had returned to the house with Callie, she'd told Brandon that he would have to attend the dinner party alone. And by the time he'd gotten home, she'd packed her bags.

"I hate this house and all it represents," she'd told him. "So don't worry about me wanting to keep it in the settlement. I'll take the condo in Del Mar."

"You want a divorce because I made a mistake?" he'd asked.

He'd made a lot of mistakes.

How could a man forget his own daughter? she'd asked herself time and again.

Clearly, Brandon Masterson had never been cut out to be a father. Some men weren't.

Maybe some women hadn't been meant to be mothers, either.

Her thoughts drifted to Barbara Rucker, who'd grown up in the house on Sugar Plum Lane. There could be a hundred reasons why she'd given up her baby girl in

September of 1966. Maybe she'd been young and unmarried. Maybe she'd been unable to care for a child, not just unwilling.

Time, Amy supposed, and a little snooping would tell.

She just hoped she wouldn't regret stirring up the past.

Chapter 2

That same night, next door to the old Rucker house on Sugar Plum Lane, Maria Rodriguez knelt beside the tub and watched her three-year-old son play with his Winnie-the-Pooh bath toys.

"Boing, boing," he said, bouncing a plastic Tigger across the water's surface and causing a splatter to slosh over the edge and onto the floor.

Maria couldn't help noting that the linoleum, which had once been a bright yellow and blue pattern, had dulled with age and curled away from the cracked gray caulking around the tub, revealing a strip of plywood underneath.

She'd have to add "bathroom floor" to the growing list of things that needed to be refurbished or repaired around the house, although she had very little money to spare on fix-it projects. And she had far less time.

It seemed that there were never enough hours in the day. What she wouldn't give to be able to slip away by herself for a while, to talk to someone who could actually carry on a quality conversation. If she still worked outside the home, she'd have coworkers with whom she could connect, but as it was, she was limited to chatting with her boarders or her children, which wasn't the same.

Ever since Hilda and Walter Klinefelter, who'd become self-appointed grandparents to her children and a godsend when it came to friendship and support, had left on a three-week European cruise, Maria's days had stretched into each other. Still, she was happy for the elderly couple who'd fallen in love during their golden years. Truly.

But today, it seemed, had been more trying than usual, and she was winding down fast.

If she had a few extra minutes, she'd brew herself a cup of chamomile tea—or maybe even pour a glass of wine. Then she'd find a good book and sink into a warm bath herself. But much to her dismay, her workday was far from over.

As little Walter—Wally for short—spun toward the back of the tub and reached for a miniature Pooh, the water sloshed against the sides again, threatening to spill over.

That's what she got for asking Sara to fill the bath. Sometimes it was easier doing things herself.

"Two more minutes," she said, warning Wally that bath time was almost over.

"No, not yet!"

It was amazing, she thought. She had to drag the child kicking and screaming to the tub, then had to fight twice as hard to get him out again. She reached for the pale blue towel she'd taken out of the linen closet earlier and had left on the tile counter near the sink.

"Mommy!" five-year-old Sara screeched from the open doorway. "Danny's calling me names again!"

Maria blew out a weary sigh.

"He called me a *girl,*" the child added, crossing her arms across her chest.

"You *are* a girl, honey."

"I *know.* But Danny said it like it was a *bad* thing."

She supposed the squabble wasn't a big deal, but Danny had once been so sweet and helpful, and in the past month he'd grown surly and difficult. No matter what she did, what she said, he seemed to slip further away from the child he'd once been.

Holding back another weary sigh, she slowly got to her feet. "I'll talk to him as soon as I get your little brother out of the bathtub and help him put on his pajamas. In the meantime, go get your nightgown and a towel. It's your turn for a bath."

"Oh, *o*-kay." Sara turned and stomped off in a huff.

As her daughter padded down the hall, Maria reached into the bathtub and pulled out the plug to drain the water.

"No!" Wally screeched. "I'm not *done.*"

Maybe not, but Maria was. She lifted him from the tub, and he kicked and whined in a last-ditch attempt at defiance. Then she stood him on the floor and draped the towel around him as water pooled onto the floor.

What she wouldn't give to have someone with whom she could share the parent load, especially in the evenings, but she'd been on her own for nearly four years now. And nights were the worst.

Not that she wanted her ex-husband back.

Her children's father had been her teenage crush, but he'd proven to be anything but family oriented. And even if he'd wanted to be a solid and dependable part of their lives, he still had several years left to serve in prison following a fatal altercation with the jealous husband of the woman he'd been seeing.

He wrote occasionally, but only to Danny, since Maria had not only refused to provide him with a phony alibi, she'd let him know in no uncertain terms that she didn't want anything to do with him.

She really didn't want him contacting their son, although she understood why he would. Still, that didn't mean she had to share those letters with an eleven-year-old. So each time she received one, which wasn't all that often, she would put it away for a time when Danny was older and better able to deal with one of the dark realities of life.

"Mommy!" Sara shrieked. "He's saying it *again!* And this time he's calling me a *dumb* girl."

What was she going to do with that boy?

Maria lifted the towel-bundled toddler and carried him out of the bathroom, down the hall, and to Danny's room, where the eleven-year-old lay stretched out on his bed, his hands resting under his head, his gaze on the ceiling.

"What's going on?" she asked, shuffling Wally in her arms.

"Nothing."

Maria supposed she shouldn't be overly concerned about Danny calling Sara a dumb girl. After all, there were a lot worse things he could have called her. But something niggled at her, suggesting there was more going on in her son's life than she realized, something she ought to be aware of.

The fact that his father was in prison could cause him some concern, but he seemed to have gotten over it fairly well, once they'd moved out of town and away from the whispers in the community about a crime of passion that had gone awry.

"Do you want to talk about it?" she asked her son.

"Nope." He didn't even turn his head.

She'd expected the teen years to be rough, but wasn't that surly attitude striking a little too soon?

"Did your sister do something to annoy you?"

"Yeah." He finally turned his head, albeit briefly. "She won't leave me alone. And I don't want to play with her and her stupid dolls."

Maria tried to tell herself that the squabble was typical of siblings, that Danny was growing up and wanted some privacy, that her uneasiness was for naught.

But she couldn't help stressing anyway. Shouldn't a good mother try to "fix" whatever was bothering her child?

The telephone rang, drawing her from what was fast becoming an unpleasant nightly routine. If it was another telemarketer, she was going to scream.

She set Wally on the floor and told him to go find his Pull-Ups and the jammies she'd laid out for him. Then she hurried to her bedroom to answer before the caller hung up.

"Hello?"

"Maria, this is Barbara Davila."

"Oh, hi." Maria took a seat on the edge of the bed.

"How's Mother doing?"

Ellie had more bad days than good ones, and today hadn't been easy. But Maria didn't want to complain. Not to Barbara, the woman whose relationship with her mother had always been strained. "She's all right."

"Good. I just wanted to let you know that we think we found a tenant for the house today."

So soon?

"Do you know anything about them?"

"Not really. Just that the woman is a single mother with one child—a little girl. I'm not sure when she'll move in, but she's supposed to sign the lease and take possession tomorrow."

"But the house isn't empty. . . ." Maria

paused, hoping she hadn't overstepped her boundaries.

"The woman volunteered to pack up my mother's belongings for us, and under the circumstances, I jumped at the offer."

"I would have done that for you," Maria said.

"I'm sure you would have, but you have your hands full, don't you think?"

That was for sure.

"Well, I'd better go," Barbara said. "I just wanted to keep you in the loop."

"How's Joe today?" Maria asked. Barbara's son had suffered a heart attack a couple of weeks ago, and there'd been complications.

"He's frustrated by his slow recovery, but the doctors think he'll pull through. It'll just take time."

Time.

Maria glanced at the small alarm clock on the bureau. It was after nine. The boarders had already turned in, but the kids should have been in bed an hour ago. Would this night ever end?

Why had she offered to pack Ellie's things? Where would she have found the time to do it?

And why did she feel bad that she couldn't? It really wasn't her place.

"Well, I'll let you go," Barbara said. "But if you don't mind, I'd really appreciate it if you would keep an eye on the place and let me know if anything seems . . . well, if things are out of sorts."

Ellie Rucker's home had fallen into more disrepair than Maria's had, and to be honest, Maria was surprised they'd managed to rent it so quickly.

"Sure, I can do that. Maybe I'll take some cookies or a coffee cake next door when I see that she's moving in, and then I can introduce myself."

"Good. That will be one less thing for me to worry about."

And one more thing for Maria to heap on her plate. But Ellie Rucker had been a good friend, and she'd gone out of her way to welcome any newcomers to the neighborhood.

It was, Maria decided, one way to pay it forward.

But, Lord, how she could use a few extra hours in her day.

* * *

Eddie Gonzales was stretched out in the recliner, watching the evening news, when the phone rang.

Who could be calling at this hour?

He glanced at the time displayed on the cable box—it was almost ten o'clock—and reached for the portable receiver that rested on the lamp table. "Hello?"

Ramon, his brother, responded. "I didn't wake you, did I?"

"No. What's up?"

"I just got a call from the property manager at Fairbrook Realty. He's got a job for us on Sugar Plum Lane. I'm up to my neck with the Sanderson project, so would you mind going over there and giving them a bid?"

"Sure, I can do that."

"Ron said the yard had once been a showcase, but it's been neglected for years. He thought it would take a week or more to get it back into shape, especially since we're shorthanded right now. He thinks we'll have to repair the sprinkler system, too. But I'll let you make that call."

Eddie appreciated his brother's trust, but they'd both grown up on the Rensfield estate, where their father had been the gardener. And they'd learned the landscape trade early on, although Ramon was the one who actually owned the company.

"I'm tied up until about noon," Eddie said, thinking about the yards he mowed on Tuesdays. "But I'll take a look at it when I'm finished."

"Thanks."

Ramon didn't have to thank Eddie for anything. Not after Ramon had gone to bat for him with the parole board. His brother's connections with law enforcement, along with a job offer and family support, had been instrumental in getting him an early release.

"Hold on a minute." Eddie brought the recliner to an upright position and stood, careful not to step on Roscoe, the bushy-haired dog sprawled out on the floor. "I've got to find a pen."

He headed for the kitchen counter, where he kept his keys, cell phone, and daily log. Moments later, after he'd written down the address, as well as the name of the owner, he ended the call and returned to the living room.

Roscoe looked up, stretched out his big, lanky body, and yawned.

"You ready to go out before we turn in for the night?" Eddie reached for the leash he kept near the entrance.

The dog barked and got to his feet, his tail swishing back and forth with more excitement than he'd shown all evening.

Eddie ruffled the top of the mutt's head and rubbed his ears. Roscoe had to be one of the ugliest dogs he'd ever seen. The first time he'd laid eyes on him, he'd been a stray hanging out near the ball fields at Mulberry Park and begging for food from anyone who'd brought a picnic lunch. Eddie had given him a chunk of his bologna sandwich, but some of the mothers near the playground weren't so nice.

When Roscoe accidentally knocked a toddler to the sand and started licking peanut butter off the kid's face, the mother freaked out. Once she'd shooed the dog away and saw that her child was okay, she'd called someone and reported a dangerous dog on the loose.

But Roscoe didn't have a mean bone in his body. He'd just been starving, and not just for food. The poor guy only wanted a little human companionship, but no one at the park seemed to care.

When the animal control officer arrived, Roscoe bolted, almost as though he'd already had a couple of run-ins with the doggie law and knew that the uniformed man wasn't the kind of human friend he'd wanted.

Eddie had found himself silently cheering the stray's attempt to escape, but eventually the officer had cornered him. While he was being restrained, Roscoe had looked at Eddie, imploring him to help.

Talk about weird connections. Eddie had felt an inexplicable tug at his heart.

"What are you going to do with him?" he'd asked the officer.

"I'm taking him back to the animal shelter. Normally, after a bath and a medical exam, we put them up for adoption. You'd be surprised at the transformation some of these dogs make with a little soap and water. But in this case?" The officer turned to the mangy mutt. "I'm not betting on any big miracles."

Eddie had never been what you'd call an animal lover, but for some crazy reason, he'd followed the truck to the shelter. A dog as ugly as Roscoe wasn't likely to be adopted soon, and Eddie'd had a feeling the dog's days were numbered.

He'd had one last sobering thought about heading back to work and leaving the shelter alone, but when Roscoe had peered at him through that cage, as if saying, "Hey, buddy. How'd you like to be in here?" Eddie had given in and put down a deposit to hold him until he'd been cleaned up, neutered, and deemed adoptable.

So here he was, a reluctant dog owner.

Eddie snapped the leash onto Roscoe's collar, then opened the door only to see two men walking up the sidewalk.

Roscoe strained to rush forward—to greet them warmly, no doubt—but Eddie held him back.

"Going somewhere?" the taller of the two men asked.

Eddie stiffened at the sound of his parole officer's voice. "Just taking my dog for a walk."

"We were in the area and thought we'd stop by for a visit," Dale Kingsley said.

Eddie would never get used to the "visits" of virtual strangers who would rifle through his drawers and closet, usually leaving his house in shambles.

"I don't suppose you'd like to make yourself at home while I let the dog take care of business," he said, but he'd been out of prison long enough to know the routine. He'd be cuffed while the men searched his house, looking for anything that might be a parole violation.

They wouldn't find anything, though. He'd hated every second behind bars, and he wasn't going to risk ever going back again.

"We'll wait," Dale said. "And I'd rather you kept that dog outside. I got bit by a Rottweiler once, and I'm not about to take any chances."

Dale didn't need to worry about Roscoe doing anything other than licking him to death, but Eddie clamped his mouth shut.

It was one of the lessons he'd learned at Donovan Correctional Facility.

It was best to keep to yourself.

The next morning, Amy sat in front of Ron Paige's desk at Fairbrook Realty, a small, storefront office just two doors down from Parkside Community Church.

Ron had already run a credit check, and as expected, Amy had passed with flying colors. But she'd known she would. If there was one thing to be said about Brandon, it was that he was not only driven to succeed at the office, he was also determined to keep their FICO scores high.

"So far, so good," Ron said. "The only thing I need to do now is to check on your rental history."

"I own the house I'm currently living in. If you take a closer look at the credit report, you'll see the mortgage has always been paid on time."

Ron glanced at the pages in front of him. "Oh. You're right." He furrowed his brow, then looked up. "If you own a home, why do you want to lease the Rucker place?"

As a child, Amy used to tattle on herself, so she'd never been good at deception. Yet she managed a truthful response that would satisfy his curiosity without revealing her real motive. "I'm going through a divorce."

He nodded, as though that answered everything. Then he glanced back down at the paperwork in front of him and added, "You're lucky."

She didn't feel very lucky and couldn't help asking, "How so?"

"I've worked with people in the past who were in your situation, and their credit scores were usually a disaster."

Yeah, well, he didn't know Brandon.

And he didn't know Amy, either. She hadn't wanted a big fight; she'd just wanted out. And since she'd heard horror stories of year-long litigations in family court, she'd suggested they get one attorney and divide things right down the middle.

Not wanting a divorce in the first place, as well as the expense and hassle of one, Brandon had agreed to her terms.

All of them, actually. But then again, she'd tried hard to be fair.

"I gotta hand it to you," Ron said. "It sounds as though you two are dealing exceptionally well with your split."

Amy supposed they were. Yet again, her efforts to tiptoe around the truth and her hope that Ron would buy her explanation warmed her cheeks.

Apparently, she'd been able to pull off the deception, because by eleven o'clock she'd signed a six-month lease and had been handed the keys to the Rucker place.

"I've contacted a landscaping company to mow the lawn and trim the bushes," Ron said. "Mrs. Davila said her mom had always prided herself in a beautiful yard, but the place has been going steadily downhill for years."

Amy supposed she'd talk to the landscaper about staying on while the lease was in effect. Something told her she'd be too busy inside the house to worry about the yard.

Fifteen minutes later, she arrived on Sugar Plum Lane. She parked her car in the drive, removed several empty cardboard boxes from the backseat, and carried them down the walkway to the front door, intending to follow through on her part of the bargain. Somehow, that made what she was doing seem right.

The lockbox had yet to be removed, but she used the key she'd been given to enter.

Once inside, she inhaled the scent of dust and age, along with the hint of stale sugar and spice. She was tempted to open up the windows and air out the old Victorian, yet she also felt compelled to leave everything just the way it was.

She was reminded of the dozen or so

two-story clapboard houses that had been relocated from various sites in San Diego to Heritage Park and refurbished, the interiors decorated and furnished just as they'd been a hundred years ago, with a rope stretched across the doorways of the rooms to block people from entering or touching the displays.

But Amy was free to walk through the rooms of the Rucker place, to touch each item that had once passed through the fingers of the great-grandmother she'd never known.

She dropped the boxes onto the floor in the entry, then placed her hands on her hips and scanned the living room, with its faded blue walls edged with a floral wallpaper trim. Her gaze was drawn to a soot-stained red brick fireplace, where several framed photographs were displayed on a carved oak mantel.

Curiosity urged her to take a closer look at the people who'd meant something to Mrs. Rucker, and she crossed the room. As she lifted each frame, she studied the smiling images in an effort to see her mother in one of them.

There was, she supposed, a family resemblance. Or maybe she just wanted there to be one.

She lifted a brass frame that held a black-and-white photograph of a smiling young couple. The man had on an Army uniform, and the woman, an attractive blonde, was wearing the style of clothing worn in the 1940s.

There was something about the woman that reminded Amy of Betty Grable, the popular pinup girl during the war years. And while it was a stretch to see Jimmy Stewart in the fair-haired soldier, his tall, lanky build and a down-home grin lent credibility to her musing.

"Who are you?" she whispered. Friends of Mrs. Rucker? Other family members?

She returned the picture to its place on the mantel, and even though she supposed the framed photos were the sort of personal effects she should be wrapping in tissue and packing away, she couldn't bring herself to do so. Instead, she took a long, lingering look at each person.

Most of the photographs appeared to be thirty years old or more. Weren't there any more recent than that? Didn't Mrs. Rucker have any great-grandchildren?

The Rossi house was loaded with pictures and portraits of both Susan and Amy when they were young, and now Callie's photographs had a prominent place on tabletops and walls.

Deciding to leave the living room intact for now, Amy headed for the kitchen, then paused beside the lamp table, where the dirty china cup and saucer sat. She glanced at the Bible she'd noticed during her first visit to the house, its worn and cracked leather embossed with the name *Eleanor Rucker* in gold letters. It rested next to a television guide, the kind that came with the local newspaper. The date, she noted, was a little more than two months ago.

Was that the week when Eleanor Rucker had been frightened by imaginary hippies?

Was that how long the house had been empty?

Suspecting she might never get the answers to any of her questions, Amy carried the dirty dishes to the sink, turned on the spigot, and waited for the water to heat. After placing the stopper in the drain, she reached for a plastic bottle of lemon-scented dish soap that sat on the counter and squirted a stream under the faucet spray.

She lifted the dirty cup, but before placing it in the soapy water, she took time to study the pattern—tiny pink roses with a delicate gold trim.

She tried to imagine a special occasion, the dining room table draped with freshly starched white linen, the dishes set out with sparkling crystal goblets and polished silver.

In the middle of the table, she could easily see newly clipped rosebuds—pink to match the china pattern—carefully arranged in a vase and flanked by two long, tapered candles, the flames flickering in the evening light.

She could almost hear the hum of happy voices, of faceless family and friends.

Perhaps "Betty Grable" sat at the head of the table with her husband standing at her side, his hand resting gently on her shoulder, a smile on his face as he welcomed the guests with a Jimmy Stewart drawl.

The doorbell sounded, drawing Amy from her crazy thoughts, and she frowned.

No one knew she was here. Maybe it was the real estate agent coming to remove the lockbox and the sign. Or maybe it was a door-to-door salesman.

Either way, she shut off the water and strode to the entry. When she opened the front door, she found a petite, thirty-something Latina on the porch, holding a plate of brownies covered with plastic wrap.

The woman, who wore her long, dark hair straight, smiled warmly and introduced herself as Maria Rodriguez. She nodded to the left. “I live next door and thought I’d come over and welcome you to the neighborhood.”

Amy hadn’t counted on any visitors, nor had she intended to stretch the truth any more than she already had. Still, she took the plate of chocolate goodies and managed to introduce herself and return the woman’s smile. “These look delicious. Thank you.”

“One of the women in the neighborhood brought a lemon cake to me when I moved in. So when my son told me he’d seen our new neighbor, it seemed like the right thing to do.”

The conversation lulled. If Amy had truly been a new neighbor moving in, she might have known what to say. As it was, she felt like a fraud. So she thanked the woman again.

"I heard you have a daughter," Maria said.

Amy nodded, thinking that the web she'd begun to weave was expanding without any effort on her part, and she wasn't sure how to stop it from growing any further.

By sticking to the truth whenever she could, she supposed. "Her name is Callie. And she's five."

Maria flicked a long strand of hair over her shoulder and smiled. "I have a five-year-old, too. Her name's Sara. It'll be nice for her to have someone new to play with. There aren't too many girls living on the street."

Amy hadn't planned on bringing Callie to Sugar Plum Lane, but again she nodded. "That would be nice."

"Is she here?" Maria asked.

"No, not today. She's with a sitter."

A slow grin stretched across Maria's face, as though she understood how difficult it would be to have a child underfoot.

"I thought I'd pack up Mrs. Rucker's belongings first," Amy added.

Maria's smile faded. "I would have offered to pack up things for the Davilas. I didn't realize they were going to hire someone to do it."

Had Maria found that a little unusual, too? Either way, Amy decided to let it go. There were probably a lot of things she didn't understand, so she thought it best to change the subject. "I heard Mr. Davila had a heart attack. Is he doing all right?"

"There were some complications, but I think he's going to be fine. From what I understand, it's going to take some time."

"I'm sure his illness took the family by surprise," Amy added.

"Yes, it was completely unexpected. He was pretty active and appeared to be healthy. In fact, Ellie was supposed to move in with him and his wife, but that didn't pan out."

"Did she move in with one of her children instead?" Amy asked.

"She only had one child. A daughter. But they weren't very close."

Which meant what? That her daughter, who had to be Barbara Davila, wouldn't take the old woman into her home to live with her? Or that she couldn't for some reason?

Amy hated to ask too many questions, especially up front. Yet that's why she was here, wasn't it? To find the answers her mother had been seeking?

"Have you lived on Sugar Plum Lane very long?" she asked Maria.

"I moved in with my *tía,* or rather, my aunt, when my mother died. I spent my teenage years with her and left when I got married. But after I filed for divorce, I brought the kids and came home."

Apparently the women had several things in common. They'd both lost their mothers, and they'd wanted out of bad marriages, which left them raising their children alone.

"So you live with your *tía,*" Amy assumed, realizing Maria's aunt probably knew more about the Ruckers—or, more specifically, about Barbara Davila.

"No, not anymore. Sofia passed away a few years ago."

"I'm sorry to hear that." And for more reasons than one. Maria's aunt might have held the key to Amy's search.

"Well, I'd better let you get back to work," Maria said.

"Would you like a cup of tea?" The question rolled right off Amy's tongue without any forethought, and she wasn't entirely sure why.

Just to be hospitable?

Curiosity about the Ruckers?

The commonality she shared with the woman she'd just met?

"Actually," Maria said, "I'd love a cup of tea. Ellie would often brew a pot whenever I stopped by. But I need to get back home. I left my son in charge, and he's . . ." She sighed almost wearily. "Well, he hasn't been getting along with his sister lately."

"Before you go, can I ask you something?"

"Sure."

"I'm curious about Mrs. Rucker—Eleanor."

Maria smiled. "If she were standing here with us now, she'd insist that you call her Ellie. Everyone did."

"Then Ellie it is." Amy returned the woman's smile.

"What about her?"

"I . . . uh . . . spotted some old photographs and was curious about something. Hold on a minute." Amy turned and hurried to the mantel, snagged the picture of the soldier and the girl, and returned to the open doorway. "Do you know who these people are?"

Maria took the frame, glanced at the images, and nodded. "That's Ellie and her husband, Harold. I never met him. He died during World War Two, but he was the love of her life. That photo has been on her mantel ever since I can remember. There's another one like it near her bed."

"Didn't she ever remarry?" Amy asked, unsure why it seemed to matter.

"Yes, but only briefly. From what I understand, the marriage was a big mistake. She never talked to me about him, but I remember my aunt saying that he wasn't good to her."

"That's too bad."

"You mean that her second husband was a jerk?" Maria asked, handing back the frame.

"Oh, no." Amy straightened. "That she

lost the love of her life in the war, that she never met anyone else who could take his place."

Maria smiled. "You sound like a romantic."

"I always used to be."

"So did I, but my ex-husband took care of dimming my rose-colored glasses."

Amy's ex had done the same thing, but she hoped to find someone new someday, someone who valued his wife and child.

"Well," Maria said. "I really need to get home. Let me know when Callie gets here. I'll bring Sara by to meet her."

Amy nodded, although she couldn't do that.

How could she ask a child to help perpetuate the lie her mother had created?

Chapter 3

As Maria walked down the cracked, leaf-riddled sidewalk that led from Ellie's porch to the street, a sense of sadness slowed her steps. There was a part of her that hated to leave the house in the hands of a stranger, yet she had to admit that Amy seemed nice enough.

As she reached the picket fence that surrounded Ellie's yard, she passed through the gate that had completely broken off its hinges, turned to her right at the street, and continued home.

Before she reached the property line that separated her house from Ellie's, a white pickup pulled up and parked along the curb. The bed of the truck, she noted, was filled with a lawnmower and other gardening tools. And a green logo on the passenger door read GONZALES LANDSCAPING.

Maria didn't give the vehicle's arrival much thought until the driver, a dark-haired man in his twenties, climbed from the cab, leaving a brown, shaggy dog in the front seat. The dog barked, but it wasn't the animal that piqued her interest; it was the handsome driver with an olive complexion, a square-cut jaw, and a rugged build.

Normally, she kept her eyes averted from men, particularly those who were young and attractive. It was easier that way.

Her marriage hadn't been happy, and she was unwilling to put herself in the position of repeating the same mistake. But she couldn't help risking a second glance at the brawny man who stood about six foot two.

When he tossed her a grin, her brains turned to mush—her bones and joints, too. Yet, try as she might, she couldn't return the friendly gesture.

Or maybe she inadvertently had, since he continued toward her.

"Excuse me," he said. "Do you live here?"

Yes. No.

It was a simple question with a simpler answer, but for some reason, her words failed to form.

As their gazes met and locked, a swarm of butterflies rose up in her stomach. You'd think she'd never come face-to-face with an attractive man before, although she had to admit, this was the first time she'd ever been attracted to anyone other than her ex-husband. Ray's lies and betrayal had scarred her for good—at least, that's what she'd told herself.

The gardener nodded toward Ellie's house, and Maria's brain finally rallied.

"No, I live in the blue house." She pointed to hers just as the front door swung open.

"Mom!" Danny shouted from the porch.

She turned to her son, glad for the distraction, even if it meant trouble inside.

"Ellie's out in the backyard again," the unsmiling boy announced, "and she's calling for some guy named Harold."

"I . . . uh." Maria glanced at the landscaper. "I have to go."

"I can see that." His smile broadened, revealing a single dimple that could only mean bad news to any woman who found it charming.

What was with her inability to break eye contact, to move on?

"Our company is going to be doing some landscaping on the street," he added. "So if you're interested in getting a bid for your yard"—he reached into the back pocket of his jeans and pulled out a business card—"we'll give you or any of the other neighbors a ten-percent discount."

She couldn't afford a landscaper, no matter what kind of deal he gave her, yet she took his card anyway, fingered the embossed lettering.

"Mom!" Danny yelled again, this time louder and more insistent.

"I'm coming." Her words gave the proper response, but her feet seemed to be uncooperative.

"Keep us in mind," he said.

She nodded, afraid she'd be keeping the landscaper in mind longer than she ought to, and forced herself to head back to the house.

Shake it off, she told herself as she reached her front porch.

Danny stepped aside to allow her in.

Still, for some crazy reason, just as she started past the threshold, she stole one last peek over her shoulder, only to see that the landscaper hadn't moved either, that his eyes were still on her.

Amy had no more than returned the photograph of Ellie and Harold back to the mantel and started back to the kitchen when the doorbell rang.

Had Maria had a change of heart about the tea?

Oddly enough, Amy hoped so. She returned to the living room and answered the door only to find a tall, dark-haired man on the stoop. He appeared to be Latino, with soft brown eyes and a shy smile.

"Mrs. Masterson?" he asked.

She nodded.

"I'm Eddie with Gonzales Landscaping. I was asked to come by and look at the yard so that we can give the owner an estimate for cleaning things up around here."

"Oh, good." She tucked a strand of hair behind her ear. "It definitely needs some work."

"Do you have any dogs I should be aware of?"

"No, I don't." At least, not at this house.

"Is there anything specific in the yard that needs to be trimmed? Anything you're especially concerned about?"

"Actually, I've only done a cursory walk-through of the yard, so I can't really say. I know there's a rose garden in back, and it's in bad shape. Other than that, the lawn needs to be mowed and edged, the trees and bushes need to be trimmed."

"If you don't mind, Mrs. Masterson, I'll take a look around."

"No, not at all. But call me Amy."

"All right." As he stepped off the porch, she closed the door and returned to the kitchen, where she opened the pantry, threw out all the open containers of food, and boxed up the rest. She found an unopened bag of Kitty Delight, although she hadn't seen any other sign of a cat. Rather than pack it up with the food items, she left it on a shelf to deal with later.

After washing down the shelves, she started on the drawers, then scoured the counters.

Near the telephone, which no longer had a dial tone, she found a pink steno pad with several notations written in pencil:

Soup kitchen Friday. Vera will pick me up.

Tell Joey the washing machine is broken again.

760-555-1493–Daniel Delacourt–tomorrow afternoon here.

Dr. Ryley–new medication not working.

Odd, she thought. It wasn't the typical list, like the items she needed from the grocery store. It appeared that Ellie was keeping notes for herself, jotting down things she didn't want to forget.

Had she known her mind was failing?

Again, the doorbell rang. Amy wasn't sure how much time had passed. Fifteen or twenty minutes, she supposed.

Assuming the landscaper had finished checking out the yard and wanted to tell her he was leaving, she made her way back to the entry and swung open the door only to find her ex-husband and her daughter on the stoop.

"Brandon," was all she could say.

"What's going on?" he asked. "What are you doing here?"

She could be asking him the same question. And while she was tempted to level with him, as had been her habit in the past, she wasn't sure what kind of an explanation she owed him now that they were separated.

Yet with Callie standing in the midst of them, her bright-eyed smile proclaiming that she was certain the surprise visit had pleased them all, Amy found herself scrambling for a response.

"We're going to Chuck E. Cheese's," Callie announced.

Now, that was unexpected. Amy and Callie had always been at the bottom of Brandon's priority list. So why the change of heart?

When she shot him a quizzical glance, he shrugged. "I had some free time and thought I'd spend it with Callie."

Apparently the separation was having a positive effect on their almost nonexistent father/daughter relationship. But if he'd called ahead of time, Amy wouldn't have had to get a sitter.

Last night, she'd asked Stephanie Goldstein to watch Callie again, since they often helped each other by trading child care. But it hadn't worked out this time, and Amy had hired Sylvia Griswold to sit with her instead.

"It was just a spur-of-the-moment thing," Brandon added.

Apparently.

But it still didn't quite ring true.

"When I found Callie with Sylvia," he said, "I tried your cell, but you didn't answer."

She hadn't heard the phone ring. Had she forgotten to charge the battery?

"I asked Sylvia where you were, and she said you'd gone to Fairbrook. She mentioned Sugar Plum Lane, and so I drove by and spotted your car." Brandon scanned the porch and yard of the neglected house, his brow furrowed as though trying to connect the dots.

"Do you want to come with us to Chuck E. Cheese's?" Callie asked. "It'll be fun, Mommy."

"I'd like to, honey, but I've got some work to do here." Amy looked at her ex-husband and added, "I'm helping out a friend."

Brandon furrowed a brow, clearly perplexed, and she could understand why. When they'd been together, she'd stuck pretty close to home and always kept him in the loop, even if he hadn't seemed too interested in play dates, dance lessons, or mommy-and-me gym classes.

Footsteps crunched on the dried leaves and twigs that littered the side of the house, and they all turned to the sound and watched the landscaper approach.

The dark-haired man aimed a friendly smile her way. "Have you got a minute, Amy?"

Brandon's stance stiffened. "Is this your *friend?*"

What was he asking her? Did he think she was dating, and that she had something to hide?

Amy crossed her arms. "No, this is . . . the gardener." She felt a little guilty referring to the man by his occupation, but to be honest, he might have remembered her name, but she'd forgotten his.

The man in question reached out to greet Brandon. "I'm Eddie Gonzales. Are you Mr. Davila?"

"No." Brandon paused for a moment,

then gripped the man's hand, yet his body remained tense. "Brandon Masterson."

Eddie turned his attention back to Amy. "Is this a bad time?"

Apparently it was. And it seemed to be getting worse by the minute. "No, what's up?"

"Do you mind coming to the side of the house so I can show you something?"

"Not at all." She turned to her soon-to-be ex. "Excuse me for a moment, Brandon. I'll be right back."

A part of her enjoyed toying with him, especially since she didn't appreciate the surprise visit. But she wasn't the kind to resort to games, especially in front of their child.

She followed the gardener to the side yard, where a tree limb from the house next door hung over the wood fence. Or maybe *leaned on it* was more accurate.

"This branch needs to be cut back. As you can see, it's creating a problem. If we don't do something about it, the fence will need to be repaired or replaced. But we can't cut it without the neighbor's permission. Do you know the people who live there?"

"I just met her," Amy said. "Her name is Maria. And I don't think she'll mind. Do you want me to talk to her about it?"

"I'll do it. We've got a release form I'd like for her to sign." Eddie stepped closer to the fence and peered into Maria's yard, checking out the tree that was causing the problem.

Amy couldn't imagine Maria having a problem with Eddie trimming her tree. After all, the fence was already starting to bow from the weight.

"By the way," Eddie added, "the sprinkling system is shot. I'm not sure if Mr. Davila will want to go to the expense of tearing it out and replacing it. If not, you'll have to water the old-fashioned way."

It's not that Amy didn't like yard work, but she'd committed to a lot more than she'd planned already. And while she'd defend her actions to Brandon, she was getting drawn deeper and deeper into something she hadn't thought completely through when she'd leased the house.

"Well, I guess that's it for now." Eddie stepped away from the fence and turned, ready to head back to the front yard. "I don't want to keep you from your work or your company."

"He's not exactly company," she said as they walked. "But while you're here, can I ask you something?"

"Shoot."

"Do you know anything about rosebushes?"

"Quite a bit. Why?"

"Like I mentioned earlier, the woman who lived here had a rose garden in back. It's a scraggly mess now, but she clearly used to love it and care for it."

"I'd planned to trim and weed around it."

That wasn't exactly what she meant. "I'm not sure how much work the Davilas want you to do, but I'd be happy to pay you extra to get those bushes healthy once more. It just seems that . . ." What? she asked herself. That she somehow owed it to Ellie Rucker to put things back to rights? ". . . well, let's just say I'd like to see the roses bloom the way they should."

"You got it," Eddie said as they returned to the front yard, where Brandon and Callie waited. "I'll get some numbers to the Davilas, and we'll take it from there."

Amy nodded as Eddie headed toward his pickup.

When she returned her attention to Brandon, she said, "Why don't I give you a call on your cell? I think it's better if we talk privately about this."

"I don't like not knowing what you're up to," Brandon said as he placed a hand on Callie's shoulder.

"I'm not 'up to' anything. There's a perfectly good explanation." Well, he might not consider it a good one. But Amy wasn't moving to Fairbrook. And she wasn't dating anyone.

"Aren't you going with us?" Callie asked.

"Not today, honey. I'm afraid I can't. But have fun."

"Should I bring her back here?" Brandon asked.

"No." Amy would have to figure out a Plan B, whatever that might be. "Tell me what time you'll have her home, and I'll be there."

"How about two?" he asked.

She nodded, thinking she'd better get busy if she wanted to get any work—or any snooping—done.

* * *

Brandon drove his black late-model Mercedes through the traffic on his way to Chuck E. Cheese's, a place he'd only been to once and hadn't appreciated as much as everyone else seemed to. He preferred to eat at restaurants that didn't cater to kids.

As he stopped at the intersection of Canyon and Main, he noticed a man in blue coveralls sweeping the sidewalk in front of a café. He didn't give it much thought until he caught sight of the guy's profile. From the side, he looked familiar.

Brandon tried to check him out, but he pushed his broom around the corner, disappearing from view.

His dad?

No, it couldn't be. His old man had probably drunk himself to death by now. Besides, what would he be doing in Fairbrook? He didn't have any family or friends here.

"Daddy?"

Brandon glanced in the rearview mirror at Callie, who sat in her car seat in back. "Yes, honey?"

"How come the light is green and you're not going?"

Oh, for Pete's sake. Brandon glanced at the traffic light, saw that it wasn't going to get any greener, and started across the street.

"I can't wait to go to Chuck E. Cheese's," Callie said. "It's the funnest place in the world."

Ever since leaving Sugar Plum Lane, the little girl had been chattering up a storm. But it wasn't the child he wanted to talk to right now; it was her mother, who was clearly up to something.

The divorce had been an unexpected blow, but he'd gone along with it, thinking that a fight wasn't in anyone's best interest. Then Amy had insisted upon moving back to the townhome in Del Mar, which left him living alone in a sprawling four-bedroom executive house in La Jolla with a killer view, where he only returned at night to sleep.

Of course, he'd been sleeping like crap ever since Amy and Callie moved out. What had gotten into the woman who'd once been so levelheaded and predictable? She'd morphed into a woman he no longer knew.

"I'll call and explain," she'd told him.

But when? Next week?

He slipped on the Bluetooth, then called her cell instead. The phone rang several times before Amy finally answered.

"Hello?"

"Did you lose your phone? You were supposed to call me."

"No, I . . ."

Brandon meant to be patient. He really did. But he couldn't help pressing for an answer. "What's going on, Amy?"

She blew out a sigh, as though that simple explanation wasn't so simple after all. "Remember how I told you that my mother had been searching for her biological family?"

Vaguely, but he'd been pretty busy and hadn't paid a lot of attention to things that hadn't concerned him. He couldn't admit that, though, so he said, "Yes, I remember."

"Well, I decided to pick up the search where she left off as a tribute to her."

Brandon furrowed his brow. "I still don't get it, Amy. What are you doing? Looking for ghosts in a haunted house?"

She laughed, the lilt of her voice more of a balm on his raw and ragged emotions than anything else had been since she'd moved out, which included having more than his share of stiff drinks, slamming a fist through the wall once, and burying himself in more work.

"In a way," she admitted, "that's exactly what I'm doing."

Okay, she'd really gone off the deep end. He again glanced in the rearview mirror, making eye contact with the little girl they'd created, a beautiful child with her mommy's blond hair and expressive blue eyes.

A daughter that still bound them together, whether Amy liked it or not.

So he said, "I'm still waiting for that simple explanation you promised."

She inhaled, then let out a slow and steady breath. "I followed the trail to a woman named Barbara Rucker, who grew up in the house where you found me today."

"What'd you do? Break in?"

"No, I'm there legally."

That was a relief, although his wife was so honest that her mom used to say she wouldn't take a shortcut home. But after all they'd been through the past few months? Who knew what she'd do next.

"Who lives in the house now?" he asked.

"Actually, the neighbors think that I do."

"Excuse me?"

"I leased the place," she explained. "It's furnished and still holds Mrs. Rucker's personal belongings, so it gives me an opportunity to . . . look around."

What happened to the sensible woman he'd married, the loving mother who was a gourmet cook and had an eye for décor?

Brandon slowly shook his head. His wife—no way was he ready to throw in the towel and refer to her as his ex yet—had surely flipped. He couldn't believe what he was hearing.

"You signed a lease?" he asked. Of course she had; she'd just told him that. But for some reason, he'd thought he'd missed something. "For how long?"

"Six months. It's the least amount of time they'd agree to."

It wasn't about the money, but it still seemed like a big waste to him. "How much did that cost?"

"I can afford it."

"That's not the point."

"I wouldn't expect you to understand."

Quite frankly, once upon a time, right after a fairy-tale courtship and wedding, he'd thought Amy had been the easiest woman in the world to understand, to love and trust, to come home to. But she'd thrown him for a loop about six months ago, right about the time her mother passed away.

He'd told himself it was grief messing with her mind. But now? He didn't know what to think.

"Are you planning to move again?" he asked.

"No. I wouldn't do that to Callie."

He was glad to hear that. She'd done enough to the poor kid already—moved out of the only home she'd ever known, filed for divorce from her father. A man who'd do anything to provide for his family, by the way, but she'd thrown it all in his face.

He again glanced in the mirror, saw his daughter smiling at him, oblivious to the grown-up problems around her. "I realize you miss your mom, Amy. But to take on a search like that—"

"I didn't expect you to understand. You

hardly even knew my mother. In fact, I think you were still calling her Mrs. Barnes when she died."

He wasn't sure what she meant by that, so he spoke up in his own defense. "I used to call her Susan."

For some reason, he could imagine Amy rolling her eyes about now. She'd been doing that a lot in the past few months.

Where had they gone wrong? When had they gotten off track?

"For Pete's sake, Brandon. You even arrived late to the funeral."

He'd had to work that morning, and an important call had come in. He hadn't meant to be late. And then he'd run into traffic on Interstate 5—a fatal accident that had blocked all four lanes.

"I can't explain why this matters," Amy said. "Not so you would understand. But I have to do it. I've got this big, huge hole in my heart now that my mom's gone."

Brandon understood about holes in one's heart, gaps in one's life. He'd been dealing with that ever since Amy had dropped the bomb on him and moved out.

"What about me?" he asked. "What about *us?*"

"I'm sorry that our marriage wasn't strong enough, that we don't love each other like we once did. If it had been, if we did, we might have made it through anything."

She was probably right, but the trouble was, Brandon still loved Amy. And he feared he always would.

"What's done is done," she said.

Was it?

"Besides, I've always been in this alone."

Not by his choice, he wanted to say. But he kept his mouth shut. Things had changed; Amy had changed.

And even though he'd give anything to go back to the way things once were, she'd made it clear that she wasn't up for the trek.

Chapter 4

Barbara Davila walked along the tree-shaded sidewalk to Pacifica General Hospital with slow, deliberate steps. She'd hoped that the trips to visit her son would get easier, but they hadn't. Each day was still a struggle, and she suspected they would be until his discharge.

For almost two weeks now, Joey had been in the cardiac unit, and each time she pushed through the revolving doors into the lobby, she was swept back to a time in her life she'd tried to forget.

But maybe today would be different. There was talk of a heart bypass once his blood sugar level was acceptable, and she hoped that one day soon they'd announce he'd been stabilized, surgery had been scheduled, and he was finally on the road to recovery.

She was eager to get him home, where she could oversee his care and help him get back on his feet again.

She hadn't told him or his wife yet, although she was sure they'd be delighted, but she'd decided it would be best if he recovered at her house in Rancho Santa Fe. It was so much more spacious and comfortable than the small condo in Fairbrook where he and his wife lived. Barbara could also afford round-the-clock help and would spare no expense at making him comfortable. She just needed to get him home.

Who would have believed that something like this could have happened?

At forty-eight, Joseph Davila Jr. had appeared to be the picture of health, with a ready smile, a booming laugh, and a robust complexion. He ran every day—and worked out, too—but on the inside, where no one could see, he was a mess. And to make matters worse, his pancreas had been acting up and his heart had been a ticking bomb.

She entered the lobby, walked past the pink-frocked volunteers, made her way to the elevator, and rode it up to the third floor. While awaiting the doors to open, she wondered if she should have chosen to use the stairway for the exercise. After all, she had no idea what shape her own heart was in. But she'd worry about that later. She'd never liked hospitals and had managed to avoid them ever since her husband's recuperation at the military hospital in Honolulu, so she was in a hurry to get in and out.

Had it been anyone else, she'd have sent an expensive floral arrangement and come up with some plausible reason why she couldn't stop by for a visit. But this was Joseph Jr., her only son.

Her only child. She wouldn't—she *couldn't*—be anywhere other than here. So she pressed on and continued the forward momentum.

Whenever she found herself stressed, she'd learned to inhale deeply and blow it out, but she couldn't do that here. The medicinal smell was enough to send her running and gagging.

Besides the odor, everything about the hospital—the irritating squeak of rubber-soled shoes upon the polished linoleum, the hollow clunk of a plastic lunch tray on a cart, the blips and beeps of the machines keeping people alive—seemed to send her back in time to the mid-sixties. But she'd fought the mental spiral by forcing her thoughts on the present.

When she reached the nurses' desk, she waited for the woman on duty to glance up. When she did, Barbara said, "Good morning, Simone. How's Joey doing today?"

The dark-haired Florence Nightingale managed a smile. "About the same. His minister is with him now."

Barbara nodded, then proceeded to her son's private room. She'd never understood how Joey had come to be so religious, since he hadn't been raised in the church. Her mother had carted her off to Sunday school for as long as she could remember, and she'd refused to do that to her son.

So needless to say, Joey's faith had surprised her.

She could understand why it would flare up now, when his health and recovery were questionable, when he was facing his own mortality. But he'd held those same beliefs for years.

It probably had something to do with his grandmother's influence, which was one reason Barbara hadn't encouraged much of a relationship between her mother and her son while he was growing up. But once Joey had gotten a driver's license, there'd been no stopping him. He'd visited his grandma regularly, a practice that had continued even after he married.

In fact, as her mother slipped deeper into a fog of dementia, Joey had volunteered to take her in and let her live with him and his wife, rather than place her in a home.

Barbara had tried to talk him out of it, insisting that there were plenty of quality convalescent hospitals that were better equipped, better trained to handle Alzheimer's patients.

"If we put her there," Joey had said, "you'd never visit her."

Barbara hadn't argued that point. Everyone knew she hated medical facilities, even if they didn't have any idea why. But her mother didn't even recognize her these days anyway, so what would it hurt?

As Barbara entered Joey's private room, she spotted Craig Houston, the associate pastor of Joey's church, seated in the blue vinyl chair next to the hospital bed. When the fair-haired young man in his mid-twenties looked her way, she returned his smile.

There wasn't even the slightest resemblance between the men, since Joey had inherited his brown hair—now silver-laced at the temples—and olive complexion from his father's side of the family. Yet for a moment, seeing the two together, Barbara couldn't help wondering what her son's children might have grown up to look like had Cynthia, Joey's wife, been able to carry a pregnancy to term.

"Good morning," the pastor said. "How are you, Mrs. Davila?"

She supposed she should tell him he didn't need to be so formal, but she hated to get too chummy with a man of the cloth.

The next thing you knew, he'd be pressing her to attend Sunday services.

"You can call her Barbara," Joey said, his voice softer than it had been yesterday.

Weaker?

Oh, please, don't let him be failing, Barbara silently pleaded to no one in particular.

"Is that all right with you?" the pastor asked, his grin warm and friendly.

To call her Barbara? Not really, but she managed to revitalize her smile. "Of course." She broke eye contact with the minister and focused on her son. "I'm not going to stay long, honey. I just wanted to check on you and say hello. Any news on the surgery? Have they scheduled it?"

"Not yet."

An ache settled in her chest and fear clogged her throat, yet she tried to keep the optimism in her voice. "I'm sure we'll hear something soon."

A nurse popped into Joey's room to check his IV and take his vitals, and Barbara turned her head away. Distancing herself further, she walked to the window, where several plants and floral arrangements sat along the sill to brighten up the room. There was a basket of various plants that had been sent by one of Joey's neighbors, a vase of drooping carnations from someone at his office.

In the center of the display was a new arrival, a black ceramic vase holding a single red anthurium, an exotic, tropical flower with waxy leaves that reminded her of the many unique and colorful plants of Hawaii.

She felt herself hurtling back to 1966 all over again, and this time she couldn't stop it.

The Beatles, Bob Dylan.

Walter Cronkite, Vietnam.

The phone call that turned her life on end.

Is this Barbara Davila?

Yes.

Is Captain Joseph Davila your husband?

She'd wanted to hang up, to pretend the call hadn't come in, but she'd responded truthfully, her fingers clutched so tightly to the receiver that she'd thought her flesh would meld to plastic. *Yes.*

Your husband's plane went down.

Somehow, she'd managed to get through the heartbreaking, blood-pounding call—maybe because the caller had offered her hope by saying her husband had been seriously injured but had survived.

She'd left Joey in her mother's care that very day and had flown to Honolulu to be at Joseph's side. She supposed she should be happy that he'd returned from Vietnam, even though he'd been scarred on the right side of his face and still had to use a cane to walk. Many other soldiers and their families hadn't been so lucky.

Her mother had implied that Joseph's injury had been some sort of punishment for Barbara's rebellion.

Okay, so she hadn't actually come out and pointed her finger or said those very words, but Barbara knew her mother better than she knew anyone else in the world. And the accusation had been in her eyes.

Admittedly, for a while, Barbara's guilt had nearly consumed her, but she'd rallied; she'd had no choice.

From that moment on, she'd done everything she could to make things right, to be the best wife she could be, even though her husband had been left partially disabled.

And she'd succeeded. Hadn't she been the one to push Joseph to return to college and attend graduate school? To be all that he could be?

She'd been a devoted mother, too. The fact that she was here now was proof of that, wasn't it?

"Before I go," the minister said, drawing Barbara back to the present, "let's have a word of prayer."

She bristled, not wanting to be drawn to Joey's bedside and forced to pray. "I'm sorry. I don't have time for that. I really need to go, honey. I have an appointment and don't want to be late."

Pastor Craig looked at her as if he knew she was uneasy with the religious talk, but it wasn't as though she was a nonbeliever. She knew there was a creator, someone at the helm of fate. But it wasn't anyone she wanted to connect with. At least, not in a group setting.

"Okay, Mom." Joey cast her a knowing smile. "Thanks for coming by. We'll pray that you have a good day while we're at it."

"You're the one who needs strength and healing," she said.

Again, the young pastor nailed her with an expression that suggested he could see right through her, which was another reason she hated church and religious people. They seemed to think they had it all figured out, and they didn't.

No one did.

She made her way to her son's bedside and bent to give him a kiss on the cheek. "Take care of yourself, honey. And give me a call if there's any news. Or if you need anything at all."

Then she turned and walked out of the room as if one of the fallen angels were giving chase.

The next time Amy drove out to the house on Sugar Plum Lane, she took Callie with her. It was easier that way, she'd told herself.

Who knew when Brandon would show up again and throw off her plans?

And, quite frankly, she didn't appreciate his surprise visits.

"You're going to that old house again?" Callie asked as Amy secured her in her car seat.

"Yes, for a little while. I'm supposed to help the owners pack some things in boxes." Amy shut the rear door, then climbed behind the wheel and started the ignition.

She glanced into the rearview mirror before adjusting it and saw Callie fingering the straps of a pink Hello Kitty backpack that rested beside her car seat. The canvas pouch had been carefully packed with a coloring book, crayons, a couple of cartoon movies, and enough small toys to keep a child busy for hours.

Callie didn't appear to be eager for the adventure, though.

"It'll be fun," Amy told her. "You'll see. And on the way home, we'll stop by Roy's Burger Roundup for dinner."

"Can I get chicken sticks and fries?"

"You bet."

Ten minutes later, after parking in the driveway, Amy took Callie and several more empty boxes into the house.

As the child surveyed the living room, she frowned and scrunched up her nose. "It's all dark in here. And it smells yucky."

"There's a definite odor, but the house has been closed up for a long time. It just needs to be aired out." Amy strode toward the nearest window. "Give it a moment or two. It'll get better."

Callie dropped her backpack in the center of the floor, then plopped down beside it. "Will you turn on the lights?"

"Once I get things opened up, we won't need to do that." Amy pulled on the cord and drew back the drapes, letting in the sunlight. Then she unhooked the latch and slid open the window. There was a refreshing salt-laced breeze blowing in from the Pacific today, so that would help.

"Do you want me to put on a movie?" she asked the child.

"Okay. *The Little Mermaid.*"

Amy had brought along a DVD player, as well as some of her daughter's favorite movie cartoons. So she went out to the car to get it, then hooked it up to Ellie's television, put in the disk, and pushed Play.

While Callie settled in front of the TV screen, Amy carried a box to Ellie's bedroom so she could pack the woman's clothing and personal items.

As she progressed upstairs, the steps creaked in protest. She pressed on, using her free hand to grip the banister, which was made out of dark wood in a solid, bold style, the kind that tempted some children to use it as a slide. At least, that's what Amy might have tried to do, if she'd lived here as a girl. But something told her there hadn't been too many children in this house.

Maybe Ellie hadn't liked having little ones about.

At the top of the landing, a picture of two cherubs hung on the wall, which was the closest hint of children she'd yet to see.

Just below the angels sat an antique table, the top of which bore what had once been a lush, green pothos. But the plant, its leaves and vines now withered from lack of water, was nearly dead. It was as if Ellie had developed dementia overnight, and the family had just let the house go.

Yesterday, while cleaning out the pantry, she'd found a bag of cat food. She'd looked all over the house and yard for any other signs of a pet, but didn't see any. Hopefully, the plants were the only living things that had been abandoned.

Amy carried the pothos to the bathroom and turned on the faucet. After drenching the soil, she left the ceramic pot in the sink to drain and returned to the task at hand.

Once inside Ellie's bedroom, with its pale pink walls and white eyelet curtains, Amy scanned the furnishings. She wondered if they'd be considered antiques by anyone's standards. Some of them had to be at least forty to fifty years old.

The double bed had been covered haphazardly with a pink and white chenille spread. One edge hung noticeably lower than the other, as though it had been made by a child—someone Callie's age.

There was an indention on one of the pillows, as if Ellie might have lain down to take a rest before being taken away. Had she been feeling ill? Tired?

Had she only dreamed of hippies piping marijuana through the vents? Or had it been a full-blown hallucination?

She supposed it didn't matter.

A cedar chest sat at the foot of the bed, its varnish darkened and cracked with age. An old-style quilt with heart-shaped pieces had been folded carefully and draped over the top.

Interesting, Amy thought. The hearts were all the same size and stitched onto brown squares and quilted to a calico backing, but they had been made from a hodgepodge of fabric: satin, cotton, nylon, and flannel. Some of the material, like the pale yellow and white flannel with a baby duck print and the red gingham, appeared to have been washed many times, while the white satin hadn't.

She couldn't help running her fingers over the quilt, noting that the stitches were slightly uneven, the kind made by hand and not a machine. She wondered who'd made it. An older relative? A dear friend?

Ellie Rucker herself?

But enough woolgathering. She would never get anything done if she didn't stop dawdling. So she released the quilt and went to the closet. As she slid back the door, she spotted a gap between the hangers. Some of the woman's clothing appeared to be missing, but that would make sense if someone had moved her to a rest home.

After removing the remaining dresses, sweaters, and pants, she laid the clothing across the bed, then folded each item and placed it in a box. Next she emptied the drawers in the bureau, which was quick work. She suspected whoever had packed Ellie's essentials for her move to the home also had taken undergarments and nightgowns.

In the top drawer of the nightstand, she found a daily devotional, a white handkerchief with H.E.R. monogrammed near the edge, a booklet about angels, and a travel brochure for a cruise to Hawaii, among other things.

As Amy carefully emptied the drawer, she scanned each object before placing it in a second box. But when she withdrew a bundle of old letters, she paused. A white satin ribbon that had been tied and untied many times over held the missives together, as well as a small box of some kind. Still, she couldn't help noting the address on the top envelope, which had been sketched in a bold, cursive script.

Mrs. Eleanor Rucker
Star Route Three
Fairbrook, California
USA

It was from Private Harold Rucker.

Amy took a seat on the edge of the

bed, untied the satin, and set everything but the top envelope next to her. Then she removed the letter, unfolded the aged parchmentlike pages, and read the words.

Friday Nite

June 1, 1942

My Dearest Ellie,

I sure do miss you, Baby. I don't know how I'm going to get along without you for so long. I really do love you, Baby. All of my thoughts are of you. I can't help but think about the day when we will be together forever.

I sure hope you don't feel bad about getting married. I want you to know that I'll never regret it and hope you don't, either. I told you before that it was the smartest thing I ever did, and that's saying a lot coming from a smart guy like me.

I know there's a chance you could be pregnant, and if you are, it's all my fault. I should have taken better precautions, especially on our wedding night. But I have to tell you, Ellie, while I'd hate to have you go through something like that alone, I kind of hope you are.

Sure, I know you would rather not be. I remember you saying something about that.

So Ellie hadn't wanted children? Did she not like them? That certainly could be one reason there weren't any pictures of grandchildren in the house. At least none that were displayed.

According to the research, Eleanor Rucker was Barbara Davila's mother, so she'd at least had one child.

Amy continued to read.

I'll tell you again how I enjoyed myself that nite and how I'm looking forward to many more years of the same thing. When I get home, you will probably be just like a blushing bride again, huh? We will have been apart for so long that I'll have to start very slowly, like the first time.

Seriously, though, Ellie, I dream of the nights we spent together and of the ones in the future. No matter how distant they seem from us now, that day will come, and when it does, we will live happily together and raise as many kids as we can afford. OK?

That part didn't sound as though Ellie hadn't wanted children. Maybe it was just a matter of timing. After all, when this letter was written, Ellie was young and newly married. There was also a war raging in both Europe and the Pacific.

I love you, Baby. I know I keep saying that, but it's all I can think of. While I'm away, I'll probably write a hundred letters telling you the same things I just said, but bear with me because that's all I have to hold on to and it's all I can think about.

Well, honey, I have to go to chow in a few minutes, so I better sign off. We eat in groups, and if I miss my group, I miss chow. We only had one meal so far today, so I'm pretty hungry.

I know I'd told you that when I couldn't telephone any longer, that I would write every day, but that may not be possible. The first two days I wasn't feeling so hot, but today the sea is smoother and I feel better. Tomorrow, I'll tell you what has happened to me so far. I was going to start today with a sort of diary of what we are doing, but I got sidetracked on how much I love you, so I won't have time to do that now. I don't know whether I will mail all my letters in one package or separately, but when we hit port, I'll send them one way or another.

They're calling me, so I gotta go!

All my love, all my life,

Harold

Amy fingered the age-worn stationery that the young soldier had once held, that Ellie had cherished enough to keep near her bed. Letters that hadn't been meant for anyone's eyes but the man and his wife.

Still, she couldn't help reading the next dozen or so, which were just as touching and heartfelt as the first. But the last letter wasn't from Ellie's husband. It was from the War Department.

We regret to inform you that Private Harold E. Rucker was killed in action on June 10, 1942 . . .

The letter was as cold as it was official, and Amy couldn't imagine how Ellie must have felt when she'd received it. Had it been hand delivered, like it was often done in the movies?

But even then, it would have been a terrible blow.

Amy glanced at the box. She suspected it held a medal of some kind, and she'd been right. When she lifted the lid, she found a Purple Heart.

She ought to feel proud, patriotic, she supposed. After all, her great-grandfather had died for his country. But instead, she felt as though she'd lost someone, too.

As tears welled in her eyes and an ache settled in her heart, she sat on Ellie's bed for the longest time, grieving for the young bride who'd lost the love of her life.

Chapter 5

Gonzales Landscaping had been given the green light to start work for Mrs. Davila, so around lunchtime, Eddie drove to Sugar Plum Lane.

Earlier that morning, he'd hooked up a small trailer to his pickup so he could haul away the green waste. He figured after trimming all the trees and plants in the yard, he would end up with a couple of substantial loads.

Mrs. Davila had also decided to replace the sprinkler system, which meant there was plenty of work for him to do—at least a week's worth, if not more.

Since the landscaping company was busier than ever and his brother was short-handed, Eddie would be handling this project by himself, but that was okay. It was easier when he didn't have to deal with a lot of empty chatter. Besides, sometimes he preferred to be alone, a preference that had developed in prison and had continued after his parole.

He walked up the sidewalk to the blue house in which the attractive brunette lived with her kids. Her name, he'd been told, was Maria, but he supposed he ought to ask to speak to her husband, if he was home.

When he reached the door, he rang the bell. Moments later, a boy who was about ten or eleven answered.

"I'm Eddie with Gonzales Landscaping," he told the kid. "Are your parents home?"

"My mom is. My dad doesn't live here."

Eddie's first instinct was to tell the boy he shouldn't provide that kind of information to a virtual stranger, but he didn't think it was his place.

The kid turned his back to Eddie and called into the house, "Mom! Some guy wants to talk to you."

Moments later, footsteps sounded as Maria approached the front door. Several strands of her hair, which had been pulled back into a single braid hanging down her back, had come loose. And even though she was wearing an old pair of jeans and an oversized pink T-shirt, she was just as pretty as Eddie had remembered.

More so, actually.

When she reached the entry and their gazes met, her eyes, a soft caramel shade, locked on his. "Yes?"

Eddie introduced himself, since her son had only called her to the door.

"I'm doing some landscaping work at the Davila place," he added, "and the limb of the pepper tree in your backyard is weighing down on the fence. If we don't cut it back, it could mean a bigger, more expensive problem for you down the road."

As she nibbled on her lower lip, a V formed on her brow. "How much will that cost?"

A lot of guys might have tried to charge both neighbors, but Gonzales Landscaping didn't stoop to doing business like that, which was one of several reasons they were so busy. "It won't cost you anything.

I'll just cut the branch back, but I need your permission. I'd also like to come into your yard to do it, if that's all right."

She seemed to ponder the situation.

"Do you want me to show you the tree?" he asked.

"Maybe you'd better."

As he stepped off the porch and circled the house, Maria and her son followed him. Another little boy about the age of three also tagged along, his pudgy little legs hustling to keep up.

Before they reached the backyard, a girl in pigtails joined them. Eddie tried not to look at her, but he couldn't help sneaking a glance or two. Nor could he help noting that she had expressive brown eyes like her mommy's.

If his and Cecilia's baby had lived, she would have been about that age. But he shut out the thought, along with the grief and guilt.

"Mommy?" the girl asked. "When are we going to finish making the cookies?"

"In a few minutes," Maria said.

Once in the backyard, Eddie led the pretty mother and her pint-sized entourage to the tree and pointed out the limb that had created the problem.

"I can't believe I didn't notice this," Maria said.

"I'm sure you've got plenty to keep you busy."

The petite brunette glanced at him, and when their eyes met again, she smiled wryly, as if saying, "You have no idea just how busy I am."

It was weird, he thought, how they'd managed to communicate without saying any words. His parents had been able to do that, and it had always amazed him.

"I'm sure cutting back the branches will help," Maria said. "But won't we have to repair the fence? I mean, look at it. It's already leaning to the right. I don't want it to collapse."

"Once the weight is removed, it should be okay. But to be on the safe side, you can ask a handyman to check it out. He might want to shore up the post. If so, it shouldn't be too expensive to fix."

Again, she shot him a look, this one saying, "There isn't much money to spare." Then she returned her focus to the fence.

As they continued to stand in the yard, he caught a whiff of her scent. Something floral, he guessed, but it was so faint, it was hard to say. Still, he liked it.

The two little ones spotted a butterfly and chased after it, but the older boy remained.

Eddie couldn't help wondering if Maria was a day-care provider or whether she just had a bunch of kids. Not that it mattered.

Either way, she clearly had her hands full—and, apparently, no husband around to help her out. He wondered why, then shook off the curiosity. He didn't like people asking him questions about certain details of his life. Maria probably wasn't any different.

"So," he said, getting back on track, "do I have your permission to come into your yard and cut these limbs back?"

"Yes, of course." She stepped closer to the fence, checking out the way it bowed toward the Davilas' yard.

"Then if you don't mind, I'll go ahead and do it now." He figured it would be best to get the tree trimming out of the way before he tackled the job he came to do. He glanced at her roof and spotted a chimney. "I can haul it all away, if you want me to. Or I can cut it up into firewood and leave it for you to use. It's your call."

"I'd hate to make you go to any extra trouble. . . ."

He tossed her a crooked grin and shrugged. "It'll take me all of five minutes to cut the branch and to stack the wood. Don't give it another thought."

She let loose with a full-on smile, showing him an even prettier side of her. "I really appreciate this."

"No problem," he said, feeling a bit awkward and not quite sure why or what he ought to do about it.

"I'm going in to get the kids some lemonade," she said. "It's fresh squeezed. Can I bring you a glass, too?"

He really wasn't thirsty, but for some crazy reason, didn't want to decline. "Sure. That'd be nice. Thanks."

Again, the awkwardness seemed to wrap around them.

"Well . . ." She took a step back. "I guess I'll leave you to your work. If there's anything you need, let me know." But instead of going back to the house, she crossed the yard to where an old man sat in a rocking chair in the shade of an umbrella tree.

Eddie hadn't noticed him before, which was unusual, since he always tried to be alert and aware of his surroundings. But Maria's presence had thrown him off stride.

She said something to the man, whose craggy face lit up. Then she patted him on the forearm before heading toward the back porch.

As the old man's gaze connected with Eddie's, they nodded in a silent greeting.

"Is that your grandfather?" he asked the boy.

"Nope. He lives with us, though. And he's kind of like family. I don't know what his real name is, but we call him Captain."

Eddie waited for the kid to explain, but he didn't offer up anything else.

"Captain?" Eddie asked. "Is he retired from the military?"

"Yeah, he used to be in the Army, but not the regular one."

"Oh, yeah?" Eddie stepped away from the tree and started back for the truck, his mind on his work and not so much on the chatter.

But the boy continued to move with him, as if the two had become friends. "He was in the Salvation Army. You ever hear of that?"

"Yeah," Eddie said while walking. "But it's not the same kind of army you're probably thinking about."

"I know. But I think he was still a hero."

Their feet crunched on dried leaves and twigs, and while something told Eddie to let the subject drop, he couldn't help adding, "The Salvation Army doesn't fight wars."

"Captain said something about spiritual battles, but I don't know what he meant by that. Sometimes he gets a little mixed up."

This time, Eddie let the subject drop completely. And, thankfully, so did the kid.

As they walked along the side of the house the boy asked, "Where are you going? Are you leaving?"

"I need to get the chain saw from the truck."

"Need some help?"

Not from a kid. Ramon always stressed about workmen's comp issues and safety procedures, and he'd probably be quick to point out the child labor law, even though the two Gonzales brothers had grown up on the Rensfield estate and had worked alongside their old man for years. It's where they'd both learned the ins and outs of landscaping. And where they'd also learned how to become responsible members of the family.

But for some reason, he felt sorry for the kid and softened. "Sure, you can do something for me. But once I start up the chain saw, you'll need to stand back."

"Okay. I'll hang out with Captain and watch, if that's okay. I don't have anything else to do."

"What about your friends?" Eddie asked, thinking they'd both be better off if the kid went off to play. "Do any of them live near you?"

"Yeah, a couple of them do. But one guy, Jason, has strep throat and my mom won't let me play with him. And Bobby, the other one, is on vacation with his dad."

They walked in silence for a beat, until Eddie's curiosity won out.

"Do you ever go on vacation with your father?" Eddie asked, kicking himself the moment he did.

"Nope. Never."

So Maria's ex was completely out of the picture.

Eddie returned to the pickup, reached in back for the canvas drop cloth he used to carry the green waste from the yard to the truck and trailer, and handed it to the boy.

As they made their way back to the tree, Eddie spotted a beat-up hardball under a scraggly bush that grew near the fence. He stopped to pick it up, noticing that its once-red stitching was coming apart, and handed it to the kid. "Do you play baseball?"

"Nope. I thought about it a couple of times, but my mom can't take me to practices."

Ramon worked with kids on a special league, one that catered to kids at risk. Eddie helped him once in a while, when he had time, and he'd seen how sports could help a kid stay on the straight and narrow. And how a good man could provide a boy with a positive role model.

"My brother's a coach," Eddie said, "and sometimes he has to go pick kids up and take them home. In fact, he's happy to help out whenever he can."

"Yeah, well, my mom doesn't like to ask

people to do her favors. You know what I mean?"

Eddie nodded. His parents had been like that, too—not wanting to put anyone out.

"Some of the moms find it easier to car-pool," Eddie said.

"Yeah, well, I don't think baseball would work out for me all that much anyway."

"Why not?"

"My mom needs me to help out around here."

"Why?" Eddie wasn't sure why he bothered to ask. He and Ramon had both done more than their share of family chores when they'd been kids.

"You know, with the little kids and the old people and all."

"Old people?" Eddie shot a glance at Captain, who was seated all alone.

"Yeah. The Captain and Ellie."

"Who's Ellie? His wife?"

"Nope. She used to live next door before she got funny."

"Funny?"

"Well, not in a way that makes you laugh. But in a weird way that's kind of sad. It's also kind of a pain because we have to tell her everything, like when to get up and go to bed, when to go to the bathroom. You know."

No, he didn't know. And the boy seemed to read it in his expression.

"It's like when my mom took in other people's kids to watch. Now she's babysitting old people. But Captain's kind of cool. You should meet him."

Not today. Eddie had done enough talking. It was time to get busy. Yet he couldn't help tossing another glance at the old man, and then at the back door of Maria's house, where she'd slipped inside.

It seemed that she did indeed have her hands full.

And he had the strangest compulsion to offer to help her in any way he could.

At a quarter after two, Brandon looked up from his work and slowly shook his head. He'd nearly skipped lunch again, a habit he was trying to kick.

Six months ago, working overtime wouldn't have bothered him a bit. In fact, he used to keep snacks in his desk drawer to keep him going until the end of the day. But ever since Amy moved out, he'd been trying to turn over a new leaf.

So he logged off the computer, snatched his jacket from the hanger in the closet, and headed out of the high-rise office building to get a bite to eat.

He told Kara Grayson, his secretary, that he'd be back in a half hour or so. Then he walked out the glass doorway and made his way to the elevator. There, while he waited for one of the cars to stop on the twenty-third floor and for the doors to open, he glanced out the window that provided a view of downtown San Diego, as well as a glimpse of the harbor.

A cruise ship was docked at the Embarcadero, where it waited for passengers to board for a trip to who-knew-where.

Amy had wanted to plan a cruise for their seventh anniversary, but Brandon had put her off, saying he was too busy for a vacation.

"Maybe next year," he'd told her.

But now it looked as though they wouldn't be doing anything special to celebrate this time around, either. Amy had been adamant that their marriage was over.

How was that for luck?

All Brandon had ever wanted was to be successful, to be a good provider and someone his wife and child could be proud of. But apparently, according to Amy, he'd overdone it. Yet in spite of what she might think, he loved her and Callie. He just hadn't realized how much until she moved out of the La Jolla house and took their daughter with her.

And what made it all worse was that he didn't have a clue how to make things right, which was as unsettling as it was surprising. At work, he tackled cases all the time that had fallen apart for other attorneys. He was good at picking up the pieces, at structuring a new game plan, and moving ahead full throttle. It was a skill he'd learned early in life.

As a teenager, he'd figured out a way to move out of the squalid apartment in which he'd grown up, a way to break free from the lousy childhood he'd had. Education had been his ticket out, his only path to a better life than the one he'd known so far. So he'd taken the ball and run with it, snagging scholarships that took him all the way to law school and helped him land a position with a top firm. He'd even made partner in short order.

Everyone at Price, Feller, Goldstein,

and Masterson considered him a success and one of the top attorneys in the state. But little did they know that, these days, their boy wonder went home each night to an empty house in an upscale neighborhood, where he wandered the expansive rooms all by himself.

Of course, Jake Goldstein probably knew, since their wives were friends, but Jake hadn't said a word about it. And neither had Brandon.

What was he supposed to admit, that his beautiful wife had left him?

He could almost hear them all whispering behind his back, "What a loser, Masterson."

Brandon cringed at the thought. He hadn't failed at anything in his life, other than at marriage and family, which he blamed on his old man. If he'd had a better role model, if he'd grown up in a loving, two-parent home. . . .

He blew out a sigh and continued the ten-block walk to the harbor, where a guy ran a stand near the water and sold the best hot dogs Brandon had ever tasted. He sure had a hankering for a couple of them today.

As the red-striped umbrella that shaded the stand came into view, he heard whistling to his right and glanced toward the musical sound.

A man seated on a bench met his gaze in one of those weird, déjà vu moments, and the whistling stopped.

A homeless man, Brandon suspected.

He didn't look particularly dirty, though, but his beard and hair needed a trim, and his worn and frayed clothing suggested he'd hit upon hard times.

Brandon sympathized with guys like that, but he never gave them cash. Not when he wasn't sure how they'd spend the money. But he didn't mind buying them something to eat, so he continued on to the stand with that in mind.

He could smell the meat cooking, and his stomach growled in anticipation.

"Hey there." Hank, the middle-aged hot-dog hawker, broke into a bright-eyed grin when he spotted Brandon's approach. "How's it goin', Mr. Masterson?"

"Not bad." Brandon pointed to the plump wieners on the grill. "Give me four, and put them in two sacks."

"You got it."

Five minutes later, Brandon returned to the bus stop.

"You hungry?" he asked the shaggy-haired guy on the bench.

The man, his eyes a remarkable shade of blue, looked up and smiled as he took the bag Brandon offered. "Thanks."

Apparently assuming that Brandon meant to join him for lunch, he scooted over, freeing up a place to sit.

Usually, Brandon would have declined and headed back to the office, but for some crazy reason—hunger, most likely—he took a seat.

"That was nice of you," the guy said.

Brandon didn't respond. He'd gone through a few hungry days himself, and it was a do-unto-others sort of thing. So he looked out at the water, at a couple of noisy seagulls swooping near the surface and back up again. Then he dug into the bag for his hot dog.

"You know," the homeless man said, "it's never too late to change."

Brandon figured the stranger was sharing an epiphany he'd recently had. "You're right about that."

"Sometimes fixing a key relationship

can help you make sense of everything else in life," he added.

Brandon didn't feel the need to comment.

"It can also help a man rebuild a marriage."

Now *that* hit a little too close to home and caught Brandon's attention. "What are you talking about?"

"You got a raw deal as a kid, and it's created havoc in your interpersonal relationships ever since."

"Me?" Brandon merely stared at him. Other than his dad, no one had screwed him over. But that was in the past. And it certainly hadn't caused his breakup with Amy. So he shook off the pseudo-psychic vibe, but he couldn't quite ignore the words. "What in the world makes you think that?"

"There's a sadness about you. It's obvious to anyone who gets within a few feet of you. You look like someone who's down on his luck."

Oh, for Pete's sake. How could his rough-edged bench mate, of all people, make a leap like that?

Brandon was wearing an Armani suit

today. Okay, so he'd left the tie back in the office, but he clearly wasn't unkempt or wearing ragged clothes.

On the other hand, he risked a glance across the bench at the man who not only appeared to be struggling to get by in life, but who was probably a taco short of a combination plate.

Deciding to put some distance between them, Brandon folded the remainder of his lunch in the waxed paper in which it had been wrapped. As he got to his feet, he bit back the urge to respond, "You're one crazy dude."

What had compelled him to sit next to a guy like that in the first place?

"Believe it or not," the man added, "it's a fairly easy fix."

What was? Backpedaling? Going back in time?

Hunting down his old man only to find he'd probably drank himself to death by now?

Winning back Amy?

Brandon slowly shook his head but held his tongue. Who was giving the advice here? Who was offering whom a handout?

He turned away, intending to return to

the office where sanity reigned, only to hear the man say, "Just because you messed up once doesn't mean you have to keep doing the wrong thing."

Brandon froze in his tracks. Then he looked over his shoulder at the guy most people would classify as a total failure. "Who said I 'messed up'?"

"Didn't you?" Those blue eyes, clear and piercing, seemed to chip away at Brandon's façade, the one he'd created while in high school and had polished to perfection in college. "Everyone makes mistakes that can have an unexpected effect on the lives of others. And it's tough to correct what's already been done. But the future offers healing, if you'll open your heart. And making peace with the past is often the first step."

Brandon glanced out over the harbor, felt the sea breeze ruffle his hair. Was he suggesting that Brandon acknowledge defeat? That he make peace with what he'd done, what he'd failed to do?

Or was he just plain crazy?

"The next time you're in Fairbrook," the man said, "stop by the soup kitchen at Parkside Community Church."

Brandon stiffened. Fairbrook was only ten miles from here, but other than tracking down Amy on Sugar Plum Lane, he'd never even driven through the town; he'd never had any reason to.

"Why would I want to do that?" he asked.

"To face the past and make amends."

"With whom?" Brandon asked, chuckling in an effort to blow the guy off.

The man took another bite of his hot dog, then looked out over the water, at the ships and beyond. "You'll figure it out."

Brandon dismissed the encounter, telling himself the guy was off his rocker, that he was homeless for a reason.

"And if you *don't* catch on," the guy said, those blue eyes peeling back the last gilded layer of Brandon's armor, "talk to Pastor Craig."

"About what?"

"Just tell him Jesse sent you."

The Italian leather of Barbara's Gucci pumps clicked and tapped against the polished linoleum as she stepped off the elevator and turned left toward the cardiac unit on her way to visit Joey again.

She caught a whiff of the food cart, the scent of which mingled with the ever-present odor of disinfectant and pungent pharmaceuticals that seemed to drip from the walls.

A wave of nausea gripped her, just as it had in 1966, when she'd arrived at the hospital in Honolulu and had to face her husband for the first time since she'd done the unspeakable.

She'd thought that she'd caught an intestinal flu bug, since she'd felt absolutely fine for the first half of her pregnancy. Then as if a curse had been set in motion, the nausea had struck with a vengeance when she'd had to walk into Joseph's room.

She'd thought for sure that he would see the betrayal in her eyes. But he hadn't, and she'd considered it a stroke of luck.

The loose-fitting clothing she'd worn had covered a multitude of sins. And he'd been too wrapped up in himself—in the seriousness of his injury and the resulting depression after learning that there was a possibility he'd never walk again—to notice her bulging waistline.

Barbara had stayed in Hawaii for three

weeks that summer, then she'd returned to Fairbrook when they'd sent Joseph to a rehabilitation hospital on the mainland. Two months later, just before he was discharged from the service and sent home, she'd gone into premature labor.

Hadn't that been an even bigger stroke of luck? A sign that she'd be able to wipe the slate clean? That no one needed to ever know what she'd done?

After she'd given birth to a four-pound baby girl, a child she'd refused to look at before signing the adoption papers, the nursing staff hadn't been able to bundle her up and take her away soon enough.

Thank God Joseph had never found out.

He'd not only survived his injuries, but their marriage had survived her indiscretion.

Over the next few decades, Joseph had gone on to make something of his life. He was now a successful businessman, the CEO of an aerospace company, and seriously considering a run for Congress next year.

Barbara had no doubt he'd make it. Her husband had been destined for big things, which was why he'd been spared in Vietnam.

Thank goodness, it was behind them now, although a ghost from the past had almost ruined it six months ago.

She could nearly hear the woman's soft, almost frail voice on the phone now.

"Mrs. Davila?"

"Yes?"

"Barbara Rucker Davila?"

"Yes," she'd said again, this time louder. She'd hoped the caller would cut to the chase. She'd had an appointment for a manicure and pedicure that afternoon and needed to leave.

"I'm Susan Rossi," the woman said. "You don't know me, but I think you're my mother."

Everything Barbara had set to rights had turned topsy-turvy again, but she'd pulled out of the tailspin long enough to say, "I'm sorry. You have the wrong number. I'm not your mother. Please don't ever call this house again."

"But—"

Barbara had hung up the phone. Her heart had pounded like an old-fashioned steam locomotive, and she'd felt the blood pulsating in her ears. She'd managed to keep her secret for nearly forty-five years.

And she'd be darned if she would let it out now.

Chapter 6

The next day, as Amy drove down Sugar Plum Lane, she spotted the gardener's pickup parked in front of the house, but there was no sign of Eddie in the yard.

The lawn had been mowed and trimmed, though. And a sprinkler, which had been attached to a hose, was spraying water over the driest patch of brown grass. So Amy suspected he was in the back.

"How come we keep coming here?" Callie asked, as Amy pulled into the driveway and parked.

"Because Mommy is renting this house for a while. That means we can come by and go inside whenever we want to." Amy glanced into the rearview mirror, caught a wisp of confusion in her daughter's eyes. "I'm also packing things in boxes for the lady who used to live here."

The answer seemed to satisfy Callie for a moment, then she asked, "But we're not going to move all our stuff *again,* are we?"

"No, honey." Relocating from the sprawling, custom-built house on the bluffs in La Jolla to the three-bedroom townhome in Del Mar had been tough enough on the child.

"Good," Callie said, as she unbuckled the seat belt that secured her in her booster. "I don't like moving."

Guilt, as it was sometimes prone to do, sliced through Amy, reminding her that she'd made the decision to uproot Callie even though her mom had advised against it before she died.

"Don't you like the new house?" Amy asked.

"It's okay. I like my new room better than the old one, but I miss my swing set. It was the funnest one in the whole wide world."

Callie had spent hours playing on the

combination swing set/climbing structure, but it had been too big and bulky to move. Besides, it would have never fit in the little patio area that now served as their only yard.

"But we *do* have the community park," Amy reminded her, the tone of her voice holding a bit more enthusiasm than she felt. "And you get to play in the old backyard whenever you visit Daddy."

"Yeah, but I don't see him that much."

Actually, it seemed that Callie saw Brandon more now than ever before, since she'd usually been asleep whenever he'd decided to finally leave the office and come home.

"I wish we still lived in the other house," Callie said.

Amy didn't. The townhome was so much warmer and cozier. And while she still couldn't claim to be happy, she didn't feel nearly as sad and lonely there.

For a moment, she had to acknowledge that she still missed her mother, that she still grieved her death. And that the move hadn't changed any of that.

Now's not the time to make a decision like this, Brandon had said when Amy announced she was moving out. *Your mother just died. Leaving me isn't going to make you happy. Nothing will.*

I've wanted out of our marriage for a long time, she'd countered. *And my mom tried to talk me out of it. To be honest, since it seemed to give her peace thinking we'd worked through our problems, I put it off until after she was gone.*

I'll admit that I'm to blame for some of your unhappiness, honey. But not all of it. A lot of your misery comes from seeing your mom so sick and losing her. Divorcing me isn't going to make the grief go away.

Instead of continuing to explain her decision, Amy had clamped her mouth shut and started to pack. She'd never stood a chance arguing against a skilled attorney who could make a solid point even if he didn't believe what he was saying.

Brandon had been right, though. After she'd moved out, she still hurt. But she couldn't help believing she'd made the right decision.

When her mother died, Brandon should have realized that she would need him around more than ever. That she would covet his love, understanding, and support.

So no matter how she looked at it, he was to blame for the divorce.

As Amy shut off the ignition, she noticed Maria standing in her own yard, talking to her two youngest children.

Maria waved, and when she spotted Callie in the backseat, she placed her hand on her daughter's shoulder and guided her toward the shrubbery that divided the properties in the front.

Amy supposed there was no getting around introducing the girls now, so she got out of the car, opened the rear passenger door, and helped her daughter out. While Callie reached for her doll, Amy snatched the pink backpack and the additional packing boxes she'd brought.

"Hi," Maria said to the child. "You must be Callie. This is Sara."

The girls looked at each other and smiled shyly, but neither spoke.

"What have you got there?" Maria asked, looking at the doll Callie carried.

"This is Tina."

"I have a baby, too," Sara said, warming

up and pressing forward. "Do you want to see her?"

Callie nodded, and the dark-haired girl dashed toward the house, a ponytail swishing along her back.

"How's the packing coming along?" Maria asked Amy.

"Slower than I expected." Actually, she'd found herself taking her time, getting to know her mother's biological grandmother better. And with each moment she spent in the house, she sensed a growing connection to the woman who'd once lived in the old Victorian. It was almost eerie. Still, she wasn't about to share what she was doing with the neighbors. It was bad enough that Brandon knew what she was up to, that he thought she'd overstepped a boundary of some kind.

"If you'd like to get some work done without Callie underfoot," Maria said, "she can come over and help Sara and me roll out tortillas. I mixed up the dough early this morning, and we were going to head inside and finish them."

"I've heard making homemade tortillas isn't as easy as it looks."

Maria laughed. "These will taste good,

but we'll probably end up with some odd shapes."

Amy smiled, imagining they would. "Callie likes to cook and bake. Are you sure you don't mind?"

"Not at all. It'll be nice for Sara to have another little girl to play with for a change."

"All right. When you get finished, why don't the girls come over here and watch TV. I have a DVD player set up and several Disney movies for them to choose from."

"That sounds great."

Sara came back outside with her doll just as the gardener returned from the backyard.

"How's it going?" Amy asked Eddie.

"It's all right. I was on the side of the house and heard you two talking. It reminded me that I forgot to have Maria sign a release form for me to cut her tree yesterday."

"But you've already done the work," Maria said.

"Yeah, well. . . ." Eddie shrugged, and a crooked smile stretched across his face. "My brother is a real stickler for formalities, and it'll make my life a whole lot easier if I get the paperwork in order—even if it's after the fact."

"Then you'd better get the form." Maria's eyes glistened with humor. "I wouldn't want you to get into trouble."

As Eddie started for his pickup, Amy said, "Should I come and get the girls in an hour or so?"

"Don't worry about it. I'll bring them back when we're done."

"Then if you'll excuse me, I'll go inside and get busy."

As Amy unlocked the front door of Ellie's house and went inside, Maria watched her go.

She probably should have mentioned that Ellie was living with her. It wasn't as though it was a big secret, although Barbara thought it was.

"Don't let the new neighbors know that my mother is living with you," she'd said when she'd called to tell Maria someone was leasing the house. "I don't want them bothering her. I've hired a property manager to deal with any issues that might crop up."

Maria could understand that, but it wouldn't take more than a few moments of conversation for anyone to realize Ellie wasn't going to be able to deal with a leaky toilet or a faulty furnace. Still, Maria would look out for her as long as she could.

The trouble was, she didn't know how much longer she could keep Ellie. The poor woman's memory seemed to be fading more each day. And before long, she and the Davilas would all have to face the truth: Ellie would have to move to a convalescent hospital to live out her final days.

"Here you go," Eddie said, returning with a clipboard that had a sheet of paper attached.

Maria couldn't help noting how the sun shimmered off the dark strands of his hair, how beads of sweat and a smudge of dirt marred his brow.

He was a handsome man. And younger than she was.

Not that it mattered. Nothing would become of her fleeting attraction to him. A guy like that wouldn't want to be strapped to a single mom with three kids. And even if he did? She wouldn't risk heartbreak and disappointment again. Her ex had proven to be a loser in so many ways.

"It's a pretty standard form," Eddie said, handing it to her.

He was right, Maria decided, so she signed her name, giving Gonzales Landscaping permission to enter her yard and cut her tree limb—after the fact.

"What's the date?" she asked.

"Yesterday was Wednesday, the fourth."

She completed the form and returned the clipboard to Eddie. Sometimes her days blurred into one another. Had a week gone by already?

Barbara Davila usually stopped by on Tuesdays to see her mother, although with her son in the hospital, she'd missed a couple of weeks.

"You know," Eddie said, "my brother coaches a kids' baseball team, and I might be able to get your son on it. If so, I can take him back and forth to practices for you."

The comment, it seemed, had come out of the blue, and she couldn't help wondering why.

Yesterday, while Eddie had cut the tree limb in the backyard, Danny had stuck to him like glue. She'd glanced out the window several times and seen them talking, but hadn't thought anything of it.

Had Danny mentioned that he'd wanted to play Little League, but that it hadn't worked out?

Was that why he'd been so unhappy lately? Did he resent having to stick around the house so much of the time?

Maria crossed her arms and shifted her weight to one hip. "Did Danny put you up to asking me?"

"No, I'm afraid I came up with the idea all by myself."

"Why? He must have said something to you."

"Not really."

Did she dare tell Eddie about the problems she'd been having with her son?

Or had Danny already revealed that, giving the situation his own spin?

"I was just making conversation with him," Eddie said. "And I asked if he played baseball. He went on to say that you needed his help around the house, but that it was okay. He wasn't all that big on sports. But . . ."

"You didn't believe him?"

"Not really." Eddie studied her with an intensity that surprised her, unnerved her. "You seem uneasy about something. What's wrong?"

She'd never been one to open up to strangers, but for some reason, she couldn't hold back from this one. Maybe because Danny had already reached out to him and she hoped to find a mediator, someone who could make things go back to being the way they used to be.

"Nothing's wrong," she said. "Not really. It's just that I'm having some problems with him. He's always been a happy kid and easy to get along with. Helpful, too. But he's . . . Well, I don't know if he's unhappy, going through a rebellious stage, or both."

"Getting involved in sports might help. Of course, the team Ramon coaches is made up of kids at risk. So I'm not sure how you'd feel about having Danny play with them, but they're basically good kids. They just have a couple of strikes against them."

"They're at risk?" she asked. "For what?"

"Getting into trouble. Each of them has at least one parent in jail or in prison. So they need the structure and the outlet that baseball provides."

She stiffened. Had Danny told Eddie about his dad? About how he was serving time for killing a man? She hated to ask. Instead, she said, "The season's almost over. Isn't it?"

"Actually, the team isn't affiliated with Little League. It'll last all summer. And then they'll play football in the fall and basketball in the winter."

"Who do they play against?"

"It's a new county-wide program. Quite a few of the bigger cities have received grants to fund the league and to provide equipment. And so far, it's been a big success."

Danny must have said something, although that was surprising. As far as she knew, he usually kept that secret close to the vest. And she couldn't blame him. It had been a crushing blow to her, too. To make matters worse, she'd had to stay in L.A. to testify. The details of Ray's affair with a married woman had come out during the trial, and it had been ugly—just the kind of sordid story the media loved. The Los Angeles newspapers' and the local television stations' coverage of the trial hadn't allowed her or Danny a moment's peace or privacy.

In fact, she'd taken the kids back to Fairbrook as soon as she could. She'd needed to keep them away from the embarrassing limelight and give them time to forget.

As much as she'd like to keep the conversation away from talk about her ex, about the heartache he'd dumped on her and the kids, she couldn't help asking, "Did Danny tell you about his dad?"

"Not really. He just said that he doesn't live here. And that he doesn't see him very often."

"My ex-husband is in prison," Maria admitted.

Had the news shocked him? Or had she only imagined seeing the twitch in his eye, the tension in his jaw?

"I had no idea," he finally said. "When I mentioned the ball team and the kids at risk, I was just throwing an idea out there. I wasn't even sure if the league rules would allow him to play in the games, although I figured he could at least practice with them."

"Unfortunately, Danny qualifies to play." Her voice came out soft, resigned.

"I'm sorry," Eddie said. "Having a family member in prison is tough on everyone."

"It's just one of those things, something we've learned to live with. I was hoping Danny had pulled out of it, that he'd put it all behind him, but now I'm not so sure that he has."

"Then maybe playing with the team would help."

"It might make it worse. If he didn't mention anything to you, he might prefer to keep his ugly family secret to himself."

"I could talk to him. Maybe take him to watch the kids practice."

She wasn't sure how to voice her objections, her concerns. But maybe it would be best to level with him.

"Truthfully?" she said. "I'd rather see him run around with normal kids, those who have two parents in the home. I think it would be best if he was able to see examples of happy families."

"Before you make a decision, maybe you and Danny ought to come out to Mulberry Park and watch the kids play. My brother runs a tight ship. I think you'll be surprised to see how good he is with those boys. And at how they look up to him."

"I'll have to think about it." She'd also have to find someone to sit with Ellie and the younger kids.

Hilda and Walter weren't due back from their cruise for another ten days, so they wouldn't be around.

When someone tugged on her shirt, she glanced down to see Sara standing at her side.

"When are we going to make the tortillas?"

"Right now, honey. I'm sorry."

"Are you making them yourself?" Eddie asked.

Maria nodded. "There's nothing like warm, homemade tortillas."

"You've got that right." A smile lit his face, and she found it difficult to tear her gaze away from his.

But she'd promised to take the girls in the house. And she had to check on Ellie. There was no telling what the poor old woman might get into or where she might wander.

Sadly, Ellie Rucker wasn't the same dear neighbor that she'd once been.

Inside the Rucker house, in one of the spare bedrooms, Amy knelt beside the open closet door, where she'd found a small blue plastic storage container filled with paid bills, canceled checks, and tax returns. She'd only taken a cursory glance at them, assuming that Ellie's family would have to go through them and decide which to keep and which to shred.

Since the contents were already packed, she pulled out the entire container, got to her feet, and carried it to the area in the living room where she'd been stacking the other boxes she'd packed.

Then she returned to the closet, wondering how Ellie could have managed to fill such a small space to the brim with so many odds and ends. Someone had built shelves along the back wall, each of which was loaded with things the woman had accumulated over the years.

Amy's gaze lit on a large red carrying case adorned with hand-painted white roses. She unlatched the metal clips and opened it. Inside, she spotted a keyboard and realized it was a musical instrument of some kind.

An accordion? she wondered. She'd never seen one up close before.

Had her great-grandmother been a musician?

Apparently so.

Rather than set the instrument aside, she pulled it out of the case, unhooked the sides, and allowed it to expand. Then she slipped her arms into the straps. She didn't have a clue what to do next, but she'd had piano lessons as a child and knew her way around a keyboard. Before long, she'd gotten comfortable with the feel, with the sound, and was playing a melody by heart.

She wasn't sure how long she sat there, fiddling with the instrument and trying her hand at a simple tune. She wasn't a talented pianist as her mother had been, but she did okay. She'd never stopped to think that she and her mom might have inherited their musical skill from the family they'd never known.

After twenty minutes or so, Amy closed

up the accordion and returned it to its case. Then she took it to the living room and left it with the growing stack of items that had belonged to Ellie.

When she reentered the upstairs bedroom, which she'd begun to think of as the yellow room because of the sunny color of the walls and the old-style bedspread with a daffodil print, she spotted an interesting painting on the wall. It was a watercolor of children playing at a park on a summer day.

She hadn't paid much attention to any of the framed artwork that decorated the house, but this particular painting called to her, and she drew close enough to note that it was an original and not a print. It was also very good. She looked at the bottom corner for the name of the artist. It was painted by E. Rucker.

Ellie had been quite a woman, Amy realized, regretting that they'd never met.

But standing around bemoaning the fact wasn't doing her any good, so she returned to the closet, removed the items off the shelves, and carefully placed them in the boxes she'd brought. When she ran across a book, a journal of some kind, she stopped to open the blue floral cover and scan the pages.

To Eleanor Kathleen Gordon on her birthday—

From her loving mother

May the thoughts and dreams you write upon these pages always be happy and bright. And may all your wishes come true.

Unable to stifle her curiosity, Amy carried the journal to the bed, took a seat on the edge of the mattress, and began reading.

April 24, 1941

Today was my eighteenth birthday, and what a lovely day it was. The sun was warm, yet there was a refreshing breeze that blew in from the ocean. That, I think, is one of the nicest things about living in Fairbrook: being so close to the beach and enjoying a temperate climate all year round.

Of course, the best and nicest thing of all is having met Harold and becoming his friend.

After a birthday dinner, in which Grandma and Grandpa Carlson took part, Mother presented me with this journal in which to write my thoughts. She and Daddy also gave me an easel and watercolors. We had pot roast for dinner, my favorite meal, and a seven-layer chocolate fudge cake for dessert. What a treat!

The best surprise of all was when Harold stopped by the house to see me and asked if I'd go for a walk with him. I, of course, said, "Yes!"

Two days before, Mother had advised me to take things slow. "Don't make it too easy on that young man," she'd said. But Daddy had disagreed with her. "Girls who play hard to get sometimes don't get caught, Emma." So I took Daddy's words to heart. I can't imagine chasing Harold Rucker away by pretending to be coy.

So this afternoon, as he and I strode down Sugar Plum Lane, away from my house, his arm brushed mine several times. I wanted so badly to take the initiative, but whenever he comes near me, I get a swarm of butterflies in my tummy.

Finally, he reached for my hand, and even a flock of sparrows in the treetops seemed to sing out with joy.

As we strolled along Canyon Drive, we chatted about everything and nothing at all. There isn't anyone I'd rather be with than Harold.

And you'll never guess what happened when he brought me home.

He kissed me, and it was magic!

Amy read several more entries, getting a feel for the vivacious young woman who was a lot like some of her friends had been right after high school graduation.

Her *friends*?

What about *herself*?

At one time, Amy had been so sure about her feelings for Brandon, so confident that their marriage would last forever, that she hadn't been able to imagine them being anything other than happy.

Their kisses had been magical, too. But whatever they'd shared had been fleeting.

As she continued to read, she learned that Harold, along with a couple of his buddies, had joined the Army shortly after December 7, 1941. Ellie had been both proud of his courage and scared to death that something would happen to him.

They'd married on the tenth of December, and they'd spent their honeymoon in a cabin on Palomar Mountain. One of Harold's letters had said as much.

Needless to say, Ellie didn't go into any detail, other than to say she was blissfully happy to be Harold's wife and that she was painfully sad to know he would be shipping out soon.

February 10, 1942

When Harold gets home, he'll be happy to know that I've been saving as much money as I can so that we can buy our very own house someday. The only expenses I have are the costs of a daily RC Cola and a postage stamp. Harold doesn't write very often, but I keep his letters under my pillow, tied together with the satin ribbon from my bridal bouquet.

It seems the perfect way to keep them, don't you think?

As Amy continued to read, Ellie became so real to her that she couldn't help thinking that if they'd been the same age and if their paths had somehow been able to cross, they might have become good friends.

March 16, 1942

I went to the doctor today, and my suspicions proved true. Harold and I are going to have a baby at the end of September. I'm both scared and excited. I can't wait to tell him. I know he will be thrilled to know that he's going to be a father. As soon as I finish this entry in my journal, I'm going to write and tell him the good news.

I hope and pray that the war will be over soon, and that Harold will return home. Then we'll buy a little house in Fairbrook, where we'll raise a family. I love children, and I hope that we can have as many as we're able to afford.

Had Harold ever learned that Ellie was pregnant?

The letters Amy read yesterday suggested that he'd thought about the possibility yet didn't know for sure. Had Ellie's news reached him before he died?

Amy read on, but long before the pages in the journal were filled, Ellie's entries came to an abrupt stop.

June 13, 1942—

Harold—

My sweet Harold—

They say he was a hero, but—

I won't be writing for a while.

Tears welled in Amy's eyes and emotion clogged her throat. Harold and Ellie's relationship was the kind a couple dreamed of having, but it had ended before it had a chance to grow. And at eighteen, Ellie had been left a widow.

Amy held the journal to her chest and grieved for the young mother who would have to bear her child alone. Who'd held her hand when she'd given birth?

Probably her mother, Amy thought. When she'd been in labor with Callie, her mom had been a godsend. But it hadn't been her mother she'd wanted; it had been Brandon.

As the day had worn on, and as each contraction came on the heels of the last, she'd begun to wonder if he would even show up at the hospital. Her mom had taken her there, and Brandon was supposed to meet her as soon as he'd gotten out of court.

He'd been late, of course—as usual.

But at least she hadn't been completely alone. She supposed she should take comfort in that, but her disappointment had been palpable.

She took one last look at the journal, at the empty pages. According to the notes her mother had made during her search to find her birth family, Barbara Rucker had been born on September 19, 1942.

Amy hoped the baby girl had grown up to bring her mother joy, and that the two had been close.

Chapter 7

It was nearly noon when Barbara drove her white Jaguar into Fairbrook and turned down Main, one of the three tree-lined streets that bordered Mulberry Park. She scanned along the curb, looking for a parking space, only to find each of them taken.

She heaved a heavy sigh and drove around the block one more time, waiting for something to open up. She hadn't expected it to be this busy, but the lunch crowd was probably out in full force, getting a bite to eat at one of several trendy cafés that provided outdoor dining or shopping at one of the specialty stores that drew people from miles around.

Of all the days for her to try and squeeze in a visit to her mom, she couldn't believe she'd chosen this one. She and her husband had an important dinner party that evening with one of his political supporters, and she needed to stop at her favorite dress shop in Del Mar to pick up the new St. John Knit she was having altered. She also had a hair appointment later this afternoon.

She glanced at her wristwatch, the Rolex Joseph had given her last Christmas. She didn't have time for any of this, but due to the setback Joey had suffered last Wednesday, it had been two weeks since she'd last checked on her mother. She probably should feel guilty about neglecting her daughterly duty, but she'd called Maria periodically to ask about her, to ask whether she needed anything. At least her mom wasn't locked away in some cold, sterile convalescent hospital. Instead, she was in a private home and receiving quality care.

Besides, her mother rarely recognized anyone anymore.

As a white minivan backed out into the street, Barbara hit her brakes and uttered, "Thank goodness." Then she snagged the vacated space in front of Specks Appeal, a shop that sold designer eyeglasses.

She got out of the car, locked the door, and walked past several storefronts until she reached Petals and Stems, with its red-and-white striped awning and the colorful window display of gerbera daisies and hydrangea.

A middle-age man dressed in blue coveralls was sweeping the sidewalk in front of the building with a push broom. He glanced up when she approached, stopped working long enough for her to reach the door, and smiled, revealing a gap where one of his teeth used to be.

"Good morning," she said, making eye contact yet avoiding a full-on gaze.

"It certainly is."

A bell attached to a chain on the door tinkled as she entered the shop, with its colorful displays of plants and flowers and cool, fresh floral scents. She didn't have time to dawdle, so she made her way to the refrigerator display case, opened the glass door, and made a quick and appropriate decision: a bud vase filled with three pink roses and a couple of sprigs of baby's breath.

"Hello there." A woman with salt-and-pepper-colored hair made her way to the counter, smiling and wiping her hands upon a green full-length apron. "Can I help you?"

"Yes, thank you." Barbara carried the vase to the counter. "I'd like to purchase this."

As the woman rang up the sale, Barbara lifted her Louis Vuitton purse, set it on the countertop next to the vase, and searched for the matching wallet that held her cash and credit cards.

The man who'd been sweeping out front returned to the shop. His lips parted as if he intended to say something to the woman at the cash register, then he clamped his mouth shut.

"That'll be twenty-one dollars and fifty-three cents," the woman said.

As Barbara pulled out two twenties from her wallet, the man raked his fingers through his thinning gray hair.

"Chuck," the woman at the register said, "I'll be with you in just a minute."

While waiting for her change, Barbara lifted the bud vase to her nose and sniffed the flowers that lacked the fragrance she was used to.

"They're pretty," the woman said, "aren't they?"

"Yes, although I'm spoiled. My mother used to have a green thumb, and her roses consistently won blue ribbons at the Del Mar Fair. She raised the most beautiful and lush rosebushes in the county, if not the state. But she got arthritis in her back and had to give up gardening a few years ago."

The man—Chuck—took a couple of steps toward Barbara. "Excuse me, ma'am."

Barbara drew her purse closer to her chest as she slowly turned to him. "Yes?"

"Are you Ellie Rucker's daughter?"

"Do you know my mother?"

"I met her at the soup kitchen that's run by the church across the street. She used to come in regularly, especially at the end of the month, when she was trying to stretch her Social Security check."

Barbara's cheeks warmed, and her jaw ground shut. Her mother hadn't said anything about struggling to make ends meet.

If she had, Barbara certainly would have stepped in to help. In fact, whenever she'd asked her mom how she was doing, she'd been told that everything was fine, that the Lord provided for all her needs.

Hating to have either the man or the florist think she'd been remiss, that she'd somehow failed her elderly mother, Barbara said, "She never mentioned anything about going to the soup kitchen. If she *had* . . ."

"Ellie wasn't one to complain. But then I don't have to tell you that." The man chuckled. "She was your mom. You know her better than any of us."

Barbara forced a smile. In truth, their mother/daughter relationship hadn't been good in ages, and while Barbara wasn't happy that they'd never buried the hatchet over the disagreement they'd had more than forty years ago—had it been *that* long?—she'd been too proud to admit it, too angry to completely forgive her.

"When you see Ellie," the man added, "give her my best. Tell her that Chuck Masterson said hello, and that he's praying for her."

"I'll do that."

Chuck turned to the woman behind the counter. "Is there anything else you'd like me to do for you while I'm here, Suzette?"

"Actually, the toilet in the back is leaking. I think it needs a new valve or something. Are you any good at plumbing?"

"I'll see what I can do," he said before heading to the back of the store.

When he was out of sight, and after she counted out Barbara's change, Suzette leaned forward and whispered, "Chuck's a really nice guy. You wouldn't know it, but just three or four years ago he used to be homeless. He was also an alcoholic with a bad liver, from what I heard. But thanks to the folks at the soup kitchen, he turned his life around. Now he lives in a small trailer on the church grounds, and a lot of the merchants in the area try to keep him busy with odd jobs."

Barbara merely nodded, still dealing with the uneasy fact that her mother had been frequenting the soup kitchen rather than asking her for help.

While Chuck lifted the ceramic lid to the toilet tank and checked the valves and fittings for a leak, he overheard Suzette talking about him, about the life he used to live, about the problem he'd once had.

He probably ought to be embarrassed by the man he once was, but he was so happy with the man he'd become that it no longer mattered.

As he reached into the water-filled tank and tightened a loose valve, he thought back twenty years to the day it had all started.

Chuck and his wife had left their young son with a sitter, then driven to the mountains to go skiing with friends. They'd had a blast, then stayed for a late dinner and had a couple of drinks. Their friends decided to spend the night and encouraged them to do the same, but Chuck had to work the next day.

"Come on, baby," Marianne had said. "Let's just get a motel room and head home early in the morning. The sitter won't mind. I'll just give her a call."

"I'm fine," he'd insisted. "I want to get home tonight."

But he *hadn't* been all right. He might not have been legally drunk, but he'd dozed off behind the wheel, and the car had run off the road and slammed into a tree.

Marianne had suffered internal injuries and needed surgery upon arrival at the hospital, while Chuck ended up with a concussion, a nasty cut on his head, and multiple fractures in both legs.

The pain had been excruciating, but the guilt had been worse. Still, he might have gotten through it all just fine had the surgeons not opened up Marianne, found inoperable cancer, and given her just weeks to live.

Her last days on earth had been a nightmare he'd tried his best to forget.

After she died, the doctor quit prescribing the heavy-duty narcotics, claiming Chuck was becoming dependent. So he'd turned to alcohol to numb his pain and still the haunting memories of Marianne's heartbreaking deathbed confession.

The booze had worked—at least, that's what he'd told himself over the years. It's what he'd told his son, too, when Brandon had cried and accused him of drinking too much, when he'd told him that he needed to get a job and go to work each day like other dads.

But the boy hadn't bought Chuck's lame excuses, and when he was seventeen, he graduated from high school, snagged a scholarship to some big, impressive university—Chuck couldn't even remember which one.

How was that for being a Loser Dad?

Either way, he hadn't seen his son since, which was too bad. He'd give anything to talk to Brandon now, to apologize and try to make amends, but he wasn't sure how to find him, let alone approach him. Maybe he'd still be an embarrassment.

Chuck hadn't had a drink in nearly a year, and he had a place of his own now—no more living on the streets. But even though he'd turned his life around and was truly content for the first time he could remember, he supposed he wasn't someone Brandon could be proud of.

Most of the people who were his friends these days wouldn't have wanted to have anything to do with the old Chuck. But he wasn't the same guy he once was, and they knew it.

He'd gotten the ultimate second chance. And just as Suzette had said, he'd had those folks down at the soup kitchen to thank for it all. They'd given him more than a handout. They'd given him friendship, too. And they'd shared their faith.

It was just as if some giant heavenly lightbulb had come on, and he'd never been the same again.

Chuck just wished he could have met Pastor Craig and the folks who ran the soup kitchen years ago so he wouldn't have had to beat himself up for so long.

There was one guy in particular who'd had the most impact on him, a homeless man named Jesse. One day, while they were eating meat loaf and baked potatoes, the two sat together. Jesse had zeroed in on Chuck, peeling away the dirt and the phony smiles. He'd known things that Chuck had never shared with anyone before, things that had hurt too bad to deal with sober. Not the actual details, but he'd pegged all the feelings, all the internal struggles that had caused Chuck to turn to the bottle in the first place.

It was almost as if the guy had been psychic, although he hadn't come out and revealed anything specific—past, present, or future. He just sort of knew the root of the problem.

After that, Pastor Craig had gotten a

hold of Chuck, telling him about how much God loved him, how Jesus had died for him. And now Chuck was a new creation, a new man.

Too bad he hadn't come to grips with all of that years ago. Maybe then Brandon wouldn't have bailed out on him.

"Call the boy," Jesse had said, encouraging Chuck to reach out first. "He's in the phone book."

"Maybe someday," he'd replied, afraid to admit that he hadn't been brave enough to make that call. To risk facing his son and learning that his best foot forward wasn't anywhere good enough.

"Your life is nearly over," Jesse had said. "And what do you have to show for it?"

He didn't have squat, if you counted earthly possessions. But for the first time in forever, he had his self-respect and the assurance that everything was going to be okay—one way or another.

The day before Jesse left Fairbrook, he'd brought up the subject again. "You're about to check out of this world, Chuck. You don't have much time left for reunions."

At first, Chuck had thought the homeless man was just blowing smoke. After all, they were all on a wacky roller-coaster ride through life. But Chuck had been having a pain in his gut that wouldn't go away, and he'd stopped by the free clinic a few weeks back.

"I figure it's my liver," he'd told the doctor. "I haven't taken very good care of myself."

"Your liver isn't the problem," the doctor had said. "I'm afraid you have cancer."

Several tests later, Chuck had been given the news. He had six months—*tops.*

A lot of guys might have been shook up. But Chuck knew where he was going. And he'd been redeemed. He was more certain of that than the notion that the sun would rise tomorrow morning.

Well, that it would come up for those who were still riding the roller coaster.

It was weird, Chuck thought, as he replaced the toilet tank lid and washed his hands in the sink. He'd kind of like to have an impact on lives while he was still here, just like Jesse had done.

But his roller-coaster car was slowing to a halt, and he wasn't sure how much time he had left to ride.

* * *

After turning down Sugar Plum Lane, Barbara pulled behind a white pickup filled with landscaping tools and parked in front of the old house. She shut off her engine, but didn't get out of the car right away. Instead, she checked out the yard—the lawn and the shrubbery—noting that the gardeners were making some headway, but they had a long way to go before the grounds looked the way they should, the way she remembered.

A young Hispanic man—one of the gardeners, she assumed—was talking to a petite blonde on the porch of the old house. The woman must be the tenant, but Barbara didn't see any reason to introduce herself. She'd rather their contact be through the property management company.

So she reached for the bud vase she'd placed in the cup holder so it wouldn't tip over on the drive to Sugar Plum Lane, climbed from the car, and strode along the walkway to Maria's door with the pink roses in hand. She hoped they would give her mother a lift and provide some color for her bedroom.

When she reached the stoop, she rang

the bell. Moments later, Maria's oldest son answered.

"Come on in," he said. "I'll tell my mom you're here."

"Thank you." Barbara had no more than stepped inside when she spotted her mother seated on a beige sofa near the fireplace. Her hair, which appeared to have been freshly shampooed and colored with the steel-gray rinse she'd always favored, had been curled and combed. And she wore a splash of pink lipstick as if she'd been waiting for company.

A whisper of guilt blew through Barbara, and she wondered if her mother had been sitting like that last Tuesday, waiting for her to show up. But under the circumstances, she'd had no other choice but to postpone the visit.

Barbara made her way toward the elderly woman who appeared to be stooped, even while seated. "Hello, Mother."

Her mom seemed to be more focused on the gnarled, liver-spotted hands in her lap than on her visitor or even the talk show playing on the television.

"How are you doing today?" Barbara asked.

Ellie glanced up, her faded blue eyes lacking the spark they'd once had. "I'm okay."

Her once-white sweater had yellowed with age, and her pale green blouse was worn. The stitching was coming apart along the collar.

"Next week," Barbara said, "when I stop by, I'll bring a couple of new outfits for you to wear. Won't that be nice?"

Ellie merely looked at her.

Barbara would purchase something bright and cheery, something stylish.

Maria entered the living room, followed by two little girls. The dark-haired child was her daughter; the blonde had to be a friend or neighbor.

At the sound of children's voices, Ellie looked up and smiled. She motioned for the little blonde. "Come over here, Angel. Let me get a look at you."

Not surprising, the child froze in her tracks and glanced at her friend.

"It's all right," Maria's daughter said, nudging the girl forward. "You can talk to her. She's nice. She's just old."

The blonde took a shy step forward, and as she neared the elderly woman, Ellie reached for her hand and gave it a little pat. Then she looked at Barbara, her tired blue eyes lighting up as though she'd broken free of the Alzheimer's disease that had trapped her essence. "She's beautiful, Barbie. I knew she would be."

The poor little girl appeared to be ready to bolt, so Barbara stepped in to defuse the situation. "She *is* beautiful." Barbara removed the child's hand from her mother's grip. "What's your name, sweetheart?"

The child opened her mouth, but Ellie was the one who answered, her voice stronger than it had been in a long time. "It's Angel."

The blonde shook her head, her pigtails swishing from side to side. "No, it's not. I'm Callie."

As the child drew back to where her friend stood, Maria furrowed her brow and mouthed, "Who's Angel?"

Barbara shrugged. It wasn't a name she recognized, but her mother became so confused these days that it could have been any combination of personas from the past. It could even have been someone from a television show.

Who knew what was going on upstairs with her mother?

"Angel looks a lot like you did as a little girl," Ellie said, as if she'd suddenly recognized her daughter after all. Still, her words made no sense.

"My hair was brown," Barbara said. "Like Daddy's. Remember, Mom?"

Her mother brightened. "Harold! Of course I remember." She turned to Maria, hope springing in her eyes and voice. "Has the mailman come yet? I'm sure there will be a letter today."

"He's already been here," Maria said. "I'm afraid there wasn't any mail, Ellie."

Barbara wasn't sure why Maria played along with the old woman. It was best to tell her the truth, to make her accept reality.

As Callie and Sara left the room, Barbara turned to Maria and asked, "How's she been doing?"

"Yesterday was all right, but it's been a rough morning."

"What happened?"

"I came downstairs to tell her breakfast was ready, but she wasn't in her bed. I sent the kids out in the backyard to look for her while I went out front. I found her in the middle of the street."

"Why? What was she doing? Going home?"

"She said she was looking for Harold, that he was coming by to take her to the beach for a picnic and a day in the sun."

Barbara clucked her tongue and blew out a sigh. She wasn't sure why Joey—and Maria, too—insisted upon keeping Mother at home when she was so clearly ready for the safety an Alzheimer's care center would provide. She'd have to talk to Joey about this later and insist that it was time to move her.

"Are you going to be here a few minutes?" Maria asked.

"Yes. Why?"

"I need to walk Callie home. Would you mind keeping an eye on things? I won't be long."

"Of course not." Barbara glanced at her wristwatch. "I'll be here for at least a half hour. In fact, if you have an errand to run or need a break, I can stay for forty-five minutes or so."

"You don't mind?"

"No, it's silly for us both to be here."

"Captain is in the backyard," Maria added.

She didn't have to explain. She wanted Barbara to look out for him, too. But he was no trouble. He, at least, seemed to have all of his faculties and wasn't prone to wander.

"No problem," Barbara said. She appreciated what Maria was doing, even though she paid her for her mother's board and care. She sympathized with her, too. There had to be an easier way to earn extra money while working from home.

As Maria trailed after the girls, Barbara took a seat next to her mother on the sofa.

"She's a sweet little thing," Ellie said.

"Who?"

"Angel."

"I'm not sure I know who Angel is, Mother."

"The child my daughter gave away."

Barbara cringed at the reminder of both the mistake she'd made and the solution she'd come up with to correct it.

For more than forty years, her mother had been upset about the decision to put the baby up for adoption and had never failed to remind Barbara, one way or another. It had created untold stress on their relationship. But at least Ellie had never revealed the secret to a living soul.

But what would Barbara do if it all came out now?

It was definitely time to insist her mother be put in a home.

Chapter 8

Maria seemed like a nice person and a good mother, but Amy was still a little uneasy about letting Callie go with someone new for the first time. So when the doorbell rang, suggesting that Maria had brought Callie home, she placed the last of the books she'd been packing into a box and hurried to the door.

Maria, who stood with her youngest boy and the two girls on the stoop, held a plate covered in plastic wrap.

"Look what we brought for you, Mommy!" Callie's beaming smile announced that she'd had fun while she'd been gone.

"They're tortillas. And they're really yummy with butter and sugar on them."

"They look delicious," Amy said, taking the plate her neighbor handed to her.

Maria chuckled. "They might not be round, but I can assure you they taste good."

"Thanks for letting Callie help."

"It was a pleasure. She's a sweet little girl. It's going to be nice having you two live next door."

Amy forced a smile, yet didn't respond. She'd eventually tell Maria what she was doing, but probably not until after she'd packed all of Ellie's things and was ready to give up possession of the house and forfeit the six months' rent.

"Mommy," Callie said. "Will you put on the movie now? Sara's little brother wants to watch *Cars.* Okay?"

"Of course." Amy turned to Maria. "Do you have time for tea? I'm ready for a break from packing."

Maria seemed to give it some thought before saying, "Sure, I've got a few minutes."

"Good. Then we'll make it a quick cup."

Amy set up the movie for the kids, and

after they were seated and glued to the screen, she led Maria to the kitchen, where she put on a teakettle of water and took two china cups from the cupboard.

Next she opened the pantry in search of the tin of Earl Grey she'd brought from home. But when she noticed the Kitty Delight behind a can of Campbell's chicken noodle soup, her hands stilled. "I've been meaning to ask you something. Did Ellie have a cat?"

"She used to have an old gray tabby named Pretty Boy, but he died around Christmas time. And just before she began to . . . fail, she sort of adopted a stray that used to hang out in the neighborhood."

"Is it still around?" Maybe Amy should leave some food and water out for it.

"No, I haven't seen it."

"Did her family take it?"

"No, they wouldn't have done that. Her grandson's wife had an allergy to pet dander, which is why she kept dragging her feet about moving in with them. She hated to give up her cat. And her daughter . . . well, Barbara isn't the animal-lover type. I have no idea why the cat took off, but we live next to a canyon, and the coyotes are sometimes a problem."

"That's too bad."

"Yes, it was. Both Pretty Boy and the stray provided company for Ellie in the evenings. She didn't get many visitors."

"How sad."

"I think so, too."

"Didn't her family come by to see her?"

"Her grandson stopped by regularly, but he was pretty busy, so it wasn't all that often. And her daughter is involved with several different charity organizations. Still, you'd think that . . ." Maria paused.

"Think what?"

Maria shrugged. "I'm sorry. That was unfair of me. It's just that Ellie was a wonderful neighbor. And she was a good friend to my aunt."

"Just being in her house has convinced me that she was a special lady. I've been drawn to the paintings on her wall. She was a good artist. I even found an accordion in the closet, so I suspect she was a musician as well." Amy didn't mention the journals or the fact that Ellie might have been a writer, too.

"I'd completely forgotten about that accordion." A slow smile stretched across Maria's face. "One day, when I was a teenager living in Fairbrook with my aunt, she played for us—polka tunes, mostly. From what I understand, she taught herself to play by ear."

"Really? I play the piano, and so did my mother. But we had years of lessons." Amy wished she could reel in her words the moment they came out. She'd been thinking that Ellie had passed on some kind of musical gene, but she wasn't ready to reveal who she was and why she was here.

The teakettle on the stove began to whistle, and she got up, glad for the interruption. As she poured hot water into each cup, Maria scanned the kitchen.

"It feels weird being in this room and having tea with someone other than Ellie. We had a lot of chats in here, especially when I learned I was pregnant with Wally. She took the place of my aunt and said all the right things."

"You mean about childbirth and that sort of thing?"

Maria glanced down at the cup and

frowned as though it was a long story and not one she was proud of.

"I spent my teen years living with my aunt, Sofia. But one summer, I went to visit my cousin Rita in Los Angeles. I met a guy named Ray Huddleston there. He was a blue-eyed charmer, and one of those guys who had all the girls in the neighborhood panting at his feet." She opened her tea bag and placed it into the cup of water. "Needless to say, when he started paying attention to me, I was flattered. And after dating him for a whopping two months, he asked me to marry him, and I agreed."

She'd introduced herself as Maria Rodriguez, Amy thought. Hadn't she taken Ray's name? Or had she taken her own back after the split?

"*Tía* Sofia, my aunt, tried to talk me out of it, saying she'd seen his kind before. That he was a heartbreak waiting to happen. But I thought she was too old to know what she was talking about."

"And she wasn't?"

"Nope." Maria dunked the tea bag into the water several times, then removed it and added a spoonful of sugar from the bowl that sat on the table. "She had Ray pegged pretty well."

"Did you marry him?"

"Yes, I'm afraid I did." She took a sip from her cup. "We stayed in the L.A. area, where he had family and friends. I didn't know too many people, but that didn't matter. I loved him, and before long, I got pregnant with Danny. Ray seemed happy about it, but he was away from home a lot. I tried not to complain, telling myself he was a good provider, that a lot of women would be happy to have a guy like him."

Maria didn't need to tell Amy about the loneliness of going through a pregnancy alone. For one reason or another, Brandon had missed out on nearly all of the exciting events: hearing the heartbeat for the first time, staring at the ultrasound in awe, decorating the nursery.

"I began to hear rumors that Ray was seeing someone on the side."

"Was he?"

Maria nodded. "I confronted him, and he admitted to having an affair. He swore the woman meant nothing to him, that he loved me. And I believed him."

As far as Amy knew, Brandon hadn't

cheated on her, but she couldn't let the fact that Maria had married a real jerk make her think that she and Callie should have settled for less than they deserved.

She took a sip of her tea. "I take it things didn't get much better?"

"They did for a little while. I was determined to forgive and forget. About the time Sara was six weeks old, we were facing another anniversary. I wanted to do something special, even though we couldn't afford anything big. So I got a sitter for the kids, then went to the grocery store to pick up everything I needed for a romantic dinner at home, including candles and sparkling cider.

"On the way to the market, I saw his truck parked in front of the Starlight Motor Inn. My heart dropped into the pit of my stomach. I knew he'd done it to me again. I made a U-turn, parked next to his pickup, then banged on the door until he answered. Just as I'd suspected, there was a woman with him."

Amy reached over and placed her hand over Maria's. "I'm sorry. You deserve so much better than that."

"I know."

"How long have you been divorced?"

"Three years, but there's more to the story." Again, Maria seemed to wrestle with her memories, with the decision to share them with Amy. "About six months after I left L.A., Ray came here, apologizing and begging me to take him back. He thought we could make a fresh start in Fairbrook. My aunt had just passed away, and I was heartbroken and lonely."

"Did you? Take him back?"

"I hate to admit it, but yes. He'd only been here a few days." She blew out a weary sigh. "Just long enough to conceive Wally. And then the police showed up, looking for him."

"What had he done?"

"The woman he'd gotten involved with was married, and when her husband found out, there was an ugly fight. Things escalated, and the other man was shot. Ray claimed it was self-defense, although I can't understand why he would have had a gun in the first place."

"So they arrested him?"

"Yes. And can you believe it?" She slowly shook her head. "He had the gall to ask me to provide him with an alibi for that night. But I refused to lie for him. Now he's serving a twenty-year prison sentence."

And Amy thought *she* had problems. "I'm sorry, Maria."

"Me, too. It's been rough, but we've all put it behind us now." Maria glanced at the clock on the wall. "I hadn't meant to stay so long. Or to vent. I really should get home." She scooted back her chair and got to her feet. "I'm sorry for . . ."

Amy placed a hand on Maria's forearm and gave it an affectionate squeeze. "Don't be. The next time we have tea, I'll probably be the one venting. It's nice to think that, when I do, you'll listen to me."

"Thanks." Maria smiled, her brown eyes lighting up.

Amy wondered if she'd smile and be understanding when she learned that Amy really didn't plan on moving into Ellie's house at all. That she was only here to snoop. But maybe it wouldn't matter. Maybe they'd somehow reached a level of friendship that allowed them to share things they'd be embarrassed to tell anyone else.

She hoped so, because next time she and Maria talked, she just might let the cat out of the bag.

On her way home to relieve Barbara, Maria couldn't believe she'd opened up and let Amy know her darkest secrets. But her new neighbor had been easy to talk to, and it had been so long since she'd had someone she could confide in.

As she entered the living room, where the kids had been locked on the television screen, Wally fussed about going home before *Cars* was over.

"He's being so good," Amy said. "I don't mind if he stays."

"Are you sure?"

"Absolutely. As soon as the movie's over, I'll bring him and Sara home."

So Maria agreed, thinking that she'd come back and check on him later. As she closed the door and strode down the sidewalk, she spotted Eddie in her yard rather than in Amy's. He was pruning the hedge that ran along their shared property line.

"I appreciate you doing that," she told him, "but I can't afford to pay you."

"You don't need to. Consider it a favor. I can't very well trim one side without it looking weird, so it's no big deal."

It seemed like a big deal to her. She couldn't remember the last time someone had done something to lighten her load.

The sun glistened off the ebony strands of his hair, and when he tossed a smile her way, his eyes twinkled. She could almost imagine acting upon the attraction she felt, upon the kindness he'd shown, but it was crazy to let her thoughts stray in that direction.

Eddie was clearly the kind of guy any young woman would be lucky to date. But Maria wasn't just any young woman. She was a mother of three, with a slew of bills that kept her adding and re-adding her check register at the end of the month, hoping to make ends meet.

A breeze whipped a strand of her hair across her face, and she tucked it behind an ear.

"Mom?" Danny called from the house. "Good. You're home."

Maria tore her gaze from Eddie, relieved to have a reason to quit gaping at him. "What's the matter?"

"Nothing. I just wanted to know if I can go to Jason's house. His mom said he isn't contagious anymore."

"All right, but where's Captain?"

"He's in his room, looking for his glasses."

"Will you help him find them before you leave?"

"Aw, Mom. Do I have to do *everything* around here?"

Did she ask too much of him?

Or was he only trying to make her think that she did?

Her maternal instinct told her it was the latter. "Check outside. He was reading earlier in the lawn chair under the shade."

Danny clucked his tongue, then dashed off.

Maria looked at Eddie and shrugged, offering him a what's-a-mom-to-do? expression.

"You're a good mother," he said.

"I try, but at times like this, he makes me wonder if I'm falling short."

"That's part of a kid's wiring."

"To make his mother question herself?"

"Actually, I think it's a ploy to have his own way. But don't let self-doubt get to you."

That was easier said than done.

"If his dad was standing here right now," Eddie said, "he'd tell you the same thing."

That was doubtful, but she kept her thoughts to herself.

Moments later, Danny returned, a bit out of breath. "Captain's got his glasses. You were right. He left them outside. So can I go *now?*"

"Okay. Have fun."

But before her son could run off, Eddie placed a man-sized hand on his small shoulder. "You only have one mother, Danny. And she's got a lot on her plate. It's not too much for her to ask your help. She deserves your support and your respect."

"Yeah, but . . ."

The boy and man eyed each other, and the silence spoke volumes.

"Yes, sir," Danny said, turning to Maria. "I'm sorry, Mom."

Eddie gave him a warm grin and a pat on the back. "Thanks for doing your part. *Now* go have fun."

When he was gone, Eddie turned to Maria. "I'm sorry for interfering."

"I hate to admit it, but I'm glad you did."

Eddie studied the attractive single mom, thinking that she looked a lot like Cecelia. Shorter, though, and prettier. He supposed that was reason enough to let his interest in her slide, but he couldn't seem to help it.

"Have you given any more thought to letting Danny come with me to baseball practice on Saturday?"

She bit down on her bottom lip. "Not really, but I suppose I should. It's just that . . ." She paused as if having a hard time explaining herself.

He thought he knew what was bothering her, though. His mom had always been fussy about where he and his brother went and who they spent time with. And while he figured his mother had always been a little over the top about it, he understood the hesitancy, the maternal concern.

"The offer still stands," he said. "If you'd feel better going with us, you're more than welcome to come along."

"Truthfully?" A slow smile slipped across her face. "Yes, I'd like to go, too. But I'd have to get a sitter."

"You don't need to, but that's up to you.

There's a playground at the park, so Sara and Wally would have a good time if you brought them."

She frowned and bit down on her bottom lip again. "I wish it were that easy. My elderly houseguests need someone to look after them, so I'd have to ask a friend to stay with them. But I'm not sure whom to ask. I won't know for sure until Friday night. Maybe even Saturday morning."

"No big deal. Just let me know when you can."

"All right. Thanks for understanding."

She remained next to him, as if it wasn't that easy to walk away. As if she were as drawn to him as he was to her.

He had half a notion to ask her out while they were standing there—to dinner or a movie or something. But if it was that tough for her to get out of the house, maybe he'd have to think of something they could do without leaving.

"Well," she said, nodding toward her door. "I really need to get inside."

"Okay."

She still didn't move.

And neither did he.

There seemed to be something brewing between them, something that caused his pulse to kick up a notch, his senses to reel.

Don't fight it, he wanted to say to her. But he couldn't do that. Not when he wasn't sure if he could provide her and the kids with what they needed—and he didn't mean financially.

Finally, she took a step back, slowly spun around, and headed for the house.

As much as he ought to return his focus to his work, he watched her go, watched the veil of long, dark hair swish across her back, watched the alluring sway of her hips.

He hadn't dated much since getting out of prison. When he'd lost Cecelia and had been charged with vehicular manslaughter, he'd thought that his whole life was over. That he'd never find peace.

But after five years, the pieces had finally started coming together again.

He finished clipping Maria's side of the hedge, then scanned her yard.

What would it hurt for him to clean out that flower bed along the side of her house one day after work? Or to trim the scraggly bougainvilleas that grew wildly along the fence?

That was one way he could help her out, to make her life easier.

And a way to make sure that he would get a chance to talk to her again.

While the kids watched the cartoon movie on television, Amy headed upstairs. She figured she had an hour or so before she would have to walk Maria's children home and then drive Callie back to the townhome. That is, if they continued to watch TV quietly. Even Wally, the little boy, seemed to be enthralled with the movie.

Still, she would be checking on them periodically and listening carefully. As she reached the top of the landing, she made her way to the nearest bedroom, one she hadn't tackled yet. This room, with its pale yellow walls, was decorated much the same as the others, but she noticed an old-fashioned, pedal sewing machine sitting near the window.

Amy wondered if it really worked. Steph

Goldstein had one that was similar, but someone had taken out the machinery and made it into a plant stand.

On a table next to the antique machine, she spotted a pair of pinking shears, a pin cushion, and a thimble.

So Ellie Rucker had been a seamstress, too. Was there a talent the woman hadn't had?

Nevertheless, Amy didn't have time to waste, so she went to the closet and surveyed the items she would pack into boxes later.

Like the other two closets she'd already emptied, this one had built-in shelves for storage, too. She had to tiptoe to reach the highest shelf, which held two afghans. One was made out of autumn-colored yarn—gold, brown, and orange. The other had been knit in shades of blue.

She removed them both and placed them on the bed, then went back to work.

The next shelf held a crocheted tablecloth—off-white, she decided—and several matching doilies, which she set next to the afghans. She also found a stack of dish towels that had been pressed and wrapped in tissue. All seven of them had been embroidered with a day and chore of the week. Monday was Washday, Tuesday was Ironing Day . . .

Had they been a gift Ellie had received? Or something she'd made herself and planned to give away?

Amy supposed she'd never know, as she continued to remove all of the items the old woman had stored.

When she reached the middle shelf, she ran across another journal. Well, actually, it was only part of one. The pink cover had very few pages attached. The bulk of the book was missing. As she lifted the cover to get a better look, strings dangled from where the spine used to be.

That's weird, she thought, wondering how it had come to be separated. It looked as though it had been ripped apart, although she could be wrong.

She studied the pink cover. With a collage of antique dolls, it would definitely appeal to a little girl. Had this one belonged to Barbara? Had she kept a journal to record her thoughts and reflections, too?

Amy carried what remained of the book to the bed, took a seat on the edge of the mattress, and began to read.

No, she realized, as she looked at the very first page, it wasn't Barbara's journal. The familiar script was Ellie's.

October 3, 1942

It feels strange to be writing again. After Harold's death, it was all I could do to put one foot in front of the other. The heartache of his loss was almost unbearable, but I had to pull myself together for our child.

As the baby grew, its movements within my womb helped me keep Harold and our love alive.

Would it be a boy or a girl? I wondered time and again. Would I have a son or a daughter to love?

Thoughts and dreams of the baby we'd conceived kept me going through the dark and lonely months of summer.

Then, in the afternoon of September 18, 1942, my water broke, and I knew our baby would soon be here. All through a long, grueling night, I felt Harold with me, urging me to be strong, to hold on. And when I thought I would surely die, that the pain would never ease, Barbara Ann Rucker came into the world at dawn.

Joy comes in the morning, they say. And that was

certainly true that day. Barbara's cry was the most glorious sound I'd ever heard.

When I finally held our little girl in my arms, I couldn't imagine what my life would be like without her. What a blessing she is. And she's beautiful, too, with a cute little nose and big brown peepers like Harold's.

When Mother held her for the very first time, she smiled and said, "You're surely going to pay for your raising, Eleanor. This little girl is going to be strong willed. You mark my words."

I couldn't agree more. In just a few short weeks, Barbie already knows her own mind, and I suspect that she and I are setting out on a journey that will be one sweet adventure after another.

I'm eagerly looking forward to being a mother. My only regret is that Harold won't be here with me to help me raise our little girl. I'll love her enough for both of us, though. And I'll cheer for each of her accomplishments—her first smile, her first step, her first day of school.

I can hardly wait to see the world through her eyes.

As a mother, Amy knew just how Ellie had felt. It had been fun to watch Callie pull herself up, to see her let go and toddle off on her own two feet before taking a tumble. To see the sense of wonder in her eyes when she spotted a butterfly flutter from its perch on a pot of geraniums on the back patio.

Just as Ellie had, Amy had witnessed most of those precious firsts alone. But unlike Harold, who would have been with Ellie if he could have, Brandon had missed those moments by choice.

Amy sat there just a moment longer, holding the torn journal and sensing the almost palpable presence of the young woman who'd written each heartfelt word.

What she wouldn't give to be able to meet Ellie, to share a cup of tea with her. But she'd have to settle for walking among her things, reading her words.

As much as she'd like to continue sitting in the quiet of this particular bedroom, to study the pages of the torn journal, to hunt for the remainder of the book, she decided she'd better go downstairs and check on the kids.

The movie, which she'd seen more times than she cared to admit, was coming to an end, so she took a seat in the recliner and watched until the closing credits began to roll. Then she walked Maria's children home.

Before she reached the front door, Maria stepped onto the porch and smiled. "Thanks for bringing them back. I was just coming to get them. Did they behave for you?"

"They were great," Amy said.

"Mommy?" Sara tugged on her mother's arm. "Can Callie come in and play?"

"It's all right with me," Maria said.

"Thanks, but that won't work today. I have a few errands to run. And I also need to go to the grocery store so that I can go home and start dinner."

"Will you be back later?" Sara asked.

Amy smiled at the child. "I'm sorry, honey. Not today."

Maria placed her hands on her daughter's shoulders. "We'll have to see what tomorrow brings, *mija.*"

Amy nodded. "Have a good evening."

"You, too."

When they returned to the house, Amy told Callie it was time to pack up her toys.

Moments later, they climbed into the car, and Amy started the engine. As they backed out of the driveway, Callie pointed toward Maria's house, where a gray-haired woman, stooped with age, stood at the window and peered into the street.

"That's the lady who kept calling me Angel," Callie said. "I told her my name, but she didn't listen."

As Amy put the vehicle into Drive, she glanced back at the big bay window in time to see the figure turn away.

"Who is she?" Amy asked. "Sara's grandmother?"

"I don't know. But she was really old. Older than Grandma Rossi."

"What makes you say that?"

"Because"—Callie lifted her hands and washed them across her cheeks—"her face was *all* wrinkled. And she smelled like candy canes and medicine."

Grandma Rossi had been nearly forty when she adopted Amy's mother, so she was getting on in years. But she was pretty spunky and sharp. She also wore stylish clothes and had an active social life, so it was easy to see how Callie might consider her much younger than she was.

Still, it was impossible to guess who the old woman in the window might be. Maria had mentioned living with her aunt, who'd passed away a few years back. Was the woman another relative?

The next time Amy saw Maria, she would have to ask.

Chapter 9

Callie came down with a sore throat on Friday, so Amy stayed home with her all weekend. But she was back to normal on Monday, which was good, since Amy had a doctor's appointment.

Ever since her mother had found the lump in her breast that had turned out to be malignant, Amy had been diligent about scheduling—and keeping—a yearly physical. And today had been the day.

She wouldn't get the official results from her Pap smear for a week or two, but her gynecologist had said that everything appeared to be normal.

Callie was at the Goldsteins' that morning, an arrangement Amy and Steph had worked out months ago. But she wouldn't need to be picked up until later that afternoon. Steph was taking the girls to Roy's Burger Roundup for lunch.

So with a little time on her hands, Amy decided to stop by Sugar Plum Lane before going home. But it was more than a commitment she'd made to the landlord drawing her to the Rucker house.

From the pink floral pattern on the china to the framed watercolors on the wall and the photographs that lined the mantel, Amy had gotten a solid sense of her biological great-grandmother. And she'd found herself intrigued by the woman who'd once lived there.

As she pulled into the driveway, it was nearly twelve. She noticed that Eddie's truck wasn't parked anywhere in front.

Had he left for lunch?

She supposed it didn't matter. He was a hard worker, and the yard looked better each time she stopped by.

As she strode toward the front door and dug into her purse for the keys, eager to get started while she had a little peace and quiet, a meow tore into her solitude.

She turned to the sound and spotted a white and calico-colored cat perched along the top of the fence. It appeared to be full grown but was on the scrawny side, and she wondered if it was the stray that Ellie had adopted.

Probably not. Maria said they hadn't seen it around in quite a while.

"What's the matter?" she asked the cat.

It meowed again, this time in a long, drawn-out whine that would put a Siamese to shame.

Amy wasn't what you'd call an animal lover, but she started toward the fence, sensing something was out of sorts.

The feline jumped down, landing in the yard belonging to the neighbors Amy had yet to meet.

"Have it your way," she told the animal. "I was just trying to be friendly."

She crossed the lawn, which was looking a little more green than brown these days—thanks to Eddie—returned to the front porch, and let herself into the house. But before going upstairs to the guest room in which she'd been working, she went to the kitchen, opened the pantry, and reached for the bag of Kitty Delight.

Call her a softy, but she couldn't help pouring some of the cat food onto a small dessert plate. Next she filled a saucer with tap water and took both dishes out to the back porch, where she left them for the cat.

It wasn't the sort of thing that she'd normally do; after all, the cat might not be a stray at all. But it seemed like something that would cause Ellie to smile and nod, if she were somehow able to look over Amy's shoulder and see what she'd done.

With her act of kindness complete, Amy returned to the house, headed upstairs to the room she'd been packing, and opened the closet door. As she removed the last of the boxes stored inside, she spotted a carton in the farthermost corner. She had to practically crawl inside to remove it.

As she opened the lid of the black plastic container and peered at the contents, she couldn't help mumbling her thoughts. "Now this is interesting."

Several black-and-white photographs

had been scattered on top, one of which was a wedding picture.

The bride—definitely Ellie—wore a dress rather than a gown. But she had a small veil on her head and held a bouquet of roses.

She was ten or fifteen years older in this shot and didn't seem to be anywhere near as starry-eyed as she'd been in the photograph with Harold, the one still displayed on the mantel. Yet she was smiling just the same.

The groom, while not as young and handsome as Harold had been in his Army uniform, wore a dark suit and sported a white boutonniere in his lapel.

A girl in her early teens stood beside Ellie. She was taller, but not by more than an inch or so.

Was that Barbara?

It had to be.

She appeared to be scowling, though. Had she been unhappy about her mother's decision to remarry? Or was she just displaying the attitude of a teenager who'd rather be somewhere else?

It was hard to speculate.

Amy continued to sift through the contents of the box until she pulled out a marriage license that declared that Clayton Ronald Emery and Eleanor Kathleen Rucker had been joined in holy matrimony on February 14, 1957.

Valentine's Day. A romantic choice, Amy thought. But Maria had said that Ellie's second marriage hadn't been happy, that it hadn't lasted. Was that why she'd packed the evidence of it so far away?

As Amy went through the plastic container, she found a doctor bill—several of them, actually.

A pathology report.

Malignant.

A statement from Pacifica General Hospital.

Anesthesia.

Surgery.

Discharge instructions.

Mastectomy.

Amy's heart grew stone cold, and her fingers trembled as she realized that, like Susan, her mother, Ellie had found a lump in her breast.

She sat silent for several moments, taking it all in, absorbing the pain—physical and emotional—of a woman she'd never met, a woman with whom Amy shared some of the same genetics.

Those yearly physical exams would be even more important now.

Amy took a deep breath, then slowly exhaled as she pressed on, looking through the pictures and records her great-grandmother had set aside.

She found more photos, including a birthday party of some kind—the balloons and the candles on the cake a dead give-away.

Barbara wore a happy smile that day, yet Ellie's grin was clearly strained. Had she found the lump by then? Had she gone through the surgery yet?

Amy scanned the photographs and found one of a fishing trip. Clayton was grinning from ear to ear as he lifted a string of several good-sized trout. Yet Ellie, who stood next to him, appeared to be staring off in the distance, oblivious to her husband's pride at having snagged such a fine catch.

Near the bottom of the box, Amy withdrew a legal document dated August 4, 1962.

Eleanor Kathleen Emery, the petitioner,

had been granted a divorce on grounds of mental cruelty and irreconcilable differences.

For the longest time, Amy studied the items that had been stored in the box and considered the darkness they represented, the disappointment, the grief.

Harold's letters to his young wife, while sad and painful, had been tied with a satin ribbon and placed in the nightstand, within easy reach. Yet these memories, five years of Ellie's life, had been relegated to a black container in the far corner of a spare closet.

Had it been a conscious decision? A way to bury the painful past?

Amy assumed so, and her heart, which had already gone out to the elderly woman she'd never met, ached all the more.

What she wouldn't give to have the opportunity to talk with Ellie. To tell her she would have loved to have had the chance to know her.

At four-thirty, Brandon left the office earlier than usual, climbed behind the wheel of his car, and headed south on Interstate 5 to Del Mar.

There were a hundred reasons he

should have remained at work, should have brought dinner back to his desk so he could burn the midnight oil. But there was a better reason to leave and to return early in the morning. He needed to talk to Amy, and the pressing urge to do so had grown until he couldn't ignore it any longer.

At first, when she'd moved out, he'd believed that, given time, she'd see reason. That she'd realize a lot of her misery had come with the loss of her mother. That her grief had magnified the problems in their marriage, problems that could have easily been worked through. But more than six months had passed, and things weren't any better.

In fact, they might even be worse, and Brandon was at a complete loss, which was really starting to play havoc with his career.

He'd never lost focus before, never given less than a hundred percent to whatever case he'd been working on, but ever since Amy had walked out on him, it was a struggle to keep his mind on anything but her and Callie.

What did she want from him?

He'd never laid a hand on her that wasn't

gentle or supportive, never treated her with anything but respect. He'd worked hard and provided her with a nice house, a late-model luxury car, a closet full of expensive clothes.

A lot of women would be happy to have Brandon as a husband. And more than one had let him know that she'd thought he was a good catch, that she wouldn't mind being on the receiving end of a rebound. But Brandon didn't want another woman; he wanted Amy.

It was nearly five when he finally reached the complex where they'd first lived, the townhome where she'd recently moved in with their daughter.

Rather than take a spot in visitor parking, which would have been an irritating reminder that he no longer belonged here, that he might not be welcome, he pulled along the curb in front of their unit and shut off the ignition.

He didn't see her car, but it was probably in the garage. She was a stickler for routine and was undoubtedly inside fixing dinner.

It would be nice if she invited him to stay and eat. She was a great cook, and he'd lost about fifteen pounds since they split, finding himself tired of take-out and not interested in doing much cooking himself.

On his way up the sidewalk leading to the front door, a light ocean breeze blew in from the Pacific and whipped a hank of hair over his eye; he raked it aside. For the first time in ages, he was struck with something akin to adolescent insecurity, yet he pressed on.

Before he got a chance to ring the bell, Cookie started yelping, and moments later, footsteps sounded on the ceramic tile floor in the entry.

When Amy swung open the door, holding the little dog that thought it was a Rottweiler, she looked prettier than Brandon had ever remembered, and his heartbeat kicked up a notch.

"Brandon," she'd said softly, as if completely taken aback at seeing him.

The dog squirmed in her arms, its stub of a tail wagging like crazy. Cookie, he feared, was happier to see him than his wife was.

"Is Callie here?" he asked, thinking it would be best if he spoke to Amy alone and wondering how he was going to orchestrate it.

"She's upstairs in her room. Coloring, I think." Amy tucked a strand of hair behind her ear, revealing a pearl earring. "I'll call her down."

"No," he said. "You don't need to do that."

"Is something wrong?"

You can say that again. He probably ought to smile, to lighten the mood, but he couldn't seem to swing it. "I need to talk to you."

She glanced at her wristwatch. Was she wondering what had provoked him to leave the office so early? Or did she have someplace to go?

No, he caught the aroma of dinner cooking, and his mouth watered.

As she stepped aside, allowing him into the house, the hint of a smile finally broke free.

Score one for the home team, he thought.

She led him into the living room and indicated he should take a seat. He chose the sofa, which meant she could have joined him if she'd wanted to, but she sat on the edge of an overstuffed chair instead.

"What's up?" she asked.

"I want you to come home," he admitted. "And I'm willing to do whatever it takes to convince you that we can work things out."

"I don't want to come home."

"Okay. So we don't have to jump right back into something like that. But I'm willing to talk to a professional."

She studied him for a moment, then asked, "You mean a counselor?"

He shrugged. "I hadn't seen the value in it before." But if it helped Amy to talk it out, to come to grips with whatever had her searching for peace and happiness. . . . Hey, desperate times called for desperate measures.

"I think you'd find talking to a professional helpful," she said.

He blanched at the thought. Did she expect him to accept full responsibility for the split?

That wasn't fair.

Sure, he'd left her and Callie hanging on occasion. But it had only been due to his drive to succeed at the office, to provide for his family.

Did she have any idea how tough it was to grow up in a home where the utilities never got paid on time, where the electricity went off in the middle of a TV show? Or where a guy went in to take a shower and found that the only water, if it came out of the spigot at all, was cold? Where the pantry and the refrigerators were empty more times than not?

Chuck Masterson had been a drunk, a loser, and by the time Brandon had reached high school, he'd made up his mind to bolt the minute he could. He'd vowed that if he was ever blessed with a wife and kids, they'd never have to worry about the bills being paid, that they'd always have their hearts' desire. And, more importantly, that he'd never be an embarrassment to them.

"If you want to make an appointment for us to see a counselor," he said, "I'll find the time to go."

"You'll need to make the appointment yourself, Brandon. I'm not going to go with you. At one time, I would have. But I'm just not up for it anymore."

He opened his hands, stretched out his fingers, then rolled them into fists, trying to hold on to something just out of reach.

"What good would counseling do me if

we don't have a marriage to work on?" he asked.

"It will make it easier for you to have another relationship in the future. And it will help you relate to Callie better."

Yeah, right. Amy was implying that *he* was the one who had all the problems, that *he* was the one who needed to be "fixed." But what about her? She'd lost her mother, and while it was normal for her to grieve, she'd blamed all her misery on him, on the things she'd found lacking in their relationship.

So what about all the things in their marriage that had been right?

"I think you ought to talk to someone about your childhood," she added. "About your dad's alcoholism. I think it will help you understand why you're so driven. Why you can relate to business associates and clients, but can't relate to your own wife and child."

"Being career-minded and driven is an asset. My job isn't the fire-breathing dragon you seem to think it is. It's what provided you the ability to be a stay-at-home mother." Brandon blew out an exasperated breath. "You know Amy, I'm not the only one who needs to talk to a counselor."

"What are you saying? I had a loving home, two good parents." She stiffened. "My family wasn't dysfunctional."

"Maybe not. But you're still grieving for your mom."

"I'll always grieve for her. She wasn't just my mother, she was my best friend. I'll never get over losing her."

"That's what I mean."

She rolled her eyes.

Maybe he ought to try another approach. "Therapy isn't covered in my health plan—I checked. But I'm willing to pay whatever it costs. Let's both visit a counselor and see what he or she has to say."

"You think money solves everything."

"Well, it certainly beats not having any at all. Don't forget that it's my job, my salary and savings plans that allow you to rent a house you're not even living in."

Her eyes blazed, which was his first clue to try yet another tack—or, better yet, to let it all ride until another day. But he'd had it up to his eyebrows with her stubbornness, with her inability to see the big picture.

"For some crazy reason," he began, realizing that *crazy* had probably been a lousy word choice, but unable to reel it back now, "you're so busy chasing the past and your roots that you're not focused on the here and now, on the family you and I created."

"Don't you dare talk to me about focusing on family." She stood and crossed her arms. "I'm not going to talk to you about this anymore. Nor am I going to remind you that you almost missed my mother's funeral, which was unforgivable."

"I made it," he said, getting to his feet because he hated to be looked down upon, hated to be forced into a defensive position. "How many times are you going to throw that at me? I had a critical meeting to attend, something I couldn't cancel or postpone, even under the circumstances. But I left early."

"Yeah, well, not early enough. That was the last in a long line of disappointments that pushed our marriage over the edge. And I'm not going to set myself up for any more."

"I don't suppose you are. I've never met a woman as strong-willed and stubborn as you are."

"Look who's talking." She chuffed and crossed her arms. "I'm not the one who's stubborn. I'm just determined when I set my mind on something."

"Sometimes our greatest strengths are our greatest flaws."

"Maybe you should be the one assessing your strengths, Brandon." She walked to the door, opened it.

Clearly, that was his cue to leave.

He ought to apologize, to say something to make things right. But he, too, was stubborn and determined. And he refused to throw himself at her pretty little feet.

As he walked out of the house, he heard the door shut behind him, just a little louder than necessary.

His heart was pounding and his blood was swishing through his veins like that of a dazed boxer going down for the count. He'd really done it this time, but right now, he didn't care. He just needed to get out of there.

As he climbed into his car and slid behind the wheel, an unbidden thought came to mind, a homeless man's voice that said, *The future offers healing, if you'll open your heart. And making peace with the past is often the first step.*

Like reconciling with his father?

Yeah, right. He swore under his breath.

What in the world was he thinking? Who in their right mind reflected on the half-baked advice of a homeless man?

Besides, Brandon hadn't seen his old man in fifteen years, and he had no idea where to even look for him—if he were inclined to do so.

And he wasn't.

Chuck had very little to show for his fifty-four years on earth. Just an old fifth-wheel trailer that was parked on the edge of the church grounds and some secondhand furnishings and clothes. But he had plenty to eat, good friends, and the blessed assurance of his salvation.

He also had people who depended upon him and a job to do as long as he was physically able.

Dawn and Joe Randolph, the couple in charge of the Parkside Community Church soup kitchen, had already left for the day, and Chuck was cleaning up. He didn't need to worry about anything in the actual kitchen, though. Dawn was particular about how she wanted it cleaned and always took care of it herself.

But Chuck was in charge of wiping down tables, mopping the floors, and cleaning the restrooms, something he took pride in. As it was written in Colossians, *Whatever you do, work at it wholeheartedly as though you were doing it for the Lord and not merely for people.*

That had become his motto these days.

So while he was in the ladies' room, mopping the floor, he whistled a happy tune—a praise song, actually—when a dull ache in his side cramped up.

He paused a moment and massaged the ache, thinking that it was just a result of getting older.

Taking a moment to catch his breath, he leaned against the mop as though it were a cane. He sure seemed to get winded these days. He wondered if it was a result of the cancer, or whether that, too, was to be expected with age.

It didn't matter, he supposed.

As he got back to work and opened the door of the handicapped stall, he spotted a lady's handbag on the floor—a brown, faux leather purse that had been around the block a few times, just like most of the people who partook of the free lunches offered by Parkside Community.

He leaned the mop against the wall and stooped to pick it up, wincing from the pesky pain in his side.

Some poor woman was probably stressing out about losing her purse right this very moment, and he could understand why she would. A lot of people couldn't be trusted these days.

He checked the contents of the wallet in an effort to identify the owner—Janice French, who lived at 233 First Street, Apartment 13. Chuck had no idea how to get a hold of her, what number to call, so he would just take it to her after he locked up.

When he finished his work, he went into the kitchen to find some kind of bag or sack to put the purse in. There was no need for him to carry a lady's handbag all over town. Next he shut off the lights, locked the doors, and headed for the bus stop, which was located near the front of the church.

He didn't need to wait long for number 621, which would take him to just within a block of the apartment complex where Ms. French lived.

The bus pulled to a stop, its diesel engine humming so loud a fellow could hardly think.

When the driver opened the door, Chuck held the paper sack under one arm and gripped the handrail to steady himself as he climbed the steps.

Herb Dougherty, the robust driver who'd worked for the transit district for more than twenty years, welcomed him aboard with a hearty smile. "Hello, Chuck. How's it going today?"

"Not too bad."

"You sure?" Herb asked. "You look a little pale."

"Just a bit tired. That's all."

"Good. You going to be working at the soup kitchen on Saturday? They're having that birthday party for ol' Stan Jeffries."

"Yep. Stan's a great guy." Chuck tried to smile, although the pain in his side kept gnawing at him, urging him to take a seat.

As he made his way down the aisle, the diesel engine roared and the bus bumped and swayed as Herb drove back onto the road.

Boy oh boy, Chuck thought, taking a seat near the emergency exit in one of the only empty spots available. He tried to massage out the pain in his side and figured he would have to take a couple of aspirins or something as soon as he got home.

Two stops later, a little old lady climbed onboard. Her cane dangled over her forearm as she tried to make her way down the aisle. She scanned both sides of the bus, looking for a place to sit, but not having any luck.

A couple of teenage boys, their hair shaggy and in need of a trim, looked up. He expected one of them to give up his seat, but when neither of them did, Chuck got to his feet, clutching the paper sack to his chest and biting back a wince.

Thank goodness he'd be getting off at the next stop. Maybe he'd have to sit on the bench for a moment or two.

"Here," he told the lady. "You can have my seat."

"Thanks, young man."

He could see where she might think of him as young. And he supposed he was. Fifty-four wasn't decrepit, although it sure felt that way sometimes.

'Course, that was his own fault. He should have taken better care of himself when he was younger—drunk less, eaten better food, exercised more.

He sucked in a breath, then blew it out. His side wasn't hurting him all that bad anymore, but now his stomach was tossing and turning.

Had he eaten something bad?

He wasn't one to complain, but if there was one thing he hated, it was catching the intestinal flu or a bad case of food poisoning.

As the bus slowed to a stop, Chuck found himself leaning forward. He grabbed hold of the back of the old lady's seat to steady himself. Apparently, he gripped her hair while doing so, and she squeaked out an "Ow!"

"Sorry," he said, trying to make his way off the bus.

A wave of dizziness slowed his steps, and he blinked a couple of times, trying to shake it off so that Herb didn't think he was dawdling.

"See you on Saturday," Herb said.

"Yep. You sure will." As Chuck made his way down the steps and his first foot reached the ground, everything started to spin, and his knee buckled.

Uh-oh.

A roar sounded in his ears, and then everything went dark.

Chapter 10

Late Wednesday morning, as the sun stretched high over Fairbrook, Maria carried two glasses of lemonade out to the front porch, where Captain sat with Ellie in side-by-side rocking chairs and Wally played with his trains near their feet.

Captain, who was closing in on his ninetieth birthday, appeared to be intrigued by the child, but Ellie didn't seem to be the least bit interested.

"I hope this is sweet enough for you," Maria said as she handed them the drinks.

Captain, who wore a broad-brimmed straw hat and a blue plaid shirt, took a sip, then lowered his glass. A grin softened his wrinkled face and put a twinkle in his brown eyes. "It's just right, Maria. I haven't had lemonade like this since I was a boy."

Ellie, who'd only picked at her breakfast and had been quiet all morning, merely held her glass with both hands and stared off into the street. She'd been doing that a lot lately, traveling to some faraway place where words didn't exist.

"Wally," Maria said. "Would you like some lemonade?"

"Not now. I'm not thirsty."

That wasn't surprising. He'd had two glasses of milk at breakfast.

As the engine of an approaching vehicle sounded, Maria turned to see the postman across the street, which meant that he'd already delivered her mail.

"Jerry's here earlier than usual," Captain said. "He doesn't usually come until after lunch."

"Well, while I'm outside, I may as well get it." So Maria walked to the curb, opened her box, and pulled out a good-sized stack of mail that was sandwiched between the *PennySaver* and a packet of coupons for the smart shopper.

On her way back to the house, she thumbed through the delivery. The church newsletter came today, reminding her that Pastor Craig usually stopped by to visit Captain and Ellie on Wednesdays. She also spotted the glossy photograph of an ornate European music hall, the *Palau de la Música Catalana* in Barcelona. Assuming the postcard was from Walter and Hilda, she paused on the sidewalk to read their note.

Yesterday, Hilda wrote, *on our first day in Barcelona, Walter and I went to the art museum. Today we saw this extraordinary music hall. And tomorrow, we're going to take a tour of the Basque region. You'd love Spain, Maria. I hope you and the kids can visit someday.*

Maria's maternal grandparents had been born near the Pyrenees Mountains and had told her and her cousins a lot of stories about the small village where they'd grown up and gotten married. So going to Spain had always been a dream of hers.

She glanced at the elderly couple in the rockers and her preschool-age son, who played with his Thomas the Tank Engines on the porch beside them.

It would be a long time before she could ever travel to Europe, but that didn't mean she wasn't thrilled that her dear friends had been able to go.

She continued to sort through the mail, spotting the power bill. She was almost afraid to open it. She'd been nagging the kids about leaving the lights on, but they always forgot. And sometimes Ellie got up in the middle of the night, turning on lamps all over the house.

If Joe Davila hadn't still been in the hospital, Maria might have finally caved in and admitted that it was time to put Ellie in a convalescent hospital. But she didn't want to put any unnecessary stress on Joe and his wife.

Besides, *Tía* Sofia and Ellie had once vowed to take care of each other in their twilight years. And Maria was glad she could look out for Ellie now, on Sofia's behalf.

On those rare occasions when recognition sparked in Ellie's eyes, it was all worth it, but unfortunately, the poor woman hadn't had many meaningful conversations since Maria and Danny had found her wandering in the canyon six weeks ago.

"Good morning," a familiar male called out.

Maria didn't have to look up to know that Eddie was talking to her. As she turned toward him, her pulse slipped into a "Lady in Red" beat, and a smile swept across her face.

He was wearing jeans today. And a white T-shirt with a landscaping logo. Nothing special. Yet by the way her heart was strumming, you'd think he'd just stepped off the cover of *GQ* with a bouquet of red roses and a bottle of champagne in hand.

He strode toward his pickup, then lifted the lawnmower out of the back. She assumed that he meant to mow Amy's lawn, until he lowered it to the sidewalk and pushed it toward her house.

What was he doing? When he'd cut the tree limb in her backyard, it was because it had been hanging over the fence and into Amy's property. And she understood why he'd cut both sides of the hedge the other day.

But mowing her grass? That was clearly not a favor to Amy or the Davilas, no matter how badly her lawn needed to be cut and edged.

"I can't pay you for this," she reminded him.

"You don't have to. I'm doing it because I want to."

Their gazes locked momentarily, and she felt sixteen all over again, before the harsh realities of life had chased away any romantic notions.

Still, she couldn't deny the sparks of attraction that went off whenever she spotted Eddie, whenever he looked her way.

"Mom," Danny called from the front door. "Where'd you put my Padres shirt?"

So much for thoughts of youthful innocence and carefree flirtation. She turned to her son. "I threw it out a couple of days ago."

"What!?" He plopped his hands on his hips. "Why did you do *that?*"

"It had a big tear under the sleeve, and there were a couple of stains on the front."

"But it was my *favorite* shirt! Why didn't you ask me first?"

Before she could respond, Captain

piped up. "When I was your age, I'd have gotten my backside smacked for talking to my mother like that. You're lucky you have a mom to do the laundry and to fold your clothes, son."

Danny only appeared to be the slightest bit contrite, and Maria blew out a sigh. She wasn't one to coddle her children and allow them to get away with being disrespectful, but deep in her heart, she realized her oldest son was struggling with something. Something she needed to address. That is, if she could figure out what it was. And he wasn't talking.

"Do you have a baseball mitt and a ball?" Eddie asked the boy.

"Yeah. In my closet. Why?"

"Because after I finish mowing the yard, I thought it might be fun to play catch for a little while."

Danny tossed him a why-not? shrug. "Sure. That would be cool." Then he disappeared into the house.

Maria took a few steps toward the man. "Thanks, Eddie. I appreciate you spending some time with him. But Captain's right. He shouldn't talk to me like that."

"I know. And I plan to bring that up after

we throw the ball around a bit, if it's okay with you."

She wasn't sure how to respond to his offer, to his understanding and support.

Should she jump on it?

Or turn it down? After all, the kids weren't his responsibility.

"When my brother and I were younger," Eddie added, "and we'd done something wrong, our father would say, 'Get in the car, *mijo.* We're going for a ride.' And then, when he had us alone, he'd let us know that we'd disappointed him."

"I used to get a little walk," Captain said. "Out to the woodshed, where my father took off his belt and let the leather do the talking on my hind end. But he only had to do it once or twice."

Eddie smiled. "I didn't need too many of those kind of talks. My dad had a way about him that made us want to obey, to make him proud. My brother uses that same approach with the boys on his team, and it seems to work. Those kids would do anything for him. In fact, a couple of the mothers said their sons' grades are improving and they've even started cleaning their rooms without being told."

If there'd ever been any question in Maria's mind of whether Eddie was a decent guy, whether he'd make a good husband and father, there wasn't any longer.

She tried to tell herself that she was too heavy-duty for him, that he could—and *should*—find another woman. But right now, as he prepared to mow her yard and planned to take her son under his wing, she found herself backpedaling. Reconsidering.

She couldn't help thinking that Eddie was different. That he might give a single mom with three kids more than a second glance. And she hoped that he would.

He'd invited Danny to baseball practice last Saturday, but she hadn't found a sitter and wanted to observe the first time. She had no idea how she'd pull it off, but she was determined to go next Saturday, even if she had to call the church and ask if they could find someone to sit with Ellie and Captain for an hour or two.

As Eddie started the lawnmower and Maria headed back to the house, Amy drove up and parked in her driveway.

Maria hoped her new neighbor didn't

think that she was trying to get a landscape freebie on behalf of the Davilas.

So she waited for Amy to climb out of her car, then went to meet her.

As Amy shut off the ignition, she noticed Maria in her front yard and waved. Then, after sliding out from behind the wheel, she opened the rear passenger door for Callie.

"Good morning," Maria called out as she approached the shrubs that separated the two yards.

"It is, isn't it?" Amy scanned her surroundings, taking note of the warmth of the sun and the melodious sound of birds chirping.

"Is Sara here?" Callie asked Maria. "And can she come over and play? I brought my Candy Land game today."

Maria smiled. "She's inside, picking up her toys. But yes, she can play as soon as she's finished."

Amy glanced at Maria's porch, where an elderly couple sat in rocking chairs. She wondered if the old woman was the one who had talked to Callie the other day.

"Do you have company?" she asked.

"Not exactly. That's Ellie and Captain. They're my boarders."

"Ellie?" Amy froze in mid-step. The world around her—the birds, the mower—seemed to grow silent. "Ellie *Rucker?*"

Maria nodded. "She's been staying here."

"I didn't know. . . ." Amy, her mind reeling, tried to make sense of it. "I thought she was in long-term care."

"Well, in a sense, I guess you could say that she is. She won't be going home again. Her grandson had been making arrangements to take her to live with him until he was forced to put her in long-term care. I offered to let her stay with me until he was ready for her, but then he had his first of several heart attacks. And since Ellie was doing okay, I continued to keep her."

"You've had her all this time?"

"Yes, and it's been working out okay so far. But I know it's only temporary. I hate the idea of her going to a convalescent hospital, but we're not going to be able to put that off much longer." Maria tucked a strand of hair behind her ear. "I suppose I should have mentioned something when you first moved in, but Barbara didn't want the new tenant to bother Ellie with any problems that might come up, although, after meeting you, I realized you wouldn't do that."

Amy was still trying to wrap her mind around the knowledge that her biological great-grandmother sat on Maria's porch. She wanted to meet the woman, even if she wasn't sure what to say. Or how to introduce herself.

"Would you mind if I talked to her?" Amy asked.

"No, not at all. But don't expect much by way of a conversation. Some days are better than others, and this one hasn't been very good."

"Mommy?" Callie patted Amy's side. "Can I go inside and help Sara pick up her toys?"

"If it's okay with her mom."

"Go ahead," Maria said.

As Callie raced into the house, Amy walked to the sidewalk, then cut across a patch of Maria's lawn, which Eddie had just finished mowing.

"I hope you don't mind that Eddie's over

here," Maria said. "He wanted to do me a favor."

"No problem. I think he's getting paid for the job, not by the hour." Amy paused before approaching Ellie, who was stooped, even while sitting. Her curly white hair was combed, and she wore pink lipstick, a dab of blush, even a bit of mascara. Amy assumed that Maria had applied the makeup; Grandma Rossi sometimes had trouble getting hers on straight. And it warmed her heart to think that someone cared enough to take the time.

As Amy neared the porch, she tried to imagine this Ellie as the young bride who stood beside Harold in the black-and-white photograph on the mantel. The woman who'd taught herself to play the accordion by ear, who'd written her innermost thoughts in journals and created not only watercolors, but quilts, afghans, and hand-crocheted tablecloths.

But as Ellie stared blankly, Amy wasn't having much luck with the imagery.

"Mrs. Rucker?" Amy asked.

At the sound of her name, Ellie looked up. "Yes?"

"I'm Amy Masterson."

Ellie frowned, her gaze dulled by confusion. "I don't know you."

No, she didn't; but Amy knew her. Better than she or her family might guess.

The elderly man who was wearing a Panama hat and sitting in the other rocker leaned forward and asked, "How are you related to Ellie?"

"I . . . uh . . ." Amy hated to lie; it went against everything she believed in, everything she'd been taught. So she struggled for an answer that wouldn't be too far of a stretch. "Actually, we've never even met."

"I'm sorry for the assumption. It's just that you look a bit like her daughter, Barbara." The old man grinned, his brown eyes crinkling. "Kind of like a fair-haired second cousin, I suppose."

Suddenly feeling rude, Amy reached out her hand to the man, felt his gnarled fingers grasp hers. "I'm sorry. I should have introduced myself to you."

"No," Maria interjected. "I dropped the ball. Captain, Amy is our new neighbor." Then she turned to Amy and grinned. "This dapper gentleman is Bertram Saylors, although everyone calls him Captain."

"It's nice to meet you." Amy gave his hand a gentle squeeze before releasing it.

"The pleasure is mine." The charming old man, his skin as weathered as a piece of leather that had been left to the elements for a long time, beamed.

"Captain and Ellie have been friends for years," Maria said. "A few weeks ago, when he stopped by to visit, he mentioned that he was going to have to give up his apartment and that he wasn't sure where he'd be moving. He thought he'd feel better living in an intermediate care facility, and I offered him our spare room. Now he lives here."

The screen door swung open, and the girls bounded out.

"Can I take Sara to the other house now?" Callie asked. "We're going to play the game, and she gets to go first."

Before either of the mothers could give them the go-ahead, Ellie bent forward and clasped Callie's arm. "Angel?"

"I'm *not* Angel," Callie said. "Don't you remember?"

"Of course. I'll never forget you, honey. Now you go on inside and get your jacket. It looks like rain today."

Callie's gaze sought Amy's, silently asking, *What do I do?* And Amy's heart twisted.

It didn't seem fair. Why couldn't she have found Ellie sooner?

But life wasn't always fair.

Amy carefully withdrew her daughter's arm from the elderly woman's grip. "Thank you, Ellie. I'll make sure she stays warm and dry." Then she reached into her purse, pulled out the keys, and handed them to Callie. "Why don't you and Sara unlock the door? I'll be right behind you."

As the two girls dashed off, Maria nodded toward the house. "I'd better get inside and finish the breakfast dishes. I was sidetracked earlier this morning and want to get some work done and the house picked up before Pastor Craig comes. He usually stops by to see Ellie and Captain after he's made his hospital visits on Wednesday."

"You've certainly got your hands full," Amy said, realizing that Maria had taken on a lot for a single mom.

"There are some rewarding moments," she said.

Something told Amy they were few and far between.

"Maria is a special lady," Captain said. "But she doesn't get out very much."

"Yes, I do," the petite brunette countered. "Well, on occasion. My friends, Walter and Hilda, sometimes come by and sit with Ellie and the kids. They also run errands for me, but they're on vacation and won't get home until next week."

"If you need someone to give you a break," Amy said, "just let me know. I'd be happy to help out whenever I can."

"Really?"

The offer had rolled off Amy's tongue without her giving it any thought, but she nodded. "Yes, really." Maria had no idea there was a biological connection, and Amy wasn't going to mention it now, but looking out for Ellie seemed like the right thing to do.

Maria bit down on her bottom lip, then asked, "I don't suppose you'd be able to stay at the house for a couple of hours on Saturday, would you?"

"Sure. What time?"

"From about ten until noon?"

"That works for me."

"You have no idea how much I appreciate this."

Amy smiled. "I think it's wonderful that you've tried to keep Ellie in a loving and familiar environment. There aren't many people who would."

"Well, it seems to me that you're one of those people, too."

Was she?

Amy had no idea why she'd gotten so involved. She supposed it made her feel better about what she was doing.

And maybe it would help ease some of the awkwardness when Maria found out that she and Amy weren't neighbors at all.

Chuck didn't remember much about how he got to the hospital. He was told that he'd been brought in by an ambulance, but that entire afternoon was pretty much a blur to him now.

Apparently, while getting off the bus, he'd passed out for some medical reason unrelated to the cancer and fell. But then he'd cracked his head on the curb, and he'd gone down for the count.

When he finally came to, he was lying on a gurney in the ER and some woman was asking him the typical questions needed to admit him: name; address; date of birth;

religious preference; nearest relative; whether he had insurance or not.

He answered each one truthfully. Well, everything except next of kin. He didn't know where Brandon was living nowadays—even if he'd wanted to give them his name. But he didn't see any reason to do that. Too much time had passed since they'd last seen each other, and there was too much murky water under the bridge.

But almost everyone had a family, and Chuck had spent enough years without one. He hated to make it sound as though he was alone in this world, which wasn't the case any longer. He had tons of close friends, most of whom either worked at or frequented the soup kitchen.

So Chuck had told the woman from the admissions department that Craig Houston, the associate pastor of Parkside Community Church, was his nearest relative.

And hey, that wasn't such a big stretch. Biblically speaking, they were brothers—joint heirs in the family of God, right?

And now here he was, banged up and as weak as a newborn kitten. He reached up, felt the bump on his noggin, fingered the stitches that held the gash together. It still smarted, and it was also the least of his troubles, but he needed to get out of here. The hospital bill was going to be outrageous, and there was no way he'd ever be able to pay it on his wages.

A knock sounded at the doorjamb that led to the busy hall, and when he turned to see who it was, he spotted Pastor Craig.

"Hey, Chuck," the fair-haired young minister said as he entered the hospital room. "I'm sorry I didn't get here sooner, but my wife and I were out to dinner when the call came in. And we didn't check our messages until morning."

"Young love, huh?" Chuck offered him a smile. He remembered those days, back when he and Marianne were first married. "Lucky you."

"My wife is pretty special. But it wasn't a romantic dinner. We went out with friends last night. Do you remember Ramon Gonzales?"

"Is he that fella who works with that youth baseball league?"

"Yes." Craig crossed the shiny tile floor and took a seat in the chair next to Chuck's bed. "But how about you? What's going on?"

Chuck made an attempt to laugh it off. "Tripped and fell while getting off the bus. I wouldn't be surprised if the transit district made me wear a football helmet next time I tried to get on board. Either that or ban me for life."

For *life?* That wouldn't be all that long, Chuck supposed. The doctor had come in earlier today with the test results. The numbers hadn't made him too happy, and he'd been talking about a bone marrow transplant. But Chuck wouldn't agree to one of those.

What was the use? His liver was shot already. And since the odds were stacked against him, why go to all that time and trouble and expense?

A simple cost/benefit analysis had been enough to tell Doc Williams that ol' Chuck was going to pass.

Pass on the test, pass from this life. Hey, how about that? He was getting clever with words in his old age.

But what difference did it make?

His best bet for a matching donor would

be in finding Brandon and asking him to submit to a test. But Brandon could be anywhere these days. And even if he was up for a reunion, he didn't feel like looking him up.

Okay, call him a coward. As long as Chuck didn't meet up with his son, he wouldn't have to face the fact that Brandon had probably written him off for good.

God might have forgiven Chuck for his failings—he truly believed that, too.

Trouble was, Chuck hadn't forgiven himself.

And then there was the question that had been niggling at him for years, the question a simple little blood test would answer—if Chuck had ever found the guts to pursue it.

Was Chuck truly Brandon's father?

Chapter 11

Eddie stood on one side of Maria's freshly mowed lawn and threw the baseball to Danny. The boy wound up and pitched it back.

"You've got a good arm," Eddie told him.

"You think so?"

Eddie nodded. "In fact, I think you should join my brother's baseball team. They're practicing again at Mulberry Park on Saturday at ten o'clock. Are you interested?"

"I guess, but it depends on what my mom says. And I have a feeling she's going to say no."

"I've been talking to her about it, and we might be able to work something out." Eddie glanced up at the porch to see if Maria might have come outside again, but she hadn't.

The elderly couple remained, but the man had leaned back in his chair, his fingers clasped and resting on his chest, his eyes closed and lips parted. Snoozing, Eddie suspected.

He seemed like a nice enough guy. It was obvious that he wanted to help Maria out with Danny, but Eddie figured his ideas about strict discipline might be making matters worse.

As Eddie tossed the ball back to the boy, he asked, "How good are you with a bat?"

"I'm okay. But I don't get much chance to practice."

Eddie had to reach to snag the next throw. "Does that bother you?"

"A lot of things bother me. Mostly, it's hard being the only guy living here." He shot a glance at the elderly couple on the porch. "Well, I'm not exactly the only one, but you know what I mean."

Eddie had a pretty good idea what he was getting at. “Do you miss not having your dad around here?”

Danny caught the ball Eddie had just thrown, but held it in his mitt. “He was never around all that much anyway. But he was nice to me. And a lot of times he would say, ‘Come on, Danny. Let’s you and me go to the store or to the post office,’ or things like that. And we’d leave Mom and Sara at home. I know he did something really stupid and got himself in big trouble. And that sucked for all of us. So I guess I don’t miss him. But it would be nice to have a dad around, like my friends have.”

“I can understand that,” Eddie said. “But you’re lucky in some other ways.”

“How’s that?”

“You’ve got a mom who loves you.”

“Yeah, I know.” Danny wound up and finally threw the ball back. “But she’s always giving me all these chores to do. And when . . .” He looked up at the porch. “Well, the more people who move in here, the more work she has to do and the more help she needs. I know a lot of kids who don't have to do any work at all. They just get to play all day. And they get to go fishing and join Boy Scouts and stuff like that."

"I know what you mean. My old man was the gardener on a big estate, and he had way more work than one guy was able to do alone. So my brother and I had to help him. There were a lot of times we had to miss out on fun things because we had to work on a Saturday."

"That's too bad."

"You know what, though? I learned a lot."

"Yeah, but at least you got to learn things like using tools and lawnmowers and stuff like that. I have to learn how to do dishes and the laundry. And how to clean the house."

Eddie chuckled. "So you think that some jobs are for men to do and others are for women?"

"Yeah. Don't you?"

"You ought to see my brother Ramon. He and his wife Shana are foster parents to a couple of boys who play on the baseball team. And there are a lot of nights when Shana has to work late, so he cooks dinner and cleans up the kitchen. The boys, Luis and Carlitos, help out, too. In a way, a family is a team, Danny. Sometimes you play left field, and other times you have to cover third base. That's just the way it is."

"That makes sense," Danny said. "So do you cook dinner for *your* wife?"

"I'm not married, but if I was, I'd help out doing whatever I needed to. And that won't be hard because my mom taught me some of the basics in the kitchen."

As the boy slipped into a pensive mood, Eddie dropped the subject, hoping his words would sink in.

But Danny slowly crossed the lawn to where Eddie stood. "There's something else."

"What's that?"

The boy sighed and shifted his weight to one foot. "The other day, my friend Jason was kind of messing with this older guy, a sixth grader named Doug. Jason didn't mean anything by it, you know how it is. But Doug flipped out and hit him in the nose. And it bled. When a teacher asked him about it, Jason said he sometimes gets nosebleeds. That it was no big deal. He didn't tell on Doug because . . .

Well, you know how it is. He didn't want to be called a snitch."

Eddie understood, although he didn't think it was wrong to tell on someone for hitting.

"Then the next day, Jason didn't even do anything. He was just walking to the cafeteria when Doug stopped him and told him he'd better watch his back. That one day, on the way home, he was going to kick his butt."

Scary stuff for an eleven-year-old, Eddie thought. "So then what happened?"

"At first, Jason didn't tell anyone 'cause he didn't want to be called a wimp or a sissy or anything. But then he went home and told his dad." Danny shrugged. "Well, it wasn't exactly his dad. It was his stepfather. But the guy is a cop. And he called the school, and the next thing you know, Doug quit picking on Jason."

"So, from what you're telling me, you think a dad comes in handy sometimes," Eddie said. "Even if he's only a stepfather."

"Yeah. But who am I supposed to call if something like that happens to me? My mom?" Danny shook his head. "She's just a girl. And she's big on saying sorry and turning the other cheek and that sort of thing. So if someone picks on me, I'm gonna have to fight 'em myself. Either that or get my butt kicked."

Eddie placed a hand on the boy's shoulder. "You're right, Danny. It's tough when you don't have a dad. But sometimes a male friend, like a coach or a teacher or someone like that, can step in and be the man you need."

"Well, I don't even have one of those. My teacher is Mrs. Dobbins, and she's almost as old as Ellie. What's she gonna do?" Danny slowly shook his head. "It really sucks."

"I can understand that. But you seem to be lashing out at everyone. And that doesn't seem fair. Who are you really mad at?"

Danny shrugged and clucked his tongue. "Heck, I'm not sure. My dad, I guess. My mom, too. And maybe I'm even mad at God. Isn't He supposed to fix things like this?"

"Maybe things aren't really broken. And maybe you don't need to be mad at anyone. Why don't you just take one day at a time? And if you ever have a problem with a bully, you give me a call. I'll do whatever I can to help."

"Really?"

Eddie wasn't sure what he was promising or why it felt like the right thing to do, but he nodded. "Yeah. Really. I'll give you my telephone number. You can call me anytime."

"Cool."

They continued to play catch for another ten minutes or so—more time than Eddie really had to spare. But he liked Maria's oldest son, and he wanted to help.

"I'm going to have to get back to work," Eddie finally said. "Maybe we can play catch later this afternoon. If you're going to join the team, it won't hurt to get some practice in."

"I appreciate you helping me and all," Danny said. "Especially since you're supposed to be working. I sure wouldn't want to see you get fired for being nice."

"Don't worry about it. If I was getting paid by the hour, it wouldn't be right, but I'm getting paid by the job. So it just means that I'll need to stay late today." Eddie handed over the ball, then pulled out his business card and handed it to the boy. "My cell phone number is on this. Call me anytime, even if you just want someone to talk to."

"Thanks, Eddie. This is really cool."

"Why don't you go and put the baseball gear away before your mom has to tell you to do it? That way, you'll show her that you're a responsible member of the team. And it also lets her know that you can be trusted to do the right things, even when she's not around to watch you. Trust and freedom go hand in hand."

"Okay. I'll do that. Thanks."

As the boy headed for the house, the old man, who'd apparently woken up from his nap, got up from the rocker and started down the steps. Eddie was about to turn away and go back to work when he realized Captain was heading toward him.

"Thanks for playing ball with the boy. If I got around better these days, I'd do it myself."

So Captain wasn't always going to advocate taking a don't-spare-the-rod approach and regular trips to the woodshed? That was good to know.

Eddie wasn't against an occasional spanking, but he considered it to be a last resort. "Danny's a good kid."

"You're right. He's one of the best. But he's got a man-sized chip on his shoulders these days, and he's adding a lot of extra stress to his mother's full days."

"Yeah, I know."

"Do you fancy Maria?" the old man asked.

The question came at Eddie from out of the blue, and he found himself trying to backpedal. "No. Not really. I mean, she's a pretty girl and all."

"She certainly is. And she's also got a heart of gold. That's why Ellie is staying here and not parked in some convalescent home for the rest of her days."

Eddie didn't know what to say. He'd come to that same conclusion himself, but he didn't want to show his hand to Captain. Not when he wasn't sure how to even approach Maria and actually ask her out.

"I just want to make sure your intentions are honorable," Captain continued. "She's been through a lot, and she doesn't need any more headaches."

"Adding to her trouble is the last thing I want to do. But to be honest, I would like to get to know her better."

"I can't blame you for that."

Eddie's hopes rose as he realized he'd gotten the old man's blessing. At least, it sure felt that way.

Captain straightened, as if he was going to head back to the porch and let the whole thing drop.

But he didn't.

Instead, he asked, "You ever been in trouble? Served any time?"

Hope dropped into the pit of Eddie's stomach like a load of bricks.

What should he admit? That he wasn't a bad guy? That he'd made a stupid mistake when he was a teenager? That he'd been responsible for someone's death and had been incarcerated?

"Why?" he asked instead.

"Don't know. Just a gut feeling, I guess. I used to work at a halfway house for years and saw a lot of guys come in and out."

Had Captain spotted something in Eddie's demeanor? Maybe the way he checked out his surroundings and watched his back?

Eddie tried to tell himself that what he'd done to end up in prison hadn't been as bad as what Maria's ex-husband had done, but he'd caused someone's death just the same. Still, he'd paid his debt to society.

"Danny told me you used to be involved with the Salvation Army," Eddie said.

"Yep. For more than twenty years."

"Then you ought to be familiar with concepts like forgiveness and second chances."

The old man nodded. "I certainly am."

"Well, good. Because I'm not the kid I used to be. And no matter what happens between Maria and me, I'll never intentionally hurt her or break her trust."

"Fair enough," Captain said.

Eddie hoped so, because life wasn't always fair.

He'd found that out the hard way.

Back inside the house, Maria put away the last of the breakfast dishes, then reached for the dishcloth in the sink and wrung it out. As she was wiping down the kitchen table, she realized she'd just dumped the mail on the counter and left it. So she separated it once again. After carrying the ads and junk mail to the recycling bins, she tossed them out, only to see an envelope flutter out.

It was a letter from Ray, and she'd almost thrown it away. To be honest, that's what she'd like to do with all of his correspondence—trash it or recycle it, which seemed especially fitting, since she rarely responded to him anyway.

But while she had a few minutes to herself, she pulled out a chair, took a seat at the table, and read what he had to say this time.

Dear Maria,

I hope you and the kids are doing okay. Danny hasn't written back to me yet. Will you please remind him? I know it's kind of a long drive for you, but it would be great if you could bring the kids for a visit again. It's been a long time since I've seen them.

You have no idea how lonely it gets here. On the bright side, it's given me a lot of time to think about the mistakes I've made.

By the way, my first parole hearing is on the 7th of September. There's a good chance they'll let me out if I can show them that I've got a family that needs me and kids to support. My uncle is going to tell them that he'll guarantee me work. And I figured a letter from you would help, too.

I know that I've hurt you a lot in the past. So I don't blame you for not wanting to help me. But could you please do it for the kids? You have no idea how bad it is to be locked away. I've learned my lesson, and when I get out, I plan to be the best father in the world.

Don't forget to tell Danny to write. Is he still mad at me? The last time you brought him for a visit, he let me know that I'd really let him down. I apologized, but there's not much I can do about making it up to him while I'm stuck in here. So that leads me back to the question I asked in the first place. Will you write a letter to the parole board on my behalf?

Ray

Maria had been on the receiving end of her ex-husband's song-and-dance routine too many times to fall for it again. But she truly wanted to believe him this time—at least, for the kids' sake.

She studied the familiar handwriting as if she were some kind of forensic expert and it might somehow reveal any significant changes in the man's character, but she couldn't see any difference. Maybe it wasn't so bold, so brusque. But then again, maybe that was a result of the pen he'd used or the desktop at which he'd sat.

A part of her, the part that had been lied to and betrayed, didn't care if Ray ever got out of prison. There were nights when she'd wake up in the wee hours of the morning, having dreamed they were having an angry confrontation. In each one of them, she'd screamed and railed at him until he'd bent his head in remorse. She'd wanted to hurt him as badly as he'd hurt her and the kids.

Even in her sleep, she'd remembered the embarrassment he'd rained down on them, the articles splattered across the front page of the newspaper, the television journalists and cameramen who'd followed her out of the courtroom when she'd testified for the prosecution.

Sara might have been too young to

recall any of it, but Danny hadn't been. He'd heard the whispers, the clicking tongues, felt the humiliation and shame.

Yet Maria's maternal side hoped that Ray had really made a big change, that he'd stopped being so self-centered.

Before their last separation, when he'd lived at home, he'd been a good father. But there was more to being a dad than taking the kids to the movies and buying them an occasional candy bar. A man needed to be a good role model, too, which was a level Ray might never be able to rise up to.

So how could she write a letter to the parole board for him, telling them that they should release him so he could be a part of his kids' lives?

Sometimes, when facing a difficult problem, she would go to Ellie and they'd talk about it over tea. Ellie had always known the right thing to say. And whenever they'd prayed together, Ellie's voice had resonated with peace and assurance.

But talking to Ellie wasn't going to help today.

She could go to Captain, though. He seemed to have a parental type of wisdom. So she took the letter out to the front porch, where both Captain and Ellie rested in the shade.

But Ellie's eyes held that all too familiar haze of a woman who wasn't interested in the world around her, and Captain was snoozing.

A noise sounded—metal upon metal—and she spotted Eddie, placing the lawn edger into the back of his pickup.

She couldn't talk to him, of course. Yet as their eyes met, as whatever drew her to him before pulled especially strong, she stepped off the porch and walked toward his truck. She'd mentioned Danny's father to him before. And he'd seemed to understand the effect a parent's incarceration had on a kid.

If the depths of her problems and situation frightened him off, then so be it. Better now than later.

"Do you mind if I ask you a question?" she asked.

"Not at all." He glanced at the letter she

held, clearly unsure of what she was getting at.

"I told you that my ex-husband is in prison." When he nodded, she shared what Ray had written, what he'd asked of her.

"Maybe he's sincere about making a change. There's a lot of time for thinking and reflecting when a man is behind bars."

"Yes, I'm sure you're right. And as far as the kids are concerned, I'd like to believe that he's a new man. But right before his arrest, he stopped by the house, bringing flowers for me and presents for the kids.

"He apologized wholeheartedly, making all kinds of promises. I believed him and let him move back in with us, thinking we would be able to make a new start. But when the police arrived, he asked me to lie and to provide a false alibi for him. I refused to do it, but you can see what kind of man he is."

"And you think writing a letter on his behalf would be the wrong thing to do?"

"I've been used before, Eddie. And I

can't help thinking that if he gets out early, he'll just go back to being a liar and a cheat."

"Do you still love him?" Eddie's gaze peered deep into her soul, not just seeking the truth, but demanding it.

"No. I stopped loving him right after Sara was born, and even when I decided to reconcile the last time, it was only for the sake of the kids."

He seemed to think on that for a moment. "So you wouldn't ever want to take him back?"

"Absolutely not."

Their gazes remained locked, and she could sense herself falling head over heels. . . . No. Whatever she was feeling couldn't be love; she barely knew him.

"Are you seeing anyone else?" he asked.

Uh-oh. Where was he going with that? What was he really asking?

She ought to clarify things right now, let him know that she didn't plan to ever get involved with another man again. Yet it sounded so . . . cold. So angry and bitter.

And while she might have been at that place once, she'd moved through it.

So she answered honestly. "No, I'm not."

"This probably isn't the right time, but I was wondering if you'd go out to dinner with me some night."

A sympathy date?

Or the real thing?

Her senses reeled, her head spun, and her heart melted to the point where she might have to start dog-paddling to stay afloat.

"I don't think that's a good idea," she said, raking her fingers through her hair.

The intensity in his eyes wasn't letting up. "Why not?"

Because it was the smartest thing to say, the safest choice to make, but that wasn't an answer she could share.

"I really don't know," she admitted. "I guess it's because I've resigned myself to never getting involved with another man again. I've been through too much to risk doing so again."

Eddie lifted his hand and softly ran his knuckles along her cheek, sending her pulse ripping through her veins. "I'm sorry to hear that, Maria. You deserve a lot more than what you had with Ray."

Did she?

With Eddie looking at her like that, she felt herself waffling, giving in. And it was too scary.

"I need to think about it," she said.

"Take all the time you need." His hand lowered, then dropped to his side.

She forced herself to break eye contact. Yet she still felt a connection to him and found it hard to turn away. To go back into the house where she belonged.

"I . . . uh . . . found someone to sit with Ellie and the younger kids on Saturday," she added.

"Good." A grin lit his face and sparked a gleam in his eyes. "I'll come by for you and Danny at nine-thirty so we can get to the ball fields before anyone else shows up. That'll give him and me a chance to warm up."

By the way he was beaming and her heart was soaring, you'd think that she'd agreed to the date she'd been unable to commit to just moments ago.

"We'll be ready," she said, knowing

they'd be dressed appropriately and prepared to spend an hour or two at the park.

But she wasn't sure that she'd be ready in any other sense of the word.

Chapter 12

As Barbara strode across the parking lot toward the entrance of Pacifica General Hospital, her heels crunched on the pavement grit.

Overhead, the sun shined bright and birds chattered in the treetops, suggesting that all was right in the world. She sure hoped so. After nearly two weeks of worry, she was ready for some peace of mind.

As she glanced toward the water fountain that gurgled near the entrance of the lobby, she spotted her daughter-in-law coming toward her.

Cynthia, a petite blonde in her mid-forties, waved as she approached.

If Barbara had been able to handpick a wife for her son, she would have chosen someone more vibrant, more stylish. In fact, nearly twenty years ago, when the two were dating and things appeared to be getting serious, Barbara had tried to talk Joey out of marrying the soft-spoken, unassuming young woman, thinking he could do better. But Joey had refused to listen and had gone on with the wedding.

Barbara had never expected the marriage to last, but she'd been wrong.

In the early days, she'd found several things to criticize about her daughter-in-law's habits: Cynthia's inability to keep a clean house and her refusal to hire someone to do it for her; a lack of style when it came to dressing or in decorating her home. But when Barbara had taken Joey aside to chat with him about her concerns, he'd said, "I won't allow you to talk about my wife like that, Mom."

It had been the first time Barbara had realized that she'd dropped to a secondary position in her son's life, and she'd been taken aback. She'd also been hurt, but over the years, she'd come to respect Joey for his devotion and loyalty. And more than once she'd wondered if his father would have ever done the same for her.

She wasn't sure that he would have. In spite of her best efforts, the two of them had drifted apart over the years. In fact, they'd never had the closeness that Joey and Cynthia had, which Barbara had attributed to the fact they hadn't had children and were able to spend more time together than a lot of couples.

After greeting her daughter-in-law, Barbara asked, "Have you talked to Joey today?" She'd assumed so.

"Yes, I called him while he was eating breakfast. He's doing about the same. He's also getting tired of being here."

"I can understand that." Barbara would give anything to see Joey at home, even if he had to lie in a hospital bed in the guest room and continue to take it easy.

"He's always been so active, so healthy, that this is especially trying for him."

"I'm sure it is," Barbara said. "But it's not a walk in the park for the rest of us, either."

"I know, but I think it's best if we don't

complain. I don't want to make it any harder on him than I need to."

"By the way," Barbara said, "when they do finally let him out of here, I think the two of you should come and stay at our house. I'll hire round-the-clock nursing, if the doctor thinks it's needed."

"I think he'd rather be at home. But we can talk about that later. It doesn't look as though they're going to let him out any-time soon."

Barbara's heart sank. She'd been afraid of that. As long as she thought that the doctors would either discharge him or that they would schedule the surgery at any given moment, she stayed on top of the stress and worry. "So there haven't been any major changes?"

Cynthia slowly shook her head. "Not as of yesterday afternoon."

The revolving doors spun open, and both women turned to see Pastor Craig walk out. When he recognized Cynthia, he strode right to her and gave her a hug. "How're you holding up?"

She smiled, clearly touched by the man's concern. "I'm hanging in there."

Barbara wondered what it would be like

to have someone in her corner, someone to wrap his arms around her and ask how she was doing through this trying time. Not that Joseph wasn't supportive, especially when it came to their son. It's just that he and Barbara didn't embrace all that much anymore. In fact, they rarely even touched, and she wasn't sure how or when that had all come about.

"I take it you've been inside to see Joe," Cynthia said. "Or were you here to see someone else?"

"There are a couple of other parishioners here, and I saw them all. Joe was the last one I visited. His spirits are good, and he's waiting to hear the latest lab results." Craig turned to Barbara and extended his hand. "Hello, Mrs. Davila."

She greeted him and offered him a smile. "It's nice of you to stop by and see him regularly. I know he really appreciates it."

"It's the least I can do. Joe's one of my favorite people." He smiled warmly, then added, "I saw your husband earlier. He was on his way to a meeting and stopped in to bring Joe a book he'd been talking about."

She returned his smile, surprised that

Joseph had managed to slip away during the day for a visit to their son. He'd been incredibly busy with the campaign. At least, that's what he always told her.

The pastor turned to Cynthia. "Elise Rodgers gave birth last night. It's her fourth child and her first son."

Barbara glanced at Cynthia, wondering if the news hurt. She and Joey had tried for years to have a child, but hadn't had any luck.

If Craig's announcement had struck a painful chord, Cynthia didn't let on. "The baby was early, wasn't it?"

"Three or four weeks, but everything seems to be okay. By the way, Chuck Masterson was also admitted yesterday."

"Isn't he the nice man who's the janitor at church?"

Craig nodded. "That's him. You might want to keep him in your prayers. He's having some serious health issues."

"I'll do that."

In some ways, Cynthia reminded Barbara of her mother. They both had a lot of faith and were quick to pray for others.

Not that Barbara wasn't a believer. She was, but she didn't get carried away with it. She attended church, but usually only on the important days, like Easter and Christmas. It was better that way. No one expected her to serve on any committees, attend Bible studies, or join prayer groups.

To be honest, whenever she'd had anything serious to worry or stress about in the past, she'd asked her mom to pray for her.

Her mom had often suggested they pray together, but Barbara had declined to go that far. She just didn't feel all that close to God.

Once, her mother had implied that she was probably struggling with guilt, which had really set Barbara off. For some reason, as far as her mom had been concerned, all roads led back to that fateful decision to give up the baby.

But Barbara was okay with what she'd done. It had been her only option at the time.

"Maybe you ought to come clean," her mother had once suggested, but that was the last thing in the world Barbara would do. Besides, she felt as though God knew what she'd done and why. And she figured He was okay with it.

So up until Joey's heart attack, Barbara had stopped asking her mom to pray about anything.

And afterward? When she'd really had need of her mother's prayers the most?

Her mom hadn't been coherent enough to even realize that Joey was ill.

Before leaving the townhome that morning, Amy had packed bread and lunch meat for sandwiches, as well as fruit and peanut butter cookies for dessert. So while the girls played a board game on the back porch, she fixed their lunch.

As she laid out the bread on a piece of paper towel she'd placed on the counter, she reached for the low-fat mayonnaise and paused. Callie's friend Rachel was lactose intolerant. Maybe Amy had better make sure Sara didn't have any food allergies or wasn't fussy about the things she ate. So she opened the door, where the girls had spread out their colorful game board.

Eddie was in the backyard, too, working in the rose garden, where the bushes no longer appeared to be wild and dry. Thanks to some regular watering and a bit of pruning, the leaves were brighter and a few buds had begun to open.

"Do you like turkey sandwiches?" Amy asked Sara.

The girl nodded, then reached for her purple playing piece and moved it three spaces.

Amy looked out into the rose garden and called to Eddie. "Would you like a turkey sandwich? I've got plenty."

"Thanks, but I packed a lunch today." He clipped one of the blooms, then started toward the porch. "But here, take this with you into the house." He handed her a rosebud, a dark shade of lavender.

Amy carefully gripped the stem, lifted the blossom to her nose, and took a deep whiff. She imagined Ellie relishing the fragrance of another bloom from the same bush, only on a different day in time. In a way, she supposed it was a memory they both shared. "Thank you, Eddie. It's beautiful."

"I thought so, too. You don't see many like this, and it smells good, too. The lady who used to live here must have really loved gardening. Do you have a vase you can put it in?"

"I'll find something."

As Eddie started back to work, and Amy turned to go into the house, Callie pointed to the fence. "Mommy, look! A kitty."

It was the white-and-calico cat Amy had seen yesterday.

"It's Patches," Sara said.

Amy glanced at the corner of the porch, where she'd put out food yesterday. The bowl of Kitty Delight was empty and only the saucer of water remained.

"Patches used to be Ellie's cat," Sara said, "but it ran away after Ellie moved into our house and stopped talking to people."

Amy hadn't considered how Ellie's tragic transformation from nice neighbor to a woman who'd sunk deep within herself might have affected Maria's children. Or how they might be adapting to having both Ellie and Captain move in with them.

She suspected it had certainly changed the family dynamics.

From inside the house, she heard the

doorbell. Thinking she'd better get it, she left the girls to play outside and hurried into the living room to answer.

When she swung open the door, Maria stood on the stoop. "How are the girls doing?"

"Great. I'm fixing their lunch now."

"The associate minister came by to visit Ellie and Captain. And since Wally went down for an early nap, I thought I'd come over and check on Sara while Pastor Craig is holding down the fort."

"Come on in." Amy stepped aside so Maria could enter. "Would you like a sandwich?"

"No, thanks. I already ate."

Amy led Maria past the stacks of boxes she'd begun to accumulate in the living room and took her into the kitchen. "Have a seat. It'll just take me a minute to get them settled."

"Speaking of getting settled . . ." Maria pulled out a chair and sat at the table. "Yesterday, when I told Callie that it was going to be nice having her live next door, she said that she lives in Del Mar. That she's only staying here while her mother packs boxes."

Amy's steps slowed, and she bit down on her bottom lip. She couldn't lie to Maria any longer. "If you give me a chance to feed the kids, I'll explain."

"Sure. Do you want me to put on some water for tea?"

"That's probably a good idea."

Five minutes later, the girls were taking a lunch break outside, and the mothers were sitting at Ellie's kitchen table.

Amy dropped the tea bag into her cup so it could steep in the hot water. "Callie and I aren't actually going to move into this house."

Confusion splashed across Maria's face. "I don't understand. Barbara said that you signed a lease."

"I did." Amy placed her elbows on the table and circled the china cup with her hands, but she didn't pick it up, didn't take a drink. "My mother passed away six months ago from breast cancer."

"I'm sorry to hear that." Compassion and uncertainty wrestled in Maria's expression.

"It was tough. She wasn't just my mom, she was my best friend." Amy glanced at tea brewing in her cup. "My mother was adopted when she was a newborn. And before she died, she'd been determined to find her birth mother." She looked at Maria, who didn't appear to be seeing any connection in her question and in Amy's explanation, but she continued to listen.

"I don't think a child could have had a better home than she did," Amy added. "My grandparents adored her and provided her with everything a little girl could ever want. But for some reason, she was driven to meet her birth parents and find out why they'd given her up.

"When I got married and had Callie, she seemed to put off the search for a while. And quite frankly, I was glad. I adored my grandparents and couldn't imagine how they'd feel if and when my mom uncovered her roots. I thought it would probably break my grandmother's heart."

"I can see where she might be hurt," Maria said, taking a sip from her cup.

Amy finally removed the tea bag and added a dash of sugar. "When my mom was first diagnosed with breast cancer, her compulsion to find her biological family returned, stronger than ever, and she even hired a private investigator to help."

"Did she find them?"

"No, I don't think so. I'm sure she would have said something to me if she had. The urge to find them was too strong." Amy pulled the tea bag from her cup. "After she died, I decided to continue the search for her—as a tribute, as a parting gift, I guess."

"Is *that* why you're here?" Maria asked.

Amy nodded. "While going through her belongings, I found a file with all of her notes regarding the adoption and what she'd uncovered so far. And the search led me here."

"To Ellie?" Maria asked.

"To Barbara Rucker."

Maria leaned back in her seat, taken aback by Amy's revelation. "Ellie has shared different things with me in the past, but she never mentioned Barbara giving up a baby. She must have gotten pregnant before she and Joseph married."

"There are a lot of questions and no one to really answer them for me. But when I found this house and saw that it was for sale or lease, I rented it furnished. And I offered to pack up Ellie's personal effects for the family. I'm not sure what you think about that, but it seemed the best way for me to learn about the family without encroaching on their privacy, especially with Mr. Davila being ill. Introducing myself to Barbara now might be unsettling, and I don't want to cause her any unnecessary stress."

"Have you found anything helpful?" Maria wasn't sure how she felt about Amy snooping through Ellie's belongings, uncovering secrets, but something told her Ellie would have welcomed her great-granddaughter with open arms and would have told her whatever she'd wanted to know.

"I found some letters to Ellie from Harold," Amy said. "And a journal and part of another. After reading them, I've come to realize that my great-grandmother was a wonderful woman. The kind of person I might have chosen as a friend, if we'd been of the same generation."

The women lifted their cups, but neither spoke for a while. Maria still struggled with Amy's deception, yet she couldn't say that she blamed her for taking advantage of an opportunity to get to know the Ruckers. If it hadn't been Amy packing Ellie's things, Barbara probably would have hired someone else.

Or maybe she would have asked Maria to do it. And if Maria had been the one to find those letters or the journal, she might have read them herself.

"My mom was a talented pianist," Amy said. "And when I found Ellie's accordion, I realized where her musical ability had come from."

"Did your mom look like Ellie?"

"I've found some old pictures of Ellie and Harold, but I can't say that there's any real big family resemblance. But I can see that genetics are definitely at play. My mom was also an artist."

"Then there's the breast cancer link," Maria said. "You're going to have to stay on top of that."

"I have been," Amy admitted. "But after learning about Ellie, I'll be even more careful now."

"Ellie told me that she found a lump in her breast in the late fifties, when Barbara was about sixteen years old. Ellie was afraid that she would die, but she didn't want her daughter to know how serious things were, so she tried to stay upbeat. She also kept a journal and a photo album for Barbara to remember her by."

"I didn't find those," Amy said. "Maybe she gave them to Barbara."

"Maybe. But something tells me the two of them weren't that close."

"That's surprising. From what I've found so far, Ellie adored her daughter. She saw her as a gift, a part of her and Harold."

"The teen years can be difficult," Maria said, thinking how Danny's attitude had been changing. And he still had a couple of years to go.

Again, they took a drink of tea, savored the taste while they pondered the past. Or, in Maria's case, the present.

"But Ellie pulled through," Amy said. "My mom wasn't that lucky."

"It's hard to know why some people make it and others don't. Ellie said that her entire church had been praying for her, and she believed that's why she beat the odds. She swore it was a miracle, that God had healed her."

"I've noticed that she has two Bibles," Amy said. "One upstairs on her nightstand and the other in the living room. And then she has a few plaques and wall hangings that reflect her faith."

"She lived it, too. Whenever I found myself struggling with an issue, she'd offer words of wisdom and prayer."

"Was Harold spiritual?" Amy asked.

"She never mentioned anything. But her second husband certainly wasn't."

"What makes you say that?"

"From what I understand, he never understood her church involvement."

"Is that what led to them breaking up?"

"I'm sure it created some strain on the marriage. But he was an alcoholic, and when he drank, he sometimes implied that she was only half a woman."

"That's terrible," Amy said, her expression contorting with both sympathy and disgust. "I'm glad she divorced him."

"Me, too." Maria took a drink of tea. "He didn't deserve her."

Again, they grew silent, absorbed with their own thoughts.

Finally, Amy said, "It breaks my heart to think that anyone would hurt Ellie like that, that they'd think of her as anything other than a talented woman with vibrant hopes and dreams."

Maria nodded as she thought about her old friend, the stooped and gray-haired lady whose eyes were glazed over most of the time, whose mind was locked away from those who loved and cared for her.

It was too bad that Amy hadn't been able to meet her a year or so ago, when she might have welcomed her into her heart and her home.

And for that reason, Maria no longer questioned Amy's motives for leasing the Rucker house. If she had been Amy, she might have done the same thing.

Saturday morning, Amy arrived at Ellie's house just before nine o'clock. She'd volunteered to sit with Captain and Ellie while Maria took Danny to the baseball fields at the park, but not until nine-thirty. So in the meantime, she planned to get some work done in the house. She hadn't been to Sugar Plum Lane since Wednesday, thanks to a hair appointment on Thursday and a lunch date at the playground with Rachel and Steph on Friday.

"Can I go to Sara's house and play?" Callie asked.

"No, not yet. We'll be going over there together in a little while. Why don't you color or read your books until it's time."

As Callie plopped down on the floor near the coffee table and began to spread out her crayons and her sketch pad, Amy headed upstairs to work in the last guest room.

About ten minutes later, while going through a chest of drawers, she found a little book with a pale pink satin-lined cover. In blue script across the front, it read: *Our Baby Girl.*

As she'd done numerous times before, she carried it to the bed, where she sat on the edge of the mattress and began to scan the pages.

Inside the front cover, several loose black-and-white photographs nearly slid out—pictures of Barbara as a baby and a toddler.

Amy studied each one, deciding that her own little girl bore a striking resemblance to Barbara when they were babies. They had the same heart-shaped face, expressive eyes, and dimpled smile. Callie, of course, was blond and fair, while Barbara had been a brunette, but the facial features were similar.

Amy set the photos aside and paged through the little book. Ellie had noted the dates of Barbara's first smile, her first tooth, her first steps. She'd also included a lock of curly brown hair, a birth certificate with a little footprint, and a white beaded bracelet that spelled out Baby Rucker in pink block-style letters.

The beads had caused the spine to bow out and had left an indention on the page. After she'd gone through the book, she left it on the bed and returned to the drawer, where she found a yellow-and-white crocheted baby dress and matching booties.

Had Ellie made them for her daughter? Or had they been a gift from someone else?

As Amy continued to empty the drawer, she uncovered the back cover of another torn journal, only this one was blue. Like the other portion she'd found earlier, the bulk of the pages were missing. In fact, only the last entry was attached. The handwriting was Ellie's, but the date made the entry stand out. Amy's mother had been born on that fall day in 1966.

Unable to quell her curiosity long enough to take a seat, she read it while standing before the chest of drawers.

September 19, 1966

Dear Angel,

I held you today, but only for a moment. I could hardly see your perfect little face through the tears in my eyes, and when they took you from me, it tore my heart in two. I felt as though I'd lost a piece of Harold all over again.

From now on, all the entries in my journals will be written to you, to the granddaughter I'd so wanted to keep, to raise, to love as my own.

And from now on, Angel, every one of my prayers shall include you, sweet baby. May you grow up in a loving home, with two parents who adore you. May you learn about God and how much He loves you. And someday, may you meet the grandmother who'd longed to be a part of your life.

Amy had no idea how long she'd stood there, wrapped in the love Ellie had felt for the baby that had been named Susan and adopted by Carlo and Gina Rossi. A child who'd grown up in a loving home with parents who'd adored her.

What Amy wouldn't give to be able to share Ellie's words with her mother. To let her know that she'd been loved by a wonderful woman who'd prayed for her daily.

As Amy began to read Ellie's words all over again, to bask in the love, she paused, noting something she'd breezed over the first time.

Angel.

Was that a term of endearment? A nickname? Or was it the name Ellie had given Barbara's child?

Had Ellie seen something in Callie that had made her think of the baby she'd called Angel?

Or was it just the rambling of an old woman whose mind was no longer functioning?

Chapter 13

It had only been a couple of days since Barbara had stopped by Maria's house to see her mother, yet here she was again at ten on Saturday morning.

Today's visit might be a complete waste of time, but for as long as Barbara could remember, her mother's faith had been a constant in her life. And while there were times she'd found it annoying and intrusive, it had also been a source of hope and assurance, something she could use right now.

Joey still hadn't been scheduled for the bypass surgery, and it didn't appear that it would happen anytime soon, so Barbara was more worried than ever. He was still in his forties and far too young to be struggling with such serious health issues.

He was also too young to die, and the possibility that he might shook Barbara to the core, which was why she was here, hoping for a miracle.

The trouble was, her mother's coherent days appeared to be few and far between.

Just a few weeks ago, when Barbara had told her mom about the complications that prevented the life-saving surgery Joey so desperately needed, she'd seemed to be concerned and had offered to pray for him. But by the next visit, she'd forgotten all about it.

"Pray for Joey," Barbara had urged her again, but the ever-present confusion had distorted her mother's expression.

"Who?" she'd asked, her voice frail and cracking.

"For *Joey,* Mama. He's in the hospital."

"Oh, dear. That's too bad. What happened?"

"He had a heart attack, remember?"

"But he's just a baby, Barbie."

And that had been the gist of the

conversation, so Barbara wasn't sure why she even bothered to make the attempt to ask for prayer again today. The divine connection her mom had always seemed to have had probably blown a fuse, along with the faulty synapses in her aging mind.

But maybe today she'd have a better grasp on reality and then everything would be okay. After all, if God was up there, listening to and communing with anyone, it would be Ellie Rucker.

So after parking her car at the curb in front of Maria's house, Barbara strode up the sidewalk and knocked at the door.

Moments later, an attractive blonde in her mid-twenties answered. Recognition appeared to dawn in her pretty blue eyes, although Barbara failed to make the same connection.

"Is Maria here?" Barbara asked.

"No, she took her son to baseball practice. I'm sitting with Ellie, Captain, and the kids."

Barbara was just about to introduce herself when the woman stepped aside, allowing her into the house as if she knew exactly who Barbara was and why she was here.

"I'm Amy Masterson," she said, as she closed the door behind them. "Your mom is in the living room."

The name triggered an aha! moment and Barbara realized the woman was the new tenant who lived next door and that Maria must have explained Ellie and the connection to the house.

"How's my mom doing today?" she asked.

"I've only met her once before, but she seems about the same to me."

In some cases, that might be construed as good news. But it certainly wasn't what Barbara had been hoping for.

She followed Amy into the living room, where Ellie was sitting with the old man everyone called Captain.

Ellie glanced up, but just briefly.

Barbara thought of all the times her mother had watched her intently as a child at play or had sat in the audience during an elementary school program with a proud-mama glow. All the times her innocent questions during Barbara's adolescence had been both embarrassing and annoying to a teenager hoping to break free of her mother's apron strings.

And she realized that a little of that interest would be more than welcome now. Too bad she couldn't somehow turn back the clock and relive those days with a different mindset, one in which a little hindsight worked wonders.

"She's been fairly quiet today," the old man said.

Barbara glanced at Amy, not so much for confirmation, but because she sensed the two of them had more in common than the others in the room, only to see the younger woman assessing her.

At least, it sure felt that way. Maybe she'd only imagined Amy's interest, when it was only normal curiosity, that of a tenant checking out her landlord.

Yet, deep inside, Barbara couldn't help wondering if she was making some kind of character assessment.

Was she questioning why her mother was living with a neighbor and not with her daughter?

There were a lot of reasons for that, the biggest of which was that Ellie wasn't the woman she used to be, that she couldn't be trusted to stay alone. Yet there were personal issues, too, things Barbara wouldn't ever share with others.

"I appreciate Maria helping out our family at a time like this," she said, hating herself for trying to make excuses when it really wasn't anyone's concern but her own.

"How's your son doing?" Amy asked.

"Not very well. But so far, he's holding his own."

"I'm sorry to hear that he isn't recovering as quickly as you'd hoped."

Footsteps sounded in the doorway that led to the hall, and several children entered the room—the little blond-haired girl who'd been visiting the other day, as well as Maria's two youngest.

"Mommy," the little blonde said. "Can me and Sara and Wally go outside and play?"

"Yes, but only if you stay in the backyard."

"Barbie, look." Ellie pointed a gnarled finger at the fair-haired girl. "It's Angel. She came home."

The poor kid who'd been singled out by

a crazed Ellie just a few days before now looked to her mom for some assurance.

"I'm sorry," Barbara said, apologizing for her mother's dementia. "She gets a little confused sometimes, which is why she's no longer living alone."

"I understand," Amy said. "It's okay. *Really.*"

But it wasn't okay—not at all. If truth be told, Barbara was sorry about a lot more than just her mother's comments to the child.

In her heart of hearts, she believed that, with time, she and her mother would have eventually found peace, that they might have grown close once again. But time had run out on them, and now it was too late for apologies and explanations, too late for compromise or forgiveness.

The reality that eluded Ellie these days reared up and slammed Barbara head-on, a blow that was swift and brutal.

For all intents and purposes, her mother was dead.

Tears welled in Barbara's eyes as the emotion she'd been holding back for ages pressed against her heart and rose into her throat. She blinked it all back—the guilt, the tears, the pain—but quickly realized she couldn't stay another minute. She couldn't risk breaking down in front of strangers.

She cleared her throat, hoping to break free of the emotion that had balled up inside. "I can't stay. I just wanted to say hi. I really need to go."

If Amy thought it odd that Barbara had only stopped by for a minute, she didn't say anything. And thank goodness for that.

Barbara feared that if the floodgates opened and the tears broke free, she might never stop crying. And there was no telling what might happen if she allowed herself to resurrect all the raw emotion she'd buried over the years.

As Eddie's late-model Chevy Blazer traveled along Canyon Drive on the way to Mulberry Park, Maria sat in the passenger seat, while Danny was in the back with one of the ugliest dogs Maria had ever seen.

The big, goofy-looking mutt had shaggy brown hair that covered his eyes, droopy ears, oversize paws, and, undoubtedly, the strangest mix of doggy DNA ever imagined.

She suspected there'd been a wolfhound somewhere in his questionable pedigree. And maybe a little bit of everything else.

"I hope you don't mind if Roscoe joins us," Eddie had said when he arrived at the house earlier. "He loves the park."

"Does he bite?" Maria had asked.

"Nope. He might look intimidating, but he's a big wimp."

"I think he's cool," Danny said, dropping to one knee to greet the dog and receiving a wet, sloppy lick from the tip of his chin to the bridge of his nose. "Hey, he likes me."

Eddie chuckled. "Roscoe likes everybody."

About that time, Amy arrived at the house, and Maria had thanked her again before giving her a couple of last-minute instructions.

Now she, Danny, and Eddie were on their way to the park and to what seemed like a big adventure. Maria couldn't remember the last time she'd gotten out of the house on a day when she didn't have errands to run and a schedule to keep.

Still, seated across from Eddie was a much bigger thrill than slipping off to the market or to the drugstore.

"Mom," Danny said, "can I have a dog like Roscoe?"

Maria glanced over her shoulder at her son, whose eyes were hopeful. Then she looked at the scraggly dog who sat next to him, its tongue hanging out its mouth.

A pet was out of the question since she had her hands full keeping up with the kids, Captain, and Ellie, but if she ever weakened and agreed to let Danny have a dog, it would be a small one—and one that was cute.

"I'm afraid we've been over that before," she said.

"I know. I have to wait until I'm older, but how much older do I need to be? I'm practically a teenager already. And by the time you finally let me have a pet, I'm going to be too old to play with it."

She stole a glance across the seat at Eddie, saw a grin stretched across his face, a twinkle in his eye. Something told her that some guys never get too old to enjoy a pet. But Danny didn't realize that she was already pedaling as fast as she could when it came to taking care of her boarders and the kids and keeping the house tidy, and that she didn't need to worry about holes and poop in the yard, as well as chewed-up toys and lawn chairs.

"Actually," Eddie said, "I wasn't planning on getting a dog, but Roscoe needed a home, and I felt sorry for him."

"Where did you find him?" Danny asked.

"At Mulberry Park. He'd been begging for food, and the dog catcher was after him." Eddie glanced into the rearview mirror, making eye contact with the boy.

"You were lucky to find him."

"I think Roscoe's the lucky one," Maria said. "I have a feeling he might not have fared well at the animal shelter."

"I've always had a soft spot for underdogs," Eddie said.

Was that how he saw her and Danny? As a needy mom and child? Someone to feel sorry for?

She shot another glance his way, and he flashed her a wink and a smile, turning her heart on end. Suddenly, she wasn't so sure about anything anymore.

"He's turned out to be a pretty good dog," Eddie told the boy. "But he's a lot of work. And sometimes, when I get home and would just like to take a shower, kick back, and watch TV, I have to take him out for a run instead. It's part of being a responsible pet owner."

"Hey, if that's what you're worried about, Mom, I promise to take care of a dog all by myself. I'll feed him and water him and clean up the poop and everything."

"We'll see," Maria said, hoping to cut the conversation short while staying noncommittal.

And fortunately, less than a minute later, they pulled into the parking lot near the ball fields, which would make changing the subject easy.

Eddie shut off the ignition, and they all piled out of the SUV, including the dog, who wore a red collar and matching leash.

"Can I walk Roscoe?" Danny asked.

"Sure. But why don't you run him on the grass for a while. That way, he'll behave for your mom."

Behave for her? Did Eddie expect her to dog-sit that mutt during practice?

"You don't mind keeping an eye on Roscoe, do you?"

Truthfully? Yes, but she couldn't very well tell him no. "What do I need to do?"

"Just hold on to the leash. But if you'd rather not, I'll ask one of the kids in the dugout to do it for me. It's just that they usually argue over who gets to take care of him."

Maria couldn't understand the dog's appeal to kids, or to Eddie, for that matter, but she decided to be a good sport.

Besides, she owed it to Eddie for taking her son under his wing, especially since she'd already noticed a change in Danny's attitude, and he hadn't even met the coach or the rest of the team. So she took a seat on the bleachers, where the branches of a maple tree provided a bit of shade, and watched Eddie interact with the boys who'd begun to fill the field.

When Danny returned with Roscoe, he handed her the leash, then dashed off to join practice as the dog plopped down at her feet.

A few minutes later, a red-haired woman in her mid-to-late thirties arrived with a boy who looked to be about Danny's age and took a seat next to Maria.

"Mind if I sit here?" she asked.

"Not at all. I'll scoot over so you can have some of the shade."

"Thanks." The woman gave Roscoe's ears an affectionate scratch before taking a seat, angling herself toward Maria, and pointing at the red-haired boy who'd arrived with her. "I'm Kathy Carrington, and that's Brent. Do you have a son on the team?"

"The one near the pitcher's mound talking to Eddie is mine. His name is Danny, but he's not an official team member yet. We're just checking things out."

"I did that, too. It won't take you long to see that Ramon and Eddie are great with the kids."

"I'm sure they are." A light breeze kicked a wisp of hair across Maria's cheek, and she brushed it aside.

"Brent's mom died," Kathy said, "and his dad is in prison. My husband and I have had him for about six months. Up until he joined the team, he was depressed and angry, but connecting with both Ramon and Eddie has made a big difference in his life."

"I'd assumed you were his mom," Maria said. "You both have red hair."

"Isn't that cool?" Kathy laughed. "We're not related by blood, but everyone who sees him with me assumes that we are, which is great. My husband and I are hoping to adopt him. From what I've heard, his father is seriously thinking about it, but he's not in any hurry to sign the papers. I can understand that, but he's serving a life term, and there aren't any family members willing or able to take Brent. Either way, he'll stay with us."

The engine of an approaching vehicle sounded, and Maria turned her head in time to see a Jeep Wrangler pull into a parking space near the dugout.

Kathy pointed to the Jeep. "Here comes Ramon now. He and his wife are in the process of adopting, too."

"Eddie mentioned something about his brother being a foster parent." Maria watched the man and the kids climb from the Jeep.

"Luis and Carlitos had been living with their great-grandmother, and when she got sick and couldn't care for them, Ramon and his wife took them in. It's worked out well for everyone involved, and they've got an attorney working on the paperwork now."

Ramon removed a duffel bag filled with baseball gear from the back of his vehicle, then handed it to the bigger kid. Next he pulled out three bases and gave them to the smaller boy.

As Ramon strode out to the field, where Eddie and Danny were now playing catch, he called out to his brother, and the two men greeted each other.

Maria noticed a strong resemblance, at least from a distance. Ramon wasn't quite as tall as Eddie, but he appeared to be just as well built, just as nice looking.

But she wasn't about to let Kathy catch her gawking at the men, so she forced herself to look away.

"How many other moms show up to watch practice?" she asked.

"Not too many. It's usually just me. Brent has abandonment issues, so I want him to know that I'm here for him. It's been helping, too. He's finally able to sleep through the night most of the time."

"I'm glad things are getting better," Maria said, thinking that Danny's issues no longer seemed so bad and hoping they'd soon be a thing of the past.

As the other boys began to fill the field, Danny appeared to be easily accepted as part of the team. Before long, practice got under way, and the two women grew silent as they watched.

Maria liked the way Eddie and Ramon related to the kids, especially those who'd messed up or the ones who'd shown signs of a temper or bad sportsmanship.

Never once did they belittle a child, never once did they blow up. And long before practice was over, Maria decided to let Danny join the team.

She also decided to let Eddie take her son to games and practices—if his offer was still on the table.

While Eddie helped one of the boys repair a broken lace on his mitt, Danny and Luis picked up the bases and carried them to Ramon's Jeep.

Baseball practice had gone exceptionally well today, and he hoped Maria had liked what she'd seen. Danny might not have the talent or the experience that some of the other boys had, but his heart for the game and desire to excel more than made up for it.

As Ramon headed toward the dugout, probably making a last-minute sweep to make sure the kids hadn't made a mess with sunflower seeds or left anything behind, Eddie called out to him. "Hey, Ramon. Wait up." When his brother turned around, Eddie nodded toward the bleachers. "I'd like to introduce you to Danny's mom."

"Sure. Just a second." Ramon instructed Carlitos, his youngest, to search the dugout. Then he joined Eddie, and they made their way toward Maria.

As she spotted them coming, she stood and tugged on Roscoe's leash, bringing the dog with her as she climbed from where she'd been sitting on the bleachers.

"Hey, Coach Eddie," Luis called from the pitcher's mound, where he'd joined Danny. "Can we take Roscoe for a run?"

"Yeah, he'd like that."

The boys dashed to Maria, and she handed them the leash. Then they took off for the playground, with Roscoe loping beside them.

After Eddie had introduced his brother to Maria, she said, “Kathy Carrington was sure singing your praises. She told me that Brent is really doing well since joining the team.”

“We’ve had quite a few success stories,” Eddie said.

Ramon nudged his brother with an elbow. “It was actually Eddie’s idea. He was the one who first heard about the new league that was being established through a state grant, and then he told me about it. He also knew a couple of kids who were struggling at home and needed a positive role model, and he asked me to consider being the coach. And from there, the Fairbrook Falcons just took off.”

Eddie hoped Ramon didn’t mention that he’d gotten wind of the league while in prison, and that the father of those kids had been his cellmate. Not that Eddie was keeping it a secret from Maria, but he figured it would be best if the news came from him first.

"We're only three-six in league standings," Ramon added, "but as far as making a change in the boys' lives, we're undefeated."

"If you've got room for Danny," Maria said, "and if Eddie doesn't mind helping me get him to practices and games, I'd like for him to join the team."

"No problem. He's a great kid." Ramon shot a glance at Eddie, then at Maria and back again. His eyes twinkled in a way that suggested Eddie might have more than the boy's best interests at heart, which meant there'd be a bit of an inquisition and maybe a little razzing when Maria wasn't within earshot.

"When's the next practice?" she asked.

"Wednesday at four-thirty. But there's a game on Monday evening. My wife is the team mom. I'll have her get you a schedule."

"Thanks."

"Oh," Ramon said, "we're also having a pool party a week from tomorrow. Things can get a bit wild, and Eddie and I usually get thrown into the water—clothes and all—but we have a good time."

Eddie studied Maria, saw her smile and nod in understanding. He and his brother had come to expect the dunking; it was a game the boys looked forward to.

He was glad that she approved of what they were doing and that she was going to let Danny join the team. But he was even happier to know that he'd be able to continue seeing her at practice and games when his work on the Rucker job was done.

"Well," Ramon said, "the boys and I have to get out of here. It's my wife's birthday, and we're having a party and barbecue for her at her parents' house this afternoon."

Maria blessed him with a smile. "It was nice meeting you."

"Same here." Before taking off, Ramon flashed Eddie a knowing grin, which meant that there'd definitely be a few questions coming about his assumptions and observations. Then he went to round up his sons.

That left Eddie and Maria alone, and while he felt a bit awkward and at a loss for words, he wasn't ready to end their time together, either.

"I think what you guys are doing for the boys is great," she said.

Eddie wasn't all that comfortable with her praise. Helping the team was a way to ease the last bit of guilt he still carried, a ragged remnant that seemed to dog him in spite of the time spent in prison. Even a few years of maturity and a great deal of retrospect hadn't been able to shake it.

"It's not that big a deal," he said. "My brother and I were lucky. We had a good family and great role models, so we're just paying it forward."

Yet it was more than that. When Eddie had been locked away, he'd seen how the families, particularly the children, struggled with the separations that would last year upon year, the shame, the inability to control or change a tragic web of circumstances they'd been caught up in. So when he'd heard about the intercity league that was starting up to help kids at risk, he'd encouraged Ramon to get involved. Then, once he was paroled, he'd volunteered to help coach whenever he could.

"I'm a little embarrassed to admit this,"

Maria said, "but when you first suggested that Danny play on this team, I really didn't want him involved with the children of other prisoners. I'd rather have him forget his father completely. It's tough living in the dark shadow of the man. And I'm tired of the notoriety."

Eddie glanced at his feet, wondering if she'd balk at going out with him if she knew he'd had a dark shadow and a bit of notoriety, too.

"All I've ever wanted was a happy home," she added, "a family who stayed out of trouble and off the front page of the newspaper."

That's all Eddie wanted, too.

Maybe that's what he liked about Maria. That she and the kids provided a sense of home and family. Not that he didn't get that from his parents or from Ramon, Shana, and the boys. But it wasn't the same as having a family of his own.

His life had taken a tragic and unexpected turn, but he'd paid his debt to society, even if he still blamed himself for the grief he'd caused Cecelia's family, for the guilt he still struggled with at times. And he hoped that Maria would be able to get past all that.

If so, then maybe he could, too.

Chapter 14

Amy sat on the sofa in Maria's living room with one leg tucked under her as she thumbed through a children's library book she'd found on the coffee table. She would have chosen something else to read if there'd been any options.

When a vehicle pulled up outside, she set aside *The Trouble with Penguins* and got to her feet. It was time for Maria to return, but after Barbara's surprise visit earlier, Amy didn't want to make any assumptions. So she went to the window and peered out into the street, where Eddie's SUV was idling at the curb.

Danny was the first one to open the door and enter the house. A broad grin stretched across his dirt-smudged face, suggesting he'd had a good time.

"My mom's coming in a minute," he said. "She's just saying good-bye to Eddie—I mean, to Coach."

Before Amy could respond, he blurted out, "I get to join the team. Isn't that cool?" Then he dashed off before she had a chance to agree.

Minutes later, Maria swept into the room, her mood bright and a smile dancing on her lips.

"I take it that everything went well," Amy said.

"It was great. You can't believe how nice it is to see my son happy again, even if it's just for today." Maria placed her purse on the bottom step of the stairway. "Thanks for holding down the fort."

"No problem. It's been pretty quiet. The kids are having a make-believe tea party in Sara's room, and Ellie's napping."

"What about Captain?"

"He took a book out into the backyard to read in the shade."

"I'm glad it was quiet for you."

Amy was glad, too. "By the way, Barbara stopped by to see Ellie."

"No kidding? She was just here a couple of days ago."

"I was surprised to see her, too. And the odd thing is, she was only here a minute or so. I didn't understand why she even bothered to come."

Maria scrunched her face. "She usually stays at least an hour."

"I got the feeling that she wasn't comfortable with me being here," Amy said. "I introduced myself as her tenant, so maybe that's why she took off."

"Did you tell her who you really are, who your mom was?"

"I actually considered it, but just the thought was daunting." As badly as her mother had wanted to meet Barbara, Amy should have jumped at the chance. "I'm not sure why that was. I guess because I was so caught off guard by her arrival that I couldn't figure out how to broach the subject. And even if I'd gotten up my nerve and had been able to come up with the right words, she wasn't here long enough for me to do anything other than to steal a glance at her every now and then to see if I could spot a resemblance to my mother."

"Maybe she caught you staring at her. Or maybe she's the one who noticed the resemblance."

"I doubt it. But either way, she took off out of here like a rat with its tail in a trap." And Amy had been relieved when she did. So what was with that?

"Barbara's not easy to read," Maria said. "Sometimes she comes across as cold and insensitive, then at other times, I almost feel sorry for her."

"Why?"

"I don't know. On the outside, she's got it made—a fancy house, wealth, a husband who's respected in the community. . . . But something tells me she isn't really happy."

"There's more to happiness than having possessions," Amy said, repeating the words she'd often told Brandon.

"That's true."

Footsteps sounded in the doorway, and both women turned to see Captain hobble into the room with a book in his hand.

"I think I have an idea what's bothering Barbara," he said, leaning against the doorjamb.

Amy turned to the elderly man, wanting answers, no matter where they came from. "What's that?"

"She and her mother had a falling-out years ago."

"Over what?"

"Ellie never said. She just told me that it broke her heart, and that her daughter was one of the most stubborn women the good Lord had ever made."

"Are you saying that they were never able to work through their problem?"

"Maybe they did on the outside," Captain said. "Barbara is a dutiful daughter in some ways, but it always seemed to be an obligation on her part. I'm afraid that on the inside, she never forgave Ellie."

"Never forgave her for what?" Amy asked.

"Like I said, Ellie didn't go into detail. She just let me know that something happened, and they both held each other responsible. Ellie might have had a stubborn streak, too. Who knows? But either way, it's a real shame. With her mental state what it is now, they'll never be able to completely bury the hatchet."

Amy was glad that she and her mom had never had any bad blood between them. She would have been devastated to think that their last memories had been strained or painful.

"Ellie would have been open to finding some kind of resolution or middle ground." Captain straightened, stepped away from the door frame, and eased farther into the room. "But from what she told me, Barbara hadn't been ready for that. And now Ellie's been spared from memories of the rift, and Barbara's got to deal with them on her own, knowing it can't ever be fixed."

How sad, Amy thought. With Ellie's inability to communicate, time had run out.

And speaking of time . . . She glanced at her watch. "I probably ought to get Callie."

"The kids are playing so well," Maria said. "Why don't you leave her here? I'll bring her home in a little while."

Amy didn't see any reason to correct Maria for referring to Ellie's house as "home." Not that Amy had any desire to ever move in. But she'd found a maternal presence there, a comfort that was impossible to explain.

She would have given anything to have

had a chance to meet the real Ellie. But it seemed that time had run out for her, too.

After Amy left and the front door clicked shut, Maria watched Captain make his way toward the easy chair.

"Are you hungry?" she asked. "I'm going to open a can of turkey vegetable soup and make grilled cheese sandwiches for lunch."

"Soup sounds good, but I'll probably pass on anything else. I've been having a lot of indigestion lately and don't want to overload my stomach."

For a man who was nearing ninety, Captain had always been healthy and alert. His biggest problem seemed to be mobility, although at his age, any number of things could go wrong.

"Do you want me to make a doctor's appointment for you?" she asked.

"Thanks, but that's not necessary." He lowered himself into the overstuffed chair, wincing as he did so. "How did baseball practice go?"

"Super. The coaches are great, and the boys really look up to them." She probably ought to head into the kitchen and start lunch, but something was weighing on her mind—and on her heart.

Ellie would have been her first choice of confidants, but she'd grown comfortable with Captain since he'd moved in.

"What's the matter?" he asked, apparently picking up on her worries before she even opened her mouth.

"Nothing. It's just that . . ." She took a seat at the edge of the sofa and released a weary sigh. "Well, I really like Eddie—maybe a little too much."

He chuckled. "How can you like someone too much?"

"It's not that, exactly. It's just that he's younger than I am. At least, I think he is. And he doesn't have any kids, so getting involved with me would probably cramp his style."

"So you're only looking out for *his* best interests?" Captain's eyes twinkled. "Seems to me that ought to be his decision to make."

"I know. You're right." She bit down on her bottom lip. "I'm really dragging my feet because I don't want to get involved with anyone again. I've made one heartbreaking mistake, and I don't want to make another."

"Not all men are like that ex-husband of yours." Captain leaned back in the comfort of the chair and stroked his left arm. "I doubt that you'd let yourself get involved with a playboy like Ray again."

"So you think Eddie's different?"

"I don't know him all that well, but he seems like a decent sort and worth the risk."

"I'm not a gambler, especially since any decision I make affects my kids."

"When it comes to love, sometimes you have to take a chance."

"Who said anything about *love?*"

Captain chuckled. "I've seen the way you two look at each other, and while you might not be in love, you both seem to be tiptoeing around it."

Was that what was happening?

She wanted to deny it, yet something was going on between them. That's what left her so uneasy.

Her relationship with Ray had been pure chemistry at first, and she'd mistaken it for love. And look where that had gotten her.

"Eddie and I just met," she said. "It's too soon for romance."

"Sometimes the heart has a mind of its

own, Maria." He tossed her a paternal smile. "Just take things one day at a time. There isn't any rush."

Of course there wasn't, but the more she saw Eddie, the faster her heart raced, and the more she feared she was getting caught up in a romantic whirlwind again.

"If it's meant to be, it'll all work out." Something in his words, in his gentle tone, rang true.

"Okay," she said. "I'll just play it by ear."

Or by *heart.* But that wasn't the only thing bothering her.

She leaned forward and placed her palms on her knees. "I got another letter from Ray the other day. He wants me to write to the parole board on his behalf."

"What's he want you to say?"

"That the kids need him."

"Are you going to do it?"

"I don't want to."

Captain nodded, his craggy brow furrowing as though giving her dilemma some thought. Finally, he said, "You don't have to sing his praises, you know."

She'd be hard-pressed to do that, even if he'd been a relatively good father when he'd been home and not just mediocre.

"So what's holding you back?" he asked.

"I don't want Danny to grow up with his father's values, especially when it comes to relationships."

"A lot of men make one-hundred-and-eighty-degree turnarounds when they take advantage of the prison ministries." Captain stroked his upper arm again, as though easing a tired muscle. "You know, I used to be a real hellion in my day. But then I saw the error of my ways and turned my heart and life over to Jesus. I'm walking proof that men can change."

"Yes, but I doubt that Ray's the kind to get involved with any kind of ministry."

"You'd be surprised at some of the testimonies I've heard from ex-prisoners. I'll start praying that Ray connects with a godly man."

She smiled even though she had a world of doubt. "Thanks. I'd appreciate that—for the kids' sake."

He shifted in his seat, as if he couldn't find a comfortable spot. "Does Ray get to see the children very often?"

She'd taken them to visit him on several occasions, but she'd been on edge the entire time. So now she found excuses not to make the trip. "No, he doesn't see them very often. It's a long drive, and it's hard for me to get away."

"Doesn't he want to see them?"

She couldn't lie. "Yes. He's even been trying to contact Danny, but I've been hiding the letters until he's old enough to deal with receiving them."

"You can't coddle the boy or change his reality, no matter how hard you try. And while you need to look out for his best interests, life will probably be a whole lot easier when he learns how to play the hand he's been dealt."

"Even when he's only eleven?"

Captain fingered the book in his hand, a library copy of *The Purpose Driven Life.* "I'm not saying that you need to throw the boy into something he's not able to handle, but his father made a mistake—a big one, and it's landed him in prison. He's not a part of your lives right now. Those are facts, and hiding or sugarcoating the details may not be in Danny's best interest. At least, not in the long run."

"I'm not hiding them. He's aware of what his father did and where his father is."

"Wouldn't it be better if you talked to

Danny about it? If you asked him how he felt about having a relationship with his father?"

He made it all sound so simple.

"Let me ask you this," Captain said. "And dig deep for a truthful answer. Are you trying to protect Danny? Or punish Ray?"

Her heart knotted up and thumped around in her chest like a clump of air-dried Play-Doh. She was afraid to ponder the question, let alone respond. If truth be told, the answer was, "A little of both."

She studied her elderly boarder for a moment, his thick head of white hair, his tired gray eyes, his age-lined face, the paper-thin skin of his hands. On the outside, he appeared to be at the end of his life's journey, but he'd garnered a treasure trove of wisdom along the way.

And for that reason, as well as the friendship factor, she hoped that he would be around for many more years to come.

With her quest almost over, Amy left Callie with Steph on Monday morning and returned to the house on Sugar Plum Lane.

Even though she'd packed almost all of

Ellie's personal belongings, she wasn't quite ready to hand anything over to the Realtor/property manager. She'd signed a lease for six months, and the house, as well as Ellie's essence, belonged to her until well after summer turned to fall.

She'd no more than unlocked the front door, dropped her purse on the table near the entry, and stepped into the living room when she scanned the fourteen boxes she'd stacked against the south wall.

Other than the framed photos that remained on the mantel and the quilt from Ellie's bed, which now lay on the sofa to pad the last of the breakable items, she'd packed everything.

There were still pots, pans, utensils, and appliances in the kitchen, as well as the furniture that filled the house, since Amy had leased it furnished. But the precious items had been carefully put away.

She really ought to call Ron and tell him that either he or the Ruckers could send someone to pick up the stuff at their convenience. After that was done, she really didn't have a game plan, although she had half a notion to approach Barbara on her next visit and announce who she really was, who her mother had been.

But maybe it was best to let sleeping dogs lie.

After all, her questions had been answered—at least, most of them.

As the back door creaked open and shut, Amy's heart jammed. Her first thought was that she'd imagined it, until footsteps sounded in the kitchen. Her pulse raced, and her adrenaline production skyrocketed.

Someone was in the house. But who?

One of Maria's kids?

Eddie? Barbara?

Ron Paige, the Realtor?

Any other option was too frightening to contemplate.

She backed toward the front door, her legs as stiff and spindly as a newborn fawn's, and reached for the knob, ready to dash outside. But before her escape, she called out in a deep, don't-mess-with-me tone. "Who's there?"

"It's me," a frail voice answered.

Ellie?

Amy released the knob just as the elderly woman entered the living room, her gray hair windblown, her lightweight sweater turned inside out.

She held a yellow rosebud in one hand and a house key in the other.

Amy tried to reconcile the two images she held: the young Ellie who'd once lived in the old Victorian with the woman standing before her, the ghost of a person whose mind had become her prison. But she wasn't having any luck.

Ellie's brow, already creased by age, furrowed into a craggy V, and her eyes darted back and forth as if trying to navigate through a cloudy mind.

"Who . . . are *you?*" she asked. "Why are you in my house?"

Was she having a lucid moment?

"I'm Amy. A friend of Maria's." Did she have to explain any more than that?

Ellie's head listed to the side, as if she was trying to find balance, then she straightened and her gaze brightened a couple of watts. "Of course. I remember now. Would you like to have some tea?"

Amy really should let Maria know that Ellie was here and safe, but she couldn't help thinking she'd been offered an opportunity to talk to her great-grandmother, a rare moment that might not last through a phone call.

"I'd love a cup, Ellie." She smiled. "Thanks for asking. Would you like me to fix it for us?"

"I . . ." Ellie glanced around the room, as though taking inventory, noting the boxes. Confusion toyed with her brow until she eyed the quilt on the sofa and made her way toward it. The rose dropped to the floor, completely forgotten, as she reached for the handmade blanket instead, fingering the patchwork squares made out of a hodgepodge of fabrics.

"That's pretty," Amy said, hoping the woman would remain rooted in reality. "Did you make it?"

Ellie didn't respond; she just caressed a square of pink dotted Swiss. When she looked up, she smiled. "Barbie loved her Easter dress, and she cried when she sat on that half-eaten chocolate egg."

Amy eased closer, afraid to push too hard, yet desperate to connect, to be allowed to be a part of Ellie's world, if only for a moment.

"Children grow so quickly," Ellie added.

"Yes, they do." Amy was afraid to speak, afraid to breathe.

"Barbie's going to be a woman before I know it," Ellie said, her voice wistful.

Okay, so the moment wasn't so lucid after all. But Amy was determined to have some kind of conversation, even if it was disjointed. "Did you cut the dress fabric into a quilt?"

No response.

Ellie's fingers moved to a piece of green plaid, and she studied it intently, a smile stretching across her lips. She lifted the quilt, held it against her cheek. "Harold loved that shirt."

A knock sounded at the door, and Amy had to tear herself away from the old woman to answer.

It was Maria, appearing nearly as frantic as Ellie had been when she'd entered the living room just moments before.

"Have you seen Ellie?" she asked.

"She's here, Maria. Come inside."

"Oh, thank goodness." Maria entered the house, and when she spotted Ellie, blew out a ragged breath. "I couldn't find her, and I was afraid something had happened to her."

"I meant to call you. She's only been here a minute."

They both turned to the old woman, who continued to hold the quilt against her face, rocking slowly, absorbing some kind of comfort.

"The quilt," Maria said. "She was asking for it last night, and I forgot to mention it to you. I was going to have you look for it."

"I can see that it meant a lot to her."

Maria nodded. "She was afraid that she wouldn't remember the important people and events in her life, so she made what she called a memory quilt a year or so ago. She cut satin from her wedding dress, flannel from a baby blanket her mother had made for Barbara, and fabric from some of Harold's clothing."

"That breaks my heart," Amy said.

"Mine, too."

"She must have come looking for it."

That was possible, although Amy suspected she'd just wandered into the rose garden and on into the house. That she'd stumbled upon it by chance.

Yet Amy supposed it really didn't matter. The fact that she continued to hold the quilt close suggested that there was still a ghost of the old Ellie deep inside.

Chapter 15

Armed with a small grocery list, Barbara pulled into the parking lot at the Farm Fresh Market, found a space near the entrance, and parked.

Joseph had called an hour ago, letting her know that he'd invited a group of political supporters to dinner that evening, a little detail that he'd forgotten to tell her, even though it had been on his office calendar for a week. Another woman might have snapped, but she'd held her tongue and did what she did best—scrambled to make everything right.

Thanks to Adele, her live-in housekeeper, the house was clean, the table was set, and a floral arrangement for the centerpiece had been ordered. With a little luck, the florist would have it delivered by the time Barbara got home.

It had taken three phone calls to line up a chef to prepare hors d'oeuvres and dinner, but Barbara planned to make the dessert herself—her mother's Texas chocolate cake and homemade vanilla ice cream. For some reason, her guests had always marveled over the treat, which gave the meal, as well as her candidate husband, a down-home feel.

Just as she reached for her purse, which rested on the passenger seat, her cell phone rang. She reached for it, but since she'd neglected to return it to the side pouch after she'd taken the last call, she had to dig around her wallet, cosmetic bag, and a clutter of receipts to find it.

Usually she looked at the lighted display to see who was calling first, but she was afraid she'd lose the connection if she didn't answer quickly. "Hello?"

"Barbara? It's Cynthia."

It was Joey's wife, Barbara realized.

Had her voice just cracked? "What's up, honey?"

"Joey . . ." Cynthia choked back a little sob, and Barbara's heart stalled.

"No! Don't tell me that!"

"No. . . . He's . . . not . . ." She sniffled. "It's just that he had . . . a setback. They're putting him back in ICU."

Barbara gripped the cell phone until she thought she might squeeze it in two. "I'll be right there, honey."

She pushed the End button, then dialed Joseph's office. When Marilyn Rawlings, her husband's secretary, answered, Barbara heard noise in the background, a buzz of conversation, a chuckle or two.

"I need to talk to Joseph," she said in her best don't-put-me-on-hold voice. "It's important."

"Your wife on line three," Marilyn told him.

The din of conversation stilled, and Joseph picked up the line. "Hey, Barb. How's it going?"

"Not good," she said. "Not good at all. Joey's been placed in ICU. I'm heading to the hospital now. You're going to have to cancel that dinner tonight."

"Sure," he said. "Of course. Do you want me to meet you there?"

"That would be a good idea, don't you *think?*" She hadn't meant to snap at him, but he was so caught up in his work, in the campaign strategy, that nothing else seemed to matter. Not their son, not their marriage.

For as long as she could remember, she'd been holding things together, making things right, but she was reaching her limit, and she didn't think he realized it.

"I'm sorry," she said. "I'm just so worried."

"I know. I'll get out of here as soon as I can, and I'll meet you at the hospital."

"Thanks."

Relieved that they'd found a common ground, a common crisis, she ended the call.

She hadn't meant to put a strain on the marriage she'd fought so hard and so long to keep together.

For years she'd feared that Joseph would walk out on her if he found out what she'd done while he'd been in Vietnam. And even if time might have softened the blow, she feared that he'd be crushed by her coverup, by her deception.

She'd made a deal with God, though. And she was going to spend the rest of her life making it up to everyone involved by being the best wife and mother a family ever had.

And she'd done just that, even if there were times when she'd only gone through the motions of being happy.

But if anything happened to Joey, if her son . . . Oh, dear God, she couldn't even think it.

Her eyes welled with emotion, with fear, and pain filled her chest. In a rush to get to her son's bedside, she backed out of the parking lot. But before she could blink back her tears, the Jag slammed into something rock hard, and she jerked to a sudden stop.

Oh, for Pete's sake. She glanced in the rearview mirror, expecting to see another vehicle, but spied a police patrol car instead.

How was that for luck?

Her whole life was falling apart, and now this had to happen.

Amy sat in haunting silence, grieving for the woman she'd never really met and trying to wrap her mind around what she ought to do now.

She scanned the living room, with the stacks of boxes that had left the once-cozy area as cluttered as Ellie's current mental state. Just moments ago, Maria had led the elderly woman back home. When she'd suggested they take the quilt with them, Ellie had dropped it onto the recliner as though it was a used tissue she no longer needed.

A dull ache throbbed at Amy's temples, and she massaged it away with her fingers. What more could she do here?

She'd been dragging her feet about calling the Realtor—or rather the property manager—but there was no need to dawdle any longer. Ron might as well send someone to pick up the boxes. So she dialed his number, then waited through four rings.

A click sounded, and a canned voice answered, "You've reached Ron Paige with Parkside Realty and Mar Vista Property Management Company. I'm either on another line or have stepped away from my desk. You can leave a message at the tone, or dial zero for an operator now."

Amy pressed the zero.

Another ring, another click.

A chipper female voice answered. "Parkside Realty. It's a great day to buy a new home."

"Is Ron Paige in the office?"

"He's on another line. Would you like to leave a message?"

"This is Amy Masterson. Will you have him give me a call?" She left her number, then hung up.

She glanced around the living room again. Even though she'd already set the wheels in motion and someone would soon come to pick up the boxes she'd stacked against the wall, there still didn't seem to be any hurry to pack the last of it. As weird as it might sound, Ellie's essence remained vibrant in this room as long as her things remained in the house.

But Amy couldn't hang out on Sugar Plum Lane forever, even if it was her only connection to Ellie.

She wandered to an antique curio cabinet near the fireplace, ran her fingers along the wood grain and over the lip of the trim. She studied the figurines that rested on glass shelves—a couple of Precious Moments angels and several Hummels—noticing how dusty they'd gotten.

For a moment, she thought about packing them away, then decided to take them to Maria's house instead. That way, Ellie could have them in her room, a reminder of the things that had once meant something to her.

As she turned and headed for the cabinet under the sink to get a dust rag, her gaze shifted to the photographs that lined the mantel. She probably should take those to Ellie, too.

On her way to the kitchen, she again spotted the Bible on the lamp stand. She hadn't given it much thought before; she'd just noticed the worn binding and the embossed lettering that spelled out *Eleanor Rucker* on the front cover. But she just couldn't seem to walk past it this time. So she picked it up and carried it to the sofa, where she took a seat on the cushion nearest the lamp, a place she could easily imagine Ellie sitting, the light turned on for easy reading.

As she opened the cover and flipped through the pages, she noted Ellie's handwriting in the margins, comments she'd made, scripture she'd underlined.

Amy suspected that the highlighted verses might have helped Ellie through some of the trials or struggles she'd had over the years, that they'd given her peace and assurance.

Be still and know that I am God.

Trust in the Lord.

Joy comes in the morning.

She might have taken time to read through them all if she hadn't stumbled across a couple of pieces of stationery that had been folded together and inserted between the pages, where a single passage had been highlighted. The words, "Ask and it shall be given unto you," rustled over her as she unfolded the paper and saw a list of names.

Each person mentioned had a handwritten explanation underneath.

Was this a prayer list of some kind? It certainly appeared to be.

Maria—

Lord, at times the young woman who lives next door to me is more like a daughter than the one I bore. Please bring a special man into her life, a man who will love her the way Harold loved me, a man who will respect and honor her in a way her ex-husband never did. Let him also be a good father to her kids, the kind of daddy they need.

And bless each of her children, Lord. Especially little Danny. He was the one who was more affected by his father's crime and imprisonment, the one who was hurt the most.

Amy could certainly say "Amen" to that. She wanted the same things for her new friend.

As she continued to peruse the familiar script, she noticed a name she didn't recognize.

Chuck—

I know that he was once hell-bent, Lord, but he's a good man now. And he's turned his life around. He's always got a ready smile and a servant's heart. He needs the money, yet look at all he does for the folks down at the soup kitchen. I know that I don't have to tell You that, but I pray that he will reconcile with his son. And while You're at it, will You please heal that stomach problem he has? I had an uneasy feeling when he told me about it and fear that it might be serious. Don't let him die before making amends with his only child. My heart goes out to them both, and You know why.

Amy had come to trust Ellie's intuition, so she added her own prayer for Chuck and his son before reading on.

Angel—

Dear God, bless that dear child, as well as her family—her parents, her siblings, and any children she might have. You, Lord, are the only one who knows the tears I've shed since handing her over to that woman from the adoption agency. I would have given anything to raise Angel as my own daughter, and I hope someday she will realize that. Please make sure that she was given to a family who was able to love her—perhaps even more than I would have if Barbie hadn't been so dead set against it.

After reading Ellie's journals, Amy had no doubt that Ellie had loved and wanted the baby Barbara had given up, the little girl who'd grown up to be Susan Rossi.

Was that when the rift between mother

and daughter had begun? If so, it had been going on for more than forty years, which was a long time to hold a grudge.

Still, Ellie's prayer for "Angel" had been answered many times over. It was just too bad that she hadn't been aware of that. It would have done her heart good.

Her own faith buoyed, Amy whispered, "Thanks for answering that one, Lord." Then she went on to read the other prayers on Ellie's list.

Joey and Cynthia—

Please continue to bless my dear grandson and his darling wife. He's been such a good boy, Lord. My only regret is that he never knew he had a younger sister, that the two of them didn't grow up together.

When Angel does indeed come home, as You've promised me time and again that she will, I pray that Joey will welcome her with loving arms, and that the two will become close.

Now, there was a prayer that gave Amy pause for reflection. There was no way that Joey would ever be able to meet his sister, but he could certainly meet his niece. The trouble was, Amy wasn't so sure she wanted to become a part of the Rucker family. Maybe, if Ellie had still been mentally alert, she might have felt differently.

But Ellie was no longer a factor. And Barbara seemed cool, aloof, harsh. Not at all like the daughter she'd given up.

Susan Rossi had been warm and loving. Playful, too.

And speaking of Barbara . . .

Barbara—

I don't even know what to ask for when it comes to my daughter, the heart of my heart. I loved her and doted on her to such an extent as a little girl that she grew to believe the world revolved around her and her needs. Funny how that happens. A mother can try her best to raise her child, and while we all make mistakes, we don't usually recognize them until it's too late to correct them.

I have no idea where that girl got her stubborn streak, Lord, but it will be her downfall if You don't step in and teach her how to temper it. At one time, as a little girl, she was close to You. I pray that she will turn her heart and her life back over to You, Lord. That she will come clean, with You and with Joseph.

Yes, I know why she'd like to keep things a secret, but as Pastor George said in his sermon a couple of Sundays ago, she needs to own her mistakes so she can move on. Otherwise, she'll be like that little hamster Joey used to have, running like crazy on a wheel going nowhere.

Interesting, Amy thought as she began to connect the dots. If Barbara needed to "come clean" with her husband, then it stood to reason that she'd betrayed him somehow.

Had she hidden the fact that she'd given up their child? Or that she'd been pregnant with another man's baby?

Maybe it had been a matter of infidelity, although it would have been tough to conceal a pregnancy. Wouldn't it?

Amy pondered the possibilities, then shook them off.

Did it really matter?

She supposed it did, if she were to actually approach Barbara and reveal that she was "Angel's" daughter.

But did she even want to broach the subject at all? Did she owe it to her mother to do more than just find the Ruckers?

Having no solid answers, she continued to read the last entry on the prayer list.

Me—

Last, but certainly not least, Lord, I pray that You look out for me. The elderly tend to become forgetful at times, so I hope that's all it is with me. But I'm afraid that something else is going on, and it frightens me.

I don't want to get dementia and become a burden on my family. Please don't let that happen to me. But if it's part of Your plan, I pray that You take me home before it gets bad.

A bevy of goose bumps chased up and down Amy's arms. She wasn't sure how God would choose to answer that prayer, because Ellie's mind was all but gone, and she was still here.

The familiar tone of Amy's cell phone rang, drawing her from her musing. So she tucked Ellie's list back into the Bible and went for her purse to answer the call.

It was Brandon, and his voice seemed to be lugged down by something. Despair? Weariness?

She gripped the phone tight and pressed it against her ear, trying to pick up background noises or some clue as to where he was and why he was calling. "Is something wrong?"

"Yes. I need to talk to you. Let's have dinner tonight."

"We're talking now," she said.

"Not over the phone. I need to see you in person. I'll pick you up at seven."

Whoa, she thought. *Slow down, Brandon.* A conversation over dinner sounded way too much like a date, and she wasn't up for it. Not if he had candles, soft music, and a bottle of wine in mind.

"I don't think that's a good idea," she said.

"Why not?"

Because she didn't want to go soft, didn't want to back down from the decision she'd made to go forward with her life. She still had feelings for him, but they were no longer strong enough to even attempt to work things out.

"I've already told you how I feel about reconciling," she said.

Silence stretched across the phone like a bad connection.

"Is there someone else?" he finally asked.

"No." She never would have cheated on him, and even now that they were separated, she wasn't interested in getting involved with anyone else. It was too soon.

"Then why won't you go out with me?" he asked.

"Because I don't want you to get the wrong idea."

The silence returned, and the line sparked with unspoken feelings, pain, and disappointment, creating an imaginary static.

Brandon blew out a restless sigh. "I've never met a woman as stubborn as you, Amy."

That was too bad. He might see her determination and resolve as a flaw, but she considered it an asset. She was sticking to her guns, doing the right thing. Protecting herself and her daughter from untold disappointment in the future.

"I'm sorry, Brandon. I care for you. You're the father of my daughter. But I want so much more than you're willing to give me."

"I've given you everything I possibly could. What more do you want?"

"We've been over this before. I wanted your *time.*"

"That's not a problem. You can have it—"

"Your promises aren't good enough anymore."

That prickly silence returned, threatening their conversation.

When she'd had enough of it, when she'd sensed a change of heart, when she was just about to roll over and agree to meet with him one last time, even if it was over a candlelit dinner and a glass of wine, Brandon said, "Fine. Have it your way."

His receiver slammed down like the lid of an airtight casket, and the next thing she heard was silence—the cold, shuddery kind that followed death.

Tears welled in her eyes, and a long, hard ache burrowed deep into her heart.

The first time she'd told Brandon their marriage was over, she'd been angry. But now that it was truly over and buried, all she felt was a deep and brutal sense of loss.

* * *

At his wits' end, Brandon stared at the telephone in his office, slammed his hand down on the desk and uttered a curse.

It was over. It was *really* over, and there wasn't anything he could do to fix it.

His heart rate was raging out of control, and he had the urge to get some fresh air, to escape the confines of the room that seemed to have sucked all the life out of him.

The red light on the intercom flashed and the familiar buzz sounded. His world might be spiraling out of control, but life as he knew it at the law firm was going on as usual.

He pressed the button, accepting the call from his secretary. "Yes, Kara?"

"Are you up for lunch? You don't have any appointments this afternoon, and you came in early."

That was because he'd hoped to have a dinner date with Amy tonight, and he'd wanted to cut out before five so he could pick up flowers and take a shower.

He glanced at the clock across from his desk. 1:23. He really wasn't hungry, but he wasn't going to be able to focus on anything other than Amy if he stayed here one minute longer.

Before the walls closed in on him, he said, "Sure. Why not?"

Moments later, as he was slipping on his jacket, a light rap sounded at the door he'd closed in order to have some privacy during his call to his soon-to-be ex-wife.

"Come in," he said.

Kara, a petite brunette in her mid-twenties, poked her pretty face into his office and smiled. "I thought it'd be fun to try that new bistro that just opened up down the street, Jazzy Blue's. What do you think?"

Brandon had wanted to try it, too. "Sounds good to me."

He closed his office door, then followed Kara down the hall and into the reception area. His gaze first lit upon the glossy dark curls that she sometimes wove in a twist. Today she wore her long hair loose, and it danced along her shoulders when she walked.

And speaking of walking, her hips swayed seductively side to side.

Had his secretary always been that attractive?

If so, when had he stopped noticing other women?

Chapter 16

The sun cast a lazy summer glow over the San Diego streets as Brandon walked with Kara to Jazzy Blue's.

After they turned onto Coast Highway, she nudged his arm, as if their outing had made them friends instead of coworkers. "I heard through the office grapevine that you and your wife have separated."

He really didn't want to discuss the split, although he wondered where she'd heard about it since he'd tried so hard to keep it quiet. Jake Goldstein might have spilled the beans, but he was usually pretty discreet and not prone to gossip. So maybe it had just begun to show in Brandon's eyes, in the clothing he wore—Amy used to buy all his ties and would suggest which one he ought to wear, since she was more style conscious and had a good eye for that sort of thing.

Before Brandon had hung up the phone just minutes ago, he would've been unhappy to learn that people were talking and making assumptions about his personal situation; he'd had enough of that in the past, when he'd been a kid. But now that he'd faced the fact that the marriage was really over, he supposed there wasn't any reason to keep it a secret.

Deciding that he'd pondered a response to Kara long enough, he finally said, "I'm not proud or happy about it, but Amy filed for divorce. And I guess we're going to follow through with it."

That meant talking to a family law attorney, he supposed, but he didn't want to retain anyone. Not yet. Amy had been fair so far, and he had no reason to believe things would get nasty. If they did, he'd have to hire counsel, but he didn't plan to fight.

That was odd, he realized, since he'd

had to fight so hard to get to where he was. If he hadn't, he might not have survived his childhood, gone on to college, or climbed the ranks at the firm.

They walked several more blocks before Kara spoke again. "I'm sorry to hear that, Brandon. You're a great guy, and a woman ought to thank her lucky stars to be married to you."

He ought to be flattered by the comment, and actually, he was. But did she really mean it?

In spite of having a reputation as one of the top litigators in the county, he had to admit that he still harbored a few insecurities about his worth—thanks to Chuck Masterson never caring enough to suck it up and be a real father, one a kid could depend upon. So Amy's rejection and his own sense of failure only seemed to make it all worse.

Brandon had won a full ride to UCLA and gone on to graduate from Cal Western School of Law at the top of his class. He'd also worked day and night to make partner at Price, Feller, Goldstein and now Masterson, but none of it seemed to matter at this point. He'd been with Amy for almost as long as he could remember, certainly as long as his life had held meaning, but she'd thrown a wrench into the well-oiled, carefully crafted works.

And as angry as he was, as much as he wanted to forget all about her and start fresh, he couldn't seem to let go of the memories, the dreams he'd had, all of which included her and Callie.

He couldn't help wondering what another guy in his situation might do.

Take off his wedding band, he supposed.

Would a relationship with another woman make him feel better?

He stole a gaze at Kara, noticed her chic profile, the flush on her cheeks, the hint of a grin on lips that had been artfully defined with a glossy shade of pink.

Could someone like Kara help him to set his out-of-step life back on track?

And if so, would she even want to?

As they turned right and continued along B Street, Brandon sneaked another look at the shapely brunette, a woman most men would find attractive.

Why not push the issue, take advantage of the opportunity beside him?

He looked up at the summer sky, caught the ocean breeze on his face. It didn't make sense, but he just couldn't do it, didn't want to.

When he tried to contemplate why, family values came to mind, which was a flat-out-ridiculous reason since he no longer had a family to speak of. Yet he had to admit that his father, with all his faults, had been a one-woman man. So much so, that when his mom had died, his old man had fallen completely apart.

There hadn't been anything else on the face of the earth that could take Marianne Masterson's place in Chuck's life—other than the prescription pain meds he routinely dropped and the booze he chugged.

Strangely enough, Brandon could almost understand why he'd taken that route, since he was having such a hard time calling it quits himself and letting Amy go. And for the first time in his life, he saw just what his mom's loss had done to his dad—from his father's perspective. He could see how it had crippled him, at least in the beginning, and he understood how the inability to get over it and move on with his life had eventually taken its toll. Not that Brandon planned to let it go that far, or to drink himself into a stupor each night, but he could see why someone might want to take an easy way out.

Up ahead, he spotted Jazzy Blue's, the trendy new bar and grill that several of the other attorneys had been talking about.

"I heard that they have an extensive wine list," Kara said, "and a martini bar. It might be fun to come back some evening after work. I love jazz music."

Was that an opening he ought to snatch? Should he ask if she'd like to come back with him later today? Maybe take advantage of happy hour?

If it was an opening, he couldn't quite bring himself to take advantage of it, which was pathetic, wasn't it?

At the intersection they were approaching, a homeless woman, her shoulders slumped by the weight of her plight, was pushing an overladen grocery cart along the cross street. Then she turned right and continued a slow pace in front of them.

Her unkempt hair and shabby clothes reminded Brandon of the guy named Jesse. And even though the woman hung another right and pushed her cart into an alley, disappearing from sight, his thoughts remained on Jesse.

The words the homeless man had spoken resonated in Brandon's mind as clearly right now as they'd reverberated on the city street the day they'd shared a bench near the bus stop.

Sometimes fixing a key relationship can help you make sense of everything else in life. . . . It can also help a man rebuild a marriage.

Yeah, right. He hadn't seen his old man in more than fifteen years. Even if he knew where to look for him, he couldn't imagine how patching things up with his dad would help move things along with Amy. She'd never even met the guy, so how could that affect her?

You got a raw deal as a kid, Jesse had said, *and it's created havoc in your interpersonal relationships ever since.*

Brandon had only stared at Jesse in both disbelief and annoyance. It had bothered him that a stranger had taken it upon himself to butt into another man's life. But still, the words, which held more than a semblance of truth, struck a raw chord.

It's a fairly easy fix, Jesse had added.

Brandon had complicated courtroom trials that seemed to be an easier "fix" than his relationship with Amy.

He'd laughed the guy off at that point, although the laughter had been hollow.

As if Jesse could read minds, he'd added, *Everyone makes mistakes that can have an unexpected effect on the lives of others. And it's tough to correct what's already been done. But the future offers healing, if you'll open your heart. And making peace with the past is often the first step.*

The man had clearly been crazy, one of those curbside charlatans who claimed to be psychic.

"We're here," Kara said, pointing at the eatery that was only one storefront away.

But Brandon wasn't hungry anymore, not for trendy California cuisine.

The next time you're in Fairbrook, the homeless man had said, *stop by the soup kitchen at Parkside Community Church.*

For some wild reason, that's exactly what Brandon was going to do.

As he and Kara approached the entrance to Jazzy Blue's, Brandon pulled to a stop. "I'm sorry. I can't do this. I really have to go."

She looked at him as though he was completely off his rocker, and maybe he was.

Call it a last-ditch effort to save himself, much like the terminally ill cancer patient who traveled to Mexico or Europe for an unproven and unconventional treatment, but Brandon just couldn't quite give up on his marriage.

"Where are you going?" Kara asked. "Back to the office?"

"Believe it or not, I'm leaving for the rest of the day."

She still wore a bewildered expression.

"I've got to meet with someone in Fairbrook," he added.

"Who?"

While it wasn't really any of her business, she was his secretary. She kept his schedule, did his bidding, made his excuses. So he couldn't blame her for asking.

But he couldn't bring himself to tell her that he was going to a soup kitchen and seeking out a minister named Craig.

"I'll talk to you about it when I get back."

He doubted that he really would, though. No matter what happened, or what Craig might say, Brandon couldn't see himself talking to Kara about anything other than business. Nor could he imagine pursuing anything even remotely romantic.

Not when the only woman he'd ever loved was Amy.

Already waylaid by a preventable collision with a police cruiser, Barbara didn't dare waste another minute. Her heart was racing as she gripped the steering wheel with clammy hands, yet she wouldn't risk another accident or a speeding ticket, so she drove slowly through town.

All she could think about was getting to Joey's bedside. Her son had become such a part of her that she feared she would crumble into dust without him in her life.

A few of her friends had been burdened by a ton of problems their adult children had heaped upon them: financial troubles, the custody of neglected grandkids who needed stability and love in their lives.

Some of those grown children had gone through messy and painful divorces, while others had lost jobs, abused alcohol or drugs, or had uncovered some adolescent need to "find themselves."

Either way, many of them moved back home, creating trouble for their poor parents, who'd wanted nothing more than to enjoy their retirement and who now could no longer do so.

But Barbara had been blessed with a son who was bright and successful, a man who'd made her proud.

As she reached the hospital, she looked for a place to park that was close to the entrance, but she had to drive to the far corner of the lot to find an empty space.

Apparently, Fate or someone—God,

she supposed—hadn't wanted her to arrive any sooner than she had, and she found herself tense and ready to snap in two.

She quickly climbed out of the Jag, locked the doors, then hurried toward the lobby, tucking her car keys into her purse as she went.

When she heard the jangle and clang of metal hitting pavement, she realized she had yet another hurdle to go before reaching the hospital entrance.

She grumbled under her breath as she turned to retrieve her keys and stopped dead in her tracks when she spotted a homeless man trailing her—or so it seemed.

His eyes were a stunning shade of blue, and his gaze was almost mesmerizing.

"You lost something," he said, as he stooped to pick up her key ring—a Gucci.

When he handed it over, she thanked him and dropped the keys into her purse.

"You need to own your mistakes," he said.

Was he talking about her dropping the

keys in her rush to get to the ICU? Or had she missed something?

"Excuse me?" she asked.

"Once you confess, everything will fall back into place."

Oh, for goodness sake. She should have realized that he didn't have both oars in the water. And if she needed or even wanted counseling, she'd pay top dollar for a professional.

She turned to go, eager to put some distance between them.

"I'm talking about Angel," he added.

At that, her steps froze, and she slowly turned around. Over the years, her mother had referred to the baby as Angel, and there was no way this man would know that. Unless, of course, he was one of her mother's friends, which wasn't likely.

Or was it?

She'd been shocked to find out recently that her mother had been frequenting the soup kitchen in town, so maybe they *had* known each other after all.

"Who are you?" she asked.

He didn't answer her question. Instead,

he said, "Angel found you last year, and you refused to have anything to do with her."

Barbara's heart thumped a hollow beat, and her blood turned to sludge. No one, not even her mother, had known that a woman named Susan Rossi had called Barbara out of the blue.

If her mother had known, she would have insisted, at the very least, that Barbara do something, that she seek out the younger woman and apologize for refusing to see her.

"I had no other choice," she admitted to the man. "My husband doesn't know about any of that, and if I'd reached out to her, it would have destroyed my life."

"The secret has already destroyed you in many ways."

Had it?

She tried to wrap her mind around this weird encounter with a stranger who seemed to echo her mother's voice.

Would her mom, who was only a shell of her old self, still continue to nag at her via others for the rest of her days?

You need to come clean with Joseph,

her mother had advised time and again. *It's not right for you to keep that a secret from your husband.*

If I tell him, it'll crush him, Mom. And he'll leave me.

Maybe he will, but he's your husband, your life partner. And that's his choice to make.

Barbara again studied the stranger who appeared to be a down-and-out friend of her mom. Maybe he wasn't homeless, as she'd once thought. Maybe he was actually a private investigator—the unkempt, bumbling, *Columbo* type—and Susan Rossi had hired him to speak on her behalf, to encourage a mother/daughter relationship of some kind.

If that were the case, denial wouldn't do her much good. Yet neither would establishing any kind of relationship with the woman.

Under normal circumstances, she would have shut him out with a chilling glare, dismissing both him and his nonsense. Yet there was something in his eyes that stirred something warm in her heart, swaying her to believe she might yet find the absolution that had always eluded her.

"It happened a long time ago," she finally admitted. "I made a mistake, and I put the baby up for adoption. I can't correct that now."

"Giving up the baby was a wonderful thing for you to do," the man said. "She blessed another family. But your deception is making your life miserable."

Barbara glanced at the entry of the hospital, where Joey was in ICU, where his days might be numbered, and she snapped out of whatever kind of spell the man had cast on her. "I really don't have time to talk about this now."

"I suggest you find the time," he said. "Not with me, but with God. And if you're still not comfortable praying . . ."

How did he know that she'd stopped praying years ago, that she'd felt unworthy?

". . . try talking to Craig Houston."

The associate pastor of her mother's church? Barbara shook her head, trying to shake off the conversation, trying to get back on track. She turned toward the hospital.

Joey needed her.

What was she doing hanging out in the parking lot, talking to a stranger, and a daffy one at that?

She took several steps toward the lobby, then realized that he'd probably dog her into the hospital. So she decided to ask for his business card to determine just who he was and where he worked. If he was a PI, she'd promise to meet with him at another, more convenient time—next week? Next month? Next year?

Maybe she would agree to see Susan Rossi after all, but only if both she and her PI swore to remain silent about everything, to keep the birth and the adoption a secret.

But when she turned to face him, he was gone—just as if he'd never been there in the first place.

As Brandon drove through Fairbrook, he couldn't help thinking that he was wasting his time. But somewhere down the road, he didn't want to think that he hadn't done all he could to make his marriage work, to hold his family together.

He'd never failed at anything in his life, had never allowed himself to, and he wasn't ready to give up on his marriage yet. So he'd called 411 and had gotten the number of Parkside Community Church, where the soup kitchen was located. And then he'd talked to the secretary, a woman named Rosemary, and asked for directions.

"It's a white, old-fashioned style church with a steeple, stained glass windows, and two red doors in front," she told him. "You can't miss it. We're located right across the street from the park."

Sure enough, he found it. And five minutes later, he followed the signs that pointed to a modular building at the far edge of the church grounds and entered the soup kitchen.

Several groups of people were seated at rectangular tables. A young mother sat with two children, a boy and a girl. Three old men, one wearing a patriotic hat of some kind, chuckled while drinking coffee and eating a slice of lemon meringue pie. There were, he guessed, about fifteen diners in all.

He made his way to the nearest man, the fellow with a fringe of shaggy gray hair poking out from under his red, white, and blue cap.

"Excuse me," Brandon said. "I'm looking for Pastor Craig and was told I might be able to find him here."

"Yep." The man pointed a gnarled finger toward a doorway that probably led to the actual kitchen. "He went back to help Dawn with something. He'll be out in a minute or two."

"All right. I'll wait." Brandon left the man to finish his dessert with his friends and stood off the side, near the bulletin board on the west wall that advertised the community clinic, AA meetings, a job fair, and group counseling session hosted by County Mental Health.

After giving it a quick once-over, he leaned against the wall and watched the doorway for the associate minister to return. He couldn't help wondering why Jesse hadn't told him to speak to the senior pastor. If this was some kind of divine, magical appointment, you'd think he would have been sent to talk to the head honcho.

Either way, he was again haunted by the sense that this visit was going to be a complete waste of time.

Out of the corner of his eye, he caught movement in the doorway. A closer look revealed a blond man in his mid-twenties passing into the dining area. So Brandon pushed off the wall and approached him.

"Are you Pastor Craig?" he asked.

"Yes." One glance at Brandon's expensive suit, and his expression grew serious. "What can I do for you?"

"To tell you the truth," Brandon admitted, "I'm not entirely sure. A few days ago, I met a guy down by the Embarcadero in San Diego, and he suggested I talk to you, but he didn't say why."

The minister merely looked at him, clearly puzzled. But why shouldn't he be? Brandon still didn't get it himself, and coming to Fairbrook to seek out the pastor and introduce himself on a whim wasn't the sort of thing that he usually did.

"His name was Jesse," Brandon added. "And he said to tell you hello."

At that, a full-blown smile splashed across the pastor's face. "Oh, yeah?"

"So you know him?"

"Yes, but I haven't seen him in a while. How's he doing?"

"Okay, I guess." Brandon gave a half shrug. "But what's with that guy? He seemed to be on another planet, yet he knew things. Or at least, he implied that he did."

Craig's grin grew brighter still. "Yep, you certainly met Jesse."

"What do you know about him?"

"Just that he's got a gentle spirit and a kind heart. He's wise, too."

"Doesn't look like he takes his own advice."

Craig laughed. "That's what I thought when I first met him, but you'd be surprised."

Okay. So maybe Brandon wasn't chasing his tail by coming here after all.

"So what did he say that made you decide to step out on a limb and introduce yourself to me?" Craig asked.

"Normally, I wouldn't have, but I've found myself backed into a corner, and I guess you could say that I'm grasping at a straw."

"Why don't you come with me to my office," Craig said. "Then you can start at the beginning."

Several minutes later, Brandon followed the minister out of the soup kitchen, across the lawn, and into the church office. Now he was seated on the other side of the desk from Craig.

"Obviously, Jesse made an impression on you," the minister said.

"In a way, yes. But I'd like to preface this by saying that I'm still skeptical."

"I understand. After meeting Jesse, I had a few of those moments myself, but I've learned to either trust his advice or to give it a lot of consideration." Craig leaned back in his chair, appearing to be at ease, confident. "Jesse has an uncanny ability to . . . Well, he seems to know things without being told."

It sure seemed that way to Brandon, although he wasn't going to buy into anything psychic. He didn't believe in that sort of thing, although being here might suggest that he did.

In truth, he was merely desperate to

save his marriage, what little there was left of it.

"I'm going through a divorce," he admitted, "and I'm not happy about it. I'd like to make things work, but my wife isn't willing."

The whisper of a grin settled on the minister's face. "So Jesse suggested marital counseling? With me?"

"Not exactly. It's just that he . . . Well, it sounds kind of crazy, but he seemed to know all about the split, even though I never uttered a word about it. And then, out of the blue, he told me that I needed to work on having a relationship with my dad."

"How does your father play into this?"

"That's just it," Brandon said. "I haven't seen him since I was seventeen and left for college."

"Do you have any idea where he might be now?"

Brandon leaned back, tensed. "Are you saying that you think Jesse's right? That I need to reconcile with my father before I can reconcile with my wife?" He slowly shook his head. That was wild. *Too* wild to believe.

"I'm really not sure," Craig said. "I guess it depends. But if Jesse suggested something like that to me, I'd give it some serious thought."

Brandon didn't know what to say, what to do. "My family was dysfunctional. My father spent most of my teenage years drunk, strung out on prescription pain medication that he picked up in Tijuana, and unemployed. I don't have any idea where to look for him. I'd do a Google search, but at the rate he was going downhill, he could be homeless for all I know. And his name might not show up anywhere."

Craig straightened in the chair, no longer relaxed and at ease. He leaned forward, rested his forearms on the desk, and furrowed his brow. "If that's the case, and if Jesse sent you to see me, it's possible that he knew your dad. And that he thought he might show up at our soup kitchen, if he hasn't already."

"Anything's possible, I guess."

"What's your father's name?" Craig asked.

"Chuck Masterson."

"No kidding?" That easy grin returned. "Your father is a friend of mine."

Brandon's old man ran with ministers now? That was a switch.

"Chuck's had a tough time of it," Craig said, "but he's sober now and has turned his life around. *Way* around. You'd be surprised."

Oh, Brandon would be surprised all right. But he'd also be at a loss for words. "After fifteen years, we really don't have anything to say to each other anymore."

"Don't you?"

The minister's question burrowed deep within Brandon, deeper than any of the words Jesse had said before. But Craig didn't know what it had been like growing up in that household.

"To tell you the truth," Brandon said, "I've spent my adult life trying to prove that I'm not cut from the same bolt of cloth, that I can provide for myself and my family."

The phone rang, interrupting them.

"Excuse me," Craig said. "Do you mind if I take this?"

"Not at all." It would give Brandon a moment to think, to sort through how any of this fit into his relationship—or rather his non-relationship—with Amy.

As long as he'd believed that his old man was nowhere to be found, it was easy to remain detached. Unaffected.

"This is Pastor Craig," the minister said as he took the call.

His expression, light and carefree just moments ago, grew serious again. "Oh, no. I'm *so* sorry to hear that. When?" He listened for a couple of beats, then said, "Of course. I'll be right there."

When he ended the call, he apologized. "I'd love to talk longer, but I have to leave. One of my parishioners, a shut-in I visit regularly, is in grave condition and not expected to live. Can we talk more about this another time?"

"Sure." Brandon pushed back his chair and got to his feet.

Craig stood and patted his pocket, as if checking for his car keys, then reached inside and pulled out a business card. "Here's my number and e-mail address. As we head out of the office, you can stop by my secretary's desk. Rosemary will be happy to make an appointment for us to talk again soon. In fact, I think tomorrow afternoon is wide open."

"All right." Brandon took the card. "I

may have to be in court, but I'll see what I can do."

The two men walked back to the reception area, and as Craig reached the door, Brandon said, "I hope everything works out okay."

"So do I, but it doesn't look good." Craig raked a hand through his wheat-colored hair and blew out a sigh. "It doesn't look good at all."

Chapter 17

Maria sat next to Eddie on the front porch steps, waiting for the coroner to arrive.

Just twenty minutes earlier, she'd been in the front yard, talking to Amy over the shrubbery that marked the property line and making plans to have a barbecue next Saturday afternoon.

Eddie had been working on the automatic sprinkler system in Amy's front yard, while Captain and Ellie, as they often did, sat in the two wicker rocking chairs on the porch.

"Mommy," Wally called from the open doorway, his tone stretching into a whine.

"Sara took my Spider-Man hero and won't give him back."

"Tell her I said that she needs to give him to you, and if she won't do it, tell her to come outside. I'll talk to her."

"Okay." He dashed back into the house, slamming the door behind him.

Maria thought she heard a thump of some kind, although someone down the street was mowing their lawn, and she couldn't be sure. She dismissed the sound, thinking it was due to her son's hasty exit.

A few minutes later, the preschooler returned and called out, "Mommy . . . ," then paused.

Maria looked at Amy, rolled her eyes in a what's-a-mother-to-do sort of way, knowing she was going to have to intercede.

That is, until Wally continued by asking, ". . . how come Captain is sleeping on the ground?"

Thinking that the preschooler was joking—*hoping* that he was—she stepped away from the hedge, closer to the house, and glanced over her shoulder, only to see the old man sprawled on the porch flooring, face down.

"Oh, my gosh. Call 9-1-1," she told Amy as she rushed to Captain's side.

Amy yelled for Eddie as she sprinted across her lawn and into the other house to place the call, but Maria's only thought was to get to Captain, to find out what had happened.

She knelt beside him and rolled him onto his back. He seemed to be unconscious, and his chest rose and fell unevenly. His coloring was pale, his skin clammy. Clearly, his condition was serious.

"Ellie," she said, looking at the old woman who sat on the rocker, watching it all. "What happened?"

The elderly woman didn't so much as shrug her shoulders. It was Wally who provided the only answer, if you could call it that.

"I don't know what happened, Mommy. He was just lying on the floor when I came out. How come he's not sleeping in his bed?"

Maria had always believed honesty was the best policy with everyone, including the kids, but sometimes that wasn't possible. How could she toss out words to a three-year-old like "heart attack" or "stroke" or . . . "dying?"

"I'm not sure what's going on," she said as she checked the elderly man's pulse. Irregular.

What was she supposed to do? She'd had first aid and CPR training when she was pregnant with Danny, but for some reason, she didn't seem to remember any of it. All she knew was that Captain needed medical assistance, and he needed it *now*.

Thankfully, Eddie was at her side in a second, followed by Amy. And before long, sirens sounded.

A hook and ladder truck, as well as an ambulance, pulled up in front of the house, and paramedics rushed toward her. She'd never been so glad to have the fire department located just down the street as she was right now, and she moved out of the way, giving the emergency response team room to work.

By that time, all three of her children, as well as a couple of neighbor kids, had showed up on the scene. When she turned to reassure them about what was happening, she found Eddie doing it for her.

"But what's wrong with Captain?" Wally asked.

"He isn't feeling well," Eddie told the boy. "We think it's best if the paramedics take him to the hospital so that the doctors can take care of him."

"Are they going to make him all better?" Wally asked.

"They're going to try."

Wally nodded, as though that was all he needed to hear.

Amy, whose daughter hadn't come to Sugar Plum Lane today, eased close and slipped an arm around Maria's waist. "If you want to go with him, I can stay with Ellie and the kids. I'll just ask my friend Steph to bring Callie here."

"Thanks, Amy. I'd really appreciate that. Captain doesn't have any family. It's just me and his friends at the soup kitchen."

"I'd better call Pastor Craig," Eddie said. "We should ask him to meet us at the hospital."

He was right about contacting Captain's minister. But had he said *us*? Maria turned to the man who was winning her heart through one expected kindness after another. "Are you planning to go with me?"

"You look a little pale and shaky," he said, "and I thought . . ."

She offered him a grateful smile, placed her hand on his upper arm, and gave it an affectionate stroke. Under the cotton fabric of his shirt, she felt the corded muscles of a man used to a hard and honest day's work. "Thank you, Eddie. I'd really appreciate that."

Then, while paramedics worked on Captain, she slipped past them and entered the house for her purse, which she found on the bottom step of the stairs. She also went into Captain's room and gathered up his pill bottles. The doctors would want to know what medication he was taking and the doses that had been prescribed, and she didn't want to take time to write them all down.

When she returned outside, she found that the paramedics were no longer kneeling beside Captain, no longer checking his vitals.

"What's the matter?" she asked. "Why aren't you . . . ?"

They didn't need to say a word; their sympathetic expressions said it all.

"I'm sorry," one of them, a tall, auburn-haired man, said. "He's gone."

Eddie, who'd been talking to the paramedics, drew close to Maria. "I called the church and spoke to Craig. He was going to meet us at the hospital. But I'll have Rosemary get a hold of him and ask him to come here instead."

"I'll have to contact the coroner," the paramedic added.

She glanced at Captain, who lay on the porch as if sleeping, just as Wally had said earlier. Only now it was an eternal sleep.

Were they just going to leave his body lying on the floor until the coroner arrived? She'd heard that it sometimes took hours for that to happen.

Eddie placed his hand on her shoulder, not quite a hug, but a definite show of compassion, support. "I'll stay here with you until then."

Maria nodded, then bit down on her bottom lip, trying to take it all in. Captain, who'd had oatmeal for breakfast, who'd talked about baseball and the Padres to Danny while looking over the sports section of the newspaper just an hour earlier, had died.

She glanced at Ellie, her brow furrowed. The elderly woman didn't appear to be either shocked or grieving, just confused—as usual.

Amy, who'd been standing on the lawn, away from the activity, moved closer to the porch. "I'll take the kids and Ellie next door."

That was probably for the best.

Eddie's hand, which was resting easily on Maria's shoulder, slid around her and drew her close. "Thanks, Amy. That's a good idea."

At that, Maria realized she needed to snap to, that she couldn't expect Eddie and Amy to step in and handle everything for her. But she certainly appreciated that they were willing to.

She turned and gave her new friend a hug. "Thanks, Amy. You're the best."

"So are you," Amy said as they slowly released each other. Then she gathered up the children and Ellie and took them home.

Now here Maria was, seated with Eddie on the steps of the front porch, waiting for both Craig and the coroner to arrive. She placed her hands on her knees, stroked the denim fabric of her jeans.

"Are you doing okay?" Eddie asked.

"Now that it's over, I am. Thanks for being here with me."

He placed a hand over one of hers. "Don't give it another thought."

His touch wasn't so unusual, under the circumstances. Yet his hand lingered, and she was glad that it had, because he caressed her skin with the pad of his thumb, calming her, infusing her with strength.

And at that very moment, she realized that with him by her side, she could make it through anything.

At a quarter to five, Barbara returned home from the hospital. Joseph had met her in the small waiting room off the ICU, and together they'd gone in to visit their son.

She'd tried so hard to be upbeat, to pretend that it was just a matter of time, that everything would soon be okay again, that he would have the open-heart surgery soon, that he'd be discharged and would recover like the many other people who had the same procedure.

But she hadn't been able to keep her tears at bay, especially when Joey thanked her and his father for being such wonderful parents over the years. It was almost as though he was making some kind of farewell speech, and she hadn't been ready for it.

She'd made some lame excuse to leave—saying she had to go to the ladies' room when she really hadn't needed to. And then she hadn't been able to return to his bedside.

Instead, she'd hung out in the lobby for a while, hoping to see Pastor Craig—expecting him, since he and Joey were so close—but he hadn't showed up. She'd wanted to ask him to pray for her. With his hotline to Heaven, he might be able to finagle a miracle, but apparently she was on her own with this one.

Her whole world, it seemed, was spinning out of control, and she was at a complete loss.

She'd eventually gone home, seeking not just escape, but peace and a renewal of spirit—all the things people expected to find behind the privacy of their front door. But she didn't find a bit of it today.

The fresh flowers she'd ordered from her favorite florist now adorned the dining room, as well as the entryway and the glass-topped coffee table. The aroma of the dinner that the chef had prepared for the canceled dinner filled the air.

Still, the house in which she lived, the sprawling estate that had been professionally decorated in soothing shades of beige and brown and green, provided no comfort whatsoever.

In the past, when faced with something of this magnitude, she might have turned to her mother for comfort and solace and wisdom, although she'd never been this distressed, this fearful before. But going to her mother for advice or prayer now was no longer an option.

She was on her own.

Oddly enough, the only advice she'd been offered had come from that shabby, long-haired private investigator hired by Susan Rossi.

You need to own your mistakes, he'd

said. *Once you confess, everything will fall back into place.*

Had he been right?

Was that the key? The missing piece to a jigsaw puzzle that would set everything to rights?

To be honest, she'd confessed to God time and again. And she'd made promises she'd kept—to be the best wife and mother she could be. She'd gone on to support charities, too, and had been instrumental in raising money for abused children and battered women, for the homeless, for cancer research, for . . . you name it. If it had been a worthy cause, Barbara Davila had championed it.

She'd been a good person, too. Surely that had made up for one indiscretion, one short-lived affair.

God had forgiven her, hadn't He? The fact that she'd been able to hide her pregnancy from Joseph while he'd been in the hospital in Honolulu, recovering from his injuries, was nothing short of a miracle—and an answer to her prayer. And the adoption had taken place so quickly and without a snag.

The *adoption.*

Giving up the baby was the right thing to do, the PI had said.

Yet Barbara had argued long and hard over that decision with her mother, who'd always wanted a houseful of children but had only ended up with one.

"You'll never be able to pull it off," her mother had said. "Joseph will find out anyway."

But God, it seemed, had worked that all out on Barbara's behalf; she'd been so sure of it.

"Stop seeing this baby as a part of my father and a way of keeping him alive," Barbara had argued. "It's not about my dad. And it's not about you. It's about *me.* Getting involved with that guy was a huge mistake—I admit it. Getting pregnant was a horrible complication. Keeping the baby will ruin my marriage."

"You should have thought about your marriage when you went out with Darrel Ryder in the first place," her mother had countered. "What were you thinking? Your poor husband was overseas, fighting a war."

Okay, so she'd made a bad decision and had come to regret it. But there was nothing she could do to correct that mistake after the fact. Keeping the child would mean that she'd be paying penitence for the rest of her life.

"Let me have the baby," her mother had begged. "I'll tell everyone that I had an affair and that I'm an unwed mother."

"Oh, *please,* Mom. I can't believe this is coming from you of all people, Miss Goody Two-shoes, who wouldn't tell a lie if her life depended upon it."

Still, she'd been right. Barbara *had* screwed up big time. She knew it now, but she'd also known it then. And it had all come back to haunt her nearly forty-five years later.

Yet that nightmare she'd been living paled next to losing Joey.

Ever since she'd given up the baby, she'd focused all her love, time, and energy on her son. And she was going to . . . lose him. Try as she might, she had to face that near certainty, and doing so forced her back into a corner in which she'd never expected to find herself.

For a moment, fear and guilt and impotence swirled around like a kaleidoscope of ugly colors. She did her best to let it all clear, to ponder a way out of the mess her life had become. Yet for some reason, the only thing that came to mind, the only thing that made any sense, was the comment the private investigator had made earlier today:

Your deception is making your life miserable.

Maybe it was, but she wouldn't have admitted that to the bushy-faced stranger.

When she'd told him she didn't have time to talk to him, he'd said, *I suggest you find the time. Not with me, but with God.*

As a rule, she didn't pray. To be honest, she didn't feel worthy and feared that any request or plea that she had would fall on deaf ears. So whenever times had been tough, she'd depended upon her mother's faith to get her through.

They'd talked about that once, and her mom had said, "You can't get to Heaven on your mother's coattails, Barbie. God doesn't have granddaughters."

But Barbara had blown her mom off.

Her life had been going well in those days, and she'd had almost everything in the world she could ever want.

Yet it was all a façade, wasn't it?

The deception had become so much a part of her that the ugly truth had engrained itself upon her soul.

Oh, dear God. Was that what she'd done, what she'd become?

"I'm sorry," she whispered as she sat in the midst of a professionally decorated living room that suddenly seemed dank and empty. "I made a mistake years ago by betraying my husband's trust. I broke the promise I'd made to love and honor him until death, and instead of confessing, I hid it from him. And now look at me."

While her thoughts had been directed to God, the confession she'd just made didn't seem to be enough, and she dropped to her knees beside the sofa and bowed her head in shame, in submissiveness. "I can't do it alone anymore, Lord. I've made a complete mess of it. I need You to take control of my life again. With Your help, I'll tell Joseph what I did. And I'll ask him to forgive me. If he can't, if he blows up, if he rants and raves, if he leaves me, then I'll face the consequences. But I'll face them—with You to help me."

She waited in silence to hear something, expecting a thunderous clap followed by a flash of light. Waited to feel something that would convince her that everything was going to be all right from here on out.

Yet she didn't hear or feel anything, other than a gradual sense of peace that began to settle over her, a relief that lifted from her shoulders and made her want to rise up.

"Thank you," she said as she basked in the first sense of forgiveness she'd ever really had. And for the first time in what seemed like forever, she felt worthy to be in God's presence, worthy to lay the burdens of her heart on Him. "While You're here with me, do you suppose You could spare a miracle for Joey? I won't make the mistake of telling You how or when to do it, but I'm asking You to please heal Joey, as well as our family. And I'd like You to place my world back on its axis—Your axis, Lord. Amen."

Just as though he'd been waiting out in the front yard for the spiritual dust to settle, Joseph opened the door and passed through the marble-tiled entry. "Honey? I'm home."

He entered the living room, where Barbara had been kneeling just moments before, and caught her gaze. He frowned, sensing that bad news was about to be shared. His brow, which had thickened with age and had become threaded with silver over the years, arched. "Oh, no. Is it . . . Joey?"

"No," she said. "He's not any worse. It's just that I . . ." She pointed to the cream-colored brocade sofa. "Please sit down. I have a confession to make."

"You didn't forget to transfer money into your household account again, did you?"

"I'm afraid it's worse than that." Her throat suddenly went dry and fear pounded at the back of her neck. Yet she forced herself to say what needed to be said. "I . . . uh . . ." Taking a fortifying breath, she pressed on. "I've kept a secret from you for years, Joseph. Something I'm terribly ashamed of, something I was afraid you'd never forgive me for doing."

He took a seat on the sofa and stroked the length of his left leg, which had been injured when his plane made a crash landing in Vietnam. It often bothered him when he was tired or stressed. "What's so bad that you think I'd never forgive you?"

She took another deep breath of courage, then stepped out on a limb that was sure to break. "I cheated on you when you were in the service. And I got pregnant. I gave the baby up for adoption so that you'd never know about it."

Shock, betrayal, and disbelief swam in his eyes, but he didn't utter a single word.

"I'm sorry," she added, as if those two simple words could somehow make it all right. "I was young, impulsive—selfish. And the guy meant nothing to me. I loved you. I still do. And I've tried to make it up to you over the years."

He blinked, as though trying to make sense of it all. "You're telling me about this *now?*"

"I'm sure, with the campaign coming up, you didn't need any surprises. And . . . Well, she came to see me nearly a year ago. I refused to see or talk to her, but today, a private investigator approached me, and he . . ." She paused, trying to catch a hint of Joseph's reaction, his pain, his anger.

She was met only with silence—cold, hard, brittle.

"I'm sorry," she said again. "So very sorry."

"For what?" he asked. "Cheating on me? Betraying my trust? Breaking our vows?"

"Yes, for all of that," she said. "It only happened once, and the relationship didn't last. It was a very long time ago, and I've never done anything like it since."

Joseph stood, his shoulders slumped, and he slowly shook his head. "What about the deception, Barb? We've been living a lie, and you never even once thought to tell me."

Then he did exactly what she'd always feared he would.

He walked out of the house and shut the door.

The coroner had arrived late that afternoon and released Captain's body to the funeral home. Apparently, the elderly man had planned ahead, making the arrangements with the mortuary of his choice and paying for their services in advance.

All afternoon, Eddie had stayed with Maria, keeping her company. And as strange as it might seem, there was really no other place he would have rather been.

He was sorry that Captain had died,

that the kids had seen the paramedics fail to bring him back, and that Maria had gone through it all. But death was, unfortunately, a part of life, even if people didn't like to think about it.

The kids had been a little quiet and downcast for a while, but Maria talked to them about it, telling them that Captain was happy now, that he was in a much better place. And they'd seemed to understand and to accept it.

Eddie had figured that the sooner they fell into their daily routine, the better. And while that routine really had nothing to do with him, he couldn't help wanting to hang around a little longer.

So he'd suggested they take the kids to Roy's Burger Roundup, a new burger place with an indoor playground. Maria had balked a little, until Amy, who'd been keeping the kids occupied next door, volunteered to keep Ellie while they were gone.

And now here they were, taking seats at a white Formica-covered table, while the kids dashed off to play on the indoor playground, with its colorful climbing tubes and slides.

"It's been a weird day," Maria said.

"You can say that again." Eddie studied the woman across from him. "But do you know what? Captain lived a full life, and there's no doubt in my mind where he's at right now."

"I know." She smiled at him, her pretty brown eyes glistening. "It's still sad, though."

As a tear slipped down her cheek, he reached across the table and brushed it away with his thumb, only to see another take its place. "I'm sorry, honey."

The term of endearment had just rolled right out, and while he wished he could reel it back in, she didn't seem to be bothered by it.

"You're a great guy, Eddie. I'm really glad that we . . . well, that we got to know each other."

He hoped she wasn't going to finish with some kind of breakup line, especially when they hadn't even gone on a real date yet.

She attempted a smile that shifted into an awkward, I'm-still-on-the-verge-of-tears tremble. And all Eddie could think of doing was to wrap his arms around her, to do his best to protect her.

Yet more than the table separated them, reminding him of the conversation he'd had with Captain just days before.

"I need to tell you something," he said.

"What's that?"

"Captain once asked me if my intentions were honorable when it came to you."

She smiled, cocked her head slightly to the side. "Are they?"

He nodded. "Yes. Absolutely."

She reached across the table and covered his hand with hers, letting him know that she was glad things were taking a serious romantic turn.

Yet even though Captain had passed away and couldn't take him aside right now, Eddie had the feeling the old man would have pressed him to be up front with Maria and not to hold anything back—even if the revelation caused the warmth of her touch to chill and the threads that bound them together to snap.

He supposed he owed her that much, and while he didn't like taking the risk, there was no other decent way to have an honorable relationship with her.

"There's something else I have to tell you," he said.

"What's that?"

It was his last chance to backpedal, to keep his shame to himself. But if they were going to have a lasting relationship, it needed to be honest from the start.

"When I was seventeen, I had a girlfriend who lived in Mexico, about an hour from Tijuana." He waited a beat to continue, realizing he could still change his mind about what he was about to say, but she deserved better than that—maybe she even deserved better than him.

So he took a breath and released it, buying time—or maybe courage. "It wasn't planned, and it certainly wasn't convenient, but she got pregnant. Supporting a wife and a baby was going to change my college plans, but I couldn't let her go through that alone. So I decided to bring her to Fairbrook and marry her."

Maria's touch lightened, but she didn't pull away—yet. So he pressed on. "She couldn't cross the border legally, so I decided to sneak her into the States in the trunk of my friend's car."

"Did you get caught?"

"Yeah, but not the way you might think. I was so nervous that when a car slipped up close behind me, I assumed it was a border patrol agent on my tail and drove faster. I hoped to hit the freeway, then exit before they could catch me."

Eddie's thoughts rolled back to that night, and he again felt the desperation, the fear. His hands grew clammy again, threatening to dampen the tabletop, and his stomach lurched. But he forced himself to go on, to lay it all on the table. "I sped through town, thinking that they'd send her back to Rosarito, that they'd separate us, and so I stepped on the gas. I hadn't meant to be reckless, but I'd only had my driver's license for a year or so, and . . ."

Just as if it was yesterday, Eddie could hear the skids, the crunch of metal upon metal. And his voice, heavy with the guilt he still couldn't kick, dropped an octave as he forced himself to tell it all. "I ran a red light, and someone broadsided my car, hitting the trunk and bashing it in. Cecelia was killed, and the baby, a little girl, lived only a few hours."

Maria turned his hand over and covered his palm, dampness and all, with hers. "I'm so sorry, Eddie."

"Yeah, it was tough. I . . . uh . . ." He

cleared his throat, hoping he could finish the story and praying that, when she heard the rest, she wouldn't let go, that she wouldn't pull back. "I was arrested, tried, and convicted of gross vehicular manslaughter. My attorney managed to get them to drop the federal charges of smuggling an illegal alien, but I was in prison for almost five years."

Through their tentative connection, he felt her tense, draw back.

"I know you're probably reluctant to get involved with anyone who's been in prison, but I swear to you. I never was in trouble with the law before. And I'll never be again."

She continued to only look at him, yet she hadn't let go of his hand, which he hoped was a good sign. He tried his best to read her expression, but he couldn't seem to make sense of it.

"I know you have issues about your ex-husband being incarcerated," he added. "And you don't deserve to hook up with a guy who might drag you and the kids into that sort of mess. But I'm off probation, and it's all behind me now."

At least, he sure hoped that it was. If

she couldn't accept his past, then he might never be able to completely shake it himself.

"It's a little unsettling," she said, giving his hand a warm squeeze. "But I appreciate your honesty."

"Does that mean you'll still go out with me?"

Tears welled in her eyes, and he was afraid to hear her answer. Yet her response was a nod, followed by, "Yes, Eddie. I've gotten a clear picture of the kind of man you are deep inside, and if you don't think a woman with three kids is too much for you to consider, then I'm willing to see where this goes."

Eddie's heart was swelling so big and pounding so hard, he was afraid it would burst. "You won't be sorry, Maria."

"I hope you won't be, either."

"Sorry about getting involved with you?" he asked, amazed she'd even think that might be the case.

"I'm quite a few years older than you, and—"

He lifted their clasped hands and pressed a kiss on her knuckles, silencing her it seemed before saying, "Don't believe that bill of goods that your ex may have implied. You're a wonderful woman, a loving mom. And your second husband is going to be one lucky guy."

Her eyes brightened, and her cheeks flushed.

Eddie didn't dare tell her that he had a burning desire to be that guy.

Chapter 18

After his unplanned meeting with Craig Houston had been interrupted, Brandon left the church office, drove to the beach, and parked along the busy two-lane coastal highway.

At that point, he couldn't have gone back to the office even if he'd wanted to. It would have been too awkward after bailing out on Kara at lunch.

The sun had dipped low over the ocean, and the beach crowd had thinned out, leaving the gulls to fight over any picnic scraps that had been left behind.

Out on the water, a couple of die-hard

surfers sat on their boards where the waves broke. But for the most part, the shore was deserted and provided a great respite from the trials and tribulations of life.

Brandon used to come to this very spot when he was a kid. He'd usually ride his skateboard to the bus stop, then take number 636 to the beach. It had been a good way to escape a lousy childhood, so it seemed appropriate to come here now.

Maybe a walk on the beach would help him sort through his problems, his options—what few there seemed to be.

He opened the driver's door, shed his jacket, and tossed it onto the passenger seat. Then he slipped out of his loafers and peeled off his socks. After locking his belongings in the car, he walked toward the water, eager to roll up his pants and wade along the shore.

The sand was warm, and the grains massaged his bare feet. A couple of seagulls swooped overhead and cried out as the waves ebbed and flowed.

He didn't know how long he'd walked, twenty or thirty minutes, he guessed, when his cell phone rang. He would have let it go, thinking it was someone at the office trying to reach him. But on the outside chance it was Amy, he glanced at the lighted display.

The number wasn't one he recognized, although it was local. And for some reason, he felt compelled to answer. "Hello?"

"Mr. Masterson? This is Craig Houston from Parkside Community Church."

Brandon had left a business card with the secretary, so he wasn't surprised that the minister had called him back.

"I'm sorry I had to cut you off earlier today," Craig said.

"No problem. I understand. Besides, I showed up at your office without an appointment." Who more than a busy attorney understood the ramifications of dropping in unannounced?

"Hey, if Jesse was involved in our meeting, then I'm inclined to think it was a *divine* appointment."

Brandon wasn't convinced about that, although it did seem odd that the homeless man had put two and two together and figured out that he and Chuck were related.

"Are you interested in talking to your dad?" Craig asked.

Not really, although he was still grasping at straws when it came to Amy. And if there was some connection to his lousy relationship with his father and the split from his wife, then maybe he ought to agree. "Where can I find him?"

"He's at Pacifica General Hospital."

Something told Brandon his old man hadn't landed a job there, that he might be having health problems. "What's wrong?"

"He's got cancer, and the prognosis isn't good."

The news, while startling, left him only numb. Shouldn't he feel something more than an unsettling buzz?

"I'm sorry to hear that," he finally said, still trying to sort through his reaction, to temper his response.

"He's talked to me about you on several occasions," Craig said, "and I know he'd like to see you."

Brandon didn't know what to say—not just to the minister, but to his dad, too. Under the best of circumstances, he'd be at a loss. But with the man dying?

"I'm sure things were bad when you were growing up. Chuck made it clear to me that he failed you. So I can understand if you don't want to talk to him. But I hope you consider going to visit him, especially when the window of opportunity is closing on you both."

His lack of emotion—anger, resentment, love—bothered him. Yet so did the ticking clock.

"Do you know what room he's in?" Brandon asked.

"Four-fourteen. And if you're thinking about going tonight, visiting hours are from seven to nine."

Brandon glanced at his wristwatch. What else did he have going on today? Going home to an empty house? Eating take-out and watching a boring movie on TV?

He thanked the minister, then headed back to where he'd parked his car. About twenty minutes later, he leaned against the side of his Mercedes and tried to brush the sand from his feet. Then he slipped into his shoes and socks.

The grit that remained was irritating with each step he took, but he wouldn't go home first to shower.

If he was going to check on his dad, he needed to do it before time ran out.

On his dad.

But on his marriage, too.

It had been a sad day, and Amy was glad that it was nearly over. Thank goodness Callie hadn't been around when the paramedics had tried—but failed—to save Captain's life.

As soon as Amy had realized what had happened, she'd sent the neighborhood children home and taken Sara, Danny, and Wally next door, leaving their mother to wait for the coroner.

Afterward, Eddie suggested they take Maria's kids out to dinner, which Amy thought was a good idea.

"We have Ellie to think about," Maria had reminded him. "I don't think she's up for anything like that."

"I don't mind looking after her," Amy had said. "Steph is going to bring Callie to me, so I'll just wait here until you get home."

And now here she was, seated in the living room with Ellie, who didn't seem to notice that anything was out of sync, even though there were stacks of boxes in the living room of the house that had once been hers.

Amy had fixed grilled cheese sandwiches and chicken noodle soup for dinner, but neither she nor Ellie had done more than pick at their food.

It made her wonder if, somewhere beneath the foggy surface, Ellie was aware of the fact that Captain had died, if a part of her was in mourning. Or maybe she realized that she'd reached the end of her own journey, that she would pass away one day soon.

Amy studied her great-grandmother, who sat in the brown tweed recliner. The memory quilt, which had once been folded, was now draped across the chair. The bulk of the fabric was underneath her on the seat cushion, while one corner hung over the armrest.

Ellie's arthritic hand rested atop a square of blue gingham with white eyelet trim, although she seemed oblivious to everything around her.

Next to her, on the lamp table, Ellie's Bible rested with the prayer list still folded within its pages, a silent testimony of the requests that had been answered, as well as the one that hadn't.

I don't want to get dementia and become a burden on my family. Please don't let that happen to me. But if it's part of Your plan, I pray that You take me home before it gets bad.

A cloak of sadness draped over Amy as she realized just how bad Ellie's dementia had gotten, and try as she might, she couldn't seem to shake the heavy darkness.

Ellie was still alive when Amy had located the house on Sugar Plum Lane, but she was so far removed from reality that she might as well be dead.

Amy cast a sympathetic glance at the elderly woman, whose head was bowed as though weighed down by it all, too. Her eyes were closed, her breathing slow and easy.

Why had God taken Captain today and not Ellie?

It seemed like a senseless choice. Yet rather than ponder the ins and outs of a divine plan—whatever it might be—Amy bowed her own head, clasped her hands in her lap, and offered up a prayer of her own.

"Ellie's been a good woman, a faithful

believer, yet she never got a chance to meet Angel like she wanted to. She never even learned that the baby girl was named Susan, that she grew up to be a loving daughter, a talented musician, a budding artist. . . ." Tears filled Amy's eyes. "And that she was a wonderful mother."

The grief that swelled in Amy's heart wasn't only for her mom, who she missed terribly, but for Ellie, too. The poor woman had waited nearly a half century to see her only granddaughter again, yet "Angel" had died before the two could meet.

Ellie had even tucked that request in her Bible, as though she'd been holding on to a promise—Ask and it shall be given unto you. But it hadn't worked in this case.

"What would it have hurt," Amy prayed, "to have let my mother find Ellie a year ago, when she was searching so hard for her roots? If they'd met back then, Ellie would have been more in touch with reality. And my mom would have still been alive." Guilt rose in Amy's chest, clawing its way into her throat, trying to reach for the words and pull them back.

Who was she to take God to task, to suggest that He'd been asleep on the job?

Her already bowed head slumped lower until her chin nearly touched her chest. "I'm sorry, Lord. I really didn't mean to criticize You. I know that I can only see but a moment, and You have all of eternity in mind. So even though it still doesn't make sense to me, I trust You to somehow make things right—in Your own way, in Your own time. Bless Ellie now. Give her Your peace and comfort. And when it's her time to go, welcome her home."

Amy had scarcely uttered an amen when the doorbell rang.

It was too early for Eddie and Maria's return, so she suspected it was Steph bringing Callie home. She swung open the door and realized she'd been right.

"Hi, Mommy!" her daughter said.

"Hey, sweetie. Come on in." Amy scanned the porch and lawn, then asked her friend, "Where's Rachel?"

"At home with Jake."

Before Amy could thank Steph, a swatch of fur brushed across her bare calf and she gasped. Her hand flew to her chest and she jumped aside, only to see that a blur of white and brown had rushed into the room.

"Oh, look," Callie said, "it's Patches."

The cat took a running leap, landing right in Ellie's lap, causing the unsuspecting woman to blink and lurch back in surprise.

Patches meowed and snuggled against her elderly mistress as if hoping for a loving pat, a kind word—recognition of some kind.

Poor thing, Amy thought. Ellie's dementia had taken a toll on the stray, too.

"Patches loves you," Callie said as she drew close to the old woman, showing the same kindness she'd seen Sara model.

While planning to commend her daughter later, Amy returned her gaze to Steph. "Thanks so much for keeping Callie today."

"No problem. The girls had a wonderful time together. They're more like sisters than friends." Steph craned her neck, taking a peek inside the living room. "So this is it?"

"Yeah. What do you think?"

"It's quaint and ripe with possibilities. I'm sure it would be fun to refurbish and decorate a house like this."

Amy thought so, too.

"Is that the woman?" Steph asked, indicating Ellie, who studied the cat in her lap while the child stood next to her.

"Yes, and I'd give anything to be able to have a heart-to-heart with her, but I'm afraid that's impossible. She doesn't have any idea who I am."

"I'm sorry."

"Me, too."

Steph nodded toward her car, which was parked at the curb. "Well, I really need to go. Jake's been working late this past week, and we've hardly had any time together. So he's getting Rachel ready for bed, and then, after she falls asleep, we're going to put on a movie and spend some time alone."

Amy knew firsthand how it felt to have a husband put in extra hours at the office, yet Steph seemed eager to get home and have a quiet evening with Jake.

Had Brandon been the one who'd worked late, Amy would have been primed for an argument when he got home. Then he would have defended his dedication to his job, and they would have had a quiet evening, all right—the kind silenced by anger and resentment.

"Thanks again," Amy told Steph. "I'll make it up to you someday."

"Don't worry about that. I'm glad that I could help out."

As Amy closed the door, she turned back to the living room, where Ellie sat on the recliner with Patches in her lap and a faint smile on her lips.

"You've been gone for days," the elderly woman told the stray. "And I was worried about you."

Patches hunkered down and curled into a ball, purring, no doubt, and clearly happy to be home at last.

"Ellie," Callie said. "I saw your kitty yesterday, and she climbed way up in a tree in Sara's backyard. I was scared and wanted to call the fire department to get her down."

Ellie placed a hand on Callie's cheek and blessed her with a warm smile. "Patches is a very good climber. See? She got down all by herself."

The logical response took Amy aback, and she eased closer, wondering if Ellie was having a lucid moment—and praying that she was. As she neared the sofa, one of the old floorboards squeaked and Ellie glanced up.

She scrunched her brow, and her tired blue eyes narrowed as she studied Amy with a quizzical gaze. "Have we met?"

"Yes. At Maria's house." On a whim, as Amy closed the gap between them, she added, "I'm Angel's daughter."

Ellie blinked, and something in her eyes sparked. She looked at Callie, and her head cocked slightly to the side. "Don't you mean her mother?"

Please, Amy prayed silently. *Don't let this moment fade, Lord. Let me have just one conversation with her. We—Mom and I—have waited so long.*

Amy dropped to her knees beside the recliner and reached for Ellie's frail hand. "My mother—*Angel*—was born on September nineteenth, nineteen sixty-six, at Palomar Hospital. She was adopted by Carlo and Gina Rossi, and they named her Susan."

Ellie's head listed to the other side; she was clearly confused. But what else was new? The poor woman had been having trouble making sense of things for months.

Knowing that the conversation wasn't going anywhere and convinced that she was wasting her time, Amy still couldn't help giving Ellie's hand a gentle squeeze. "Susan was the baby Barbara gave up for adoption, and I'm her daughter."

Ellie looked first at Amy, then at the child, who continued to stand beside the chair and was stroking the cat's fur.

"That's Callie," Amy said, her heart chanting, *Please, please, let her stay with us.* "She's Angel's granddaughter."

Ellie reached for a tendril of Callie's hair, letting it slide through her fingers. Then she turned to Amy, her eyes aglow. "She looks just as I'd always imagined Angel would. I only held her once, but I knew that when she grew up, she would favor Alice, Harold's baby sister. Her hair was so light, her eyes so blue. . . ."

Amy held her tongue for a moment, basking in grateful relief.

Callie, who chose that moment to wander to the coffee table, where she'd left her coloring books and markers yesterday, plopped down on the floor, unaware of the miracle that seemed to be unfolding around her.

Ellie watched the child open the box, and a warm smile softened her craggy face. "I hope Callie has the same sweet temperament as Alice had."

"She does," Amy said, sure of it, even though she had no idea who Alice was. Callie was a good kid—sweet, kindhearted—and Amy had been blessed the day she was born and placed in her arms.

"Harold's mother was never the same after Alice was struck with diphtheria and . . ." Ellie caught her breath and glanced first at Callie, then at Amy and back to the child. "Well . . . I didn't think the poor woman would ever stop grieving."

So Alice had died.

Ellie continued to watch Callie, who'd opened her coloring book to a page with fairies. Then the old woman turned in her seat, facing Amy. "Where's your mother? Is she going to stop by and see me, too?"

Amy had to tell her, yet she hated to break the news, especially when their precious connection was so fragile. But she couldn't lie. "My mother certainly wanted to meet you, but she passed away about six months ago."

Ellie's expression sank. "I'm sorry to hear that."

"But your prayers for her were answered," Amy said in a rush, hoping to keep Ellie engaged. "Angel was adopted by a wonderful couple who adored her, and she had a happy childhood, a good life."

Ellie sat back in her seat, and a wistful smile stretched across her face. "I'm so glad to hear that. I pray for her every day."

"I know you do."

Ellie's lip began to quiver, and her eyes filled with emotion. "I had to do that. It's important for a child to grow up in a loving home."

Before Amy could ponder the comment or respond, Ellie added, "I'd argued with Barbie about keeping the baby. I'd even suggested that she let me raise her, but she refused. But now, looking back, I realize then neither of us could have kept the baby. Under the circumstances, Joseph would have put two and two together. And he would have resented Angel, which wouldn't have been good."

Making the obvious leap, Amy asked, "Do you mean that he would have resented her because she wasn't his child?"

"Yes. But it would have been worse if he'd found out who her father really was."

Amy hated to press Ellie, especially when she was clearly tiptoeing on the fine line between dementia and clarity. But she needed some answers, too.

"Who was Angel's father?" Amy asked.

"I promised Barbara that I'd never tell."

"I'll keep the secret."

Ellie bit down on her bottom lip, as though struggling with the decision to end the silence, then she slowly shook her head. "You need to ask Barbara. I think she owes you that much."

Perhaps. But maybe not.

Silence stretched between them until Amy finally asked the question she'd been pondering since taking on her mother's quest. "How do you think Barbara will react when I introduce myself to her?"

"You haven't met her yet?"

"Yes, but only as a tenant. She doesn't know who I really am. And I haven't told her because, well, she seems a little . . . cold."

"That's to be expected," Ellie said. "She's built up such a wall around her secret that she's shut out all the warmth within and around her." Ellie glanced out the living room window, as if she could see something in the darkness. "But she wasn't always like that."

"What was she like before?" Amy asked. "When she was young?"

"Happy, fun loving, confident. But she was all I had, and I doted on her something fierce. I'm afraid my indulgence made her headstrong, and when she was a teenager, she rebelled. I tried to take a firm hand with her at that point, but it was too late, and she pulled away all the more."

"I'm sorry." Amy didn't know what she'd do if Callie grew up and rebelled, if she turned away from her family.

"I'll never forget one night in particular," Ellie said. "We had a terrible fight."

"What happened?"

"I used to keep journals, and Barbie found one and read it. I'd been complaining, I suppose. Not to anyone in particular, but I didn't have a husband to share those day-to-day worries with. So I put my private thoughts down on paper, and I'm afraid my reflections about Barbara back then weren't very flattering. With maturity and in retrospect, I would have said things differently, but back then, I blamed a lot of my unhappiness on Barbara's stubbornness and flaws. Yet now I realize she inherited a lot of that from me."

"You're headstrong, too?"

"Yes. I'm afraid I'm far from perfect. But it's so much easier to point out the deficiencies in others than to see the same ones in ourselves and have to deal with them."

"Barbara shouldn't have read those entries," Amy said. Yet she couldn't shake the cloying scent of hypocrisy and guilt for having done the same thing herself.

"Maybe not, but nevertheless, she was hurt by my words and furious with me. She ripped at the book until she tore it in pieces, and I . . . Well, I hate to admit this, but I said some terrible things to her that night, things I regret to this day."

"Did you apologize?"

"In a way, but I really ought to bring it up again."

Amy wasn't sure when Ellie would be able to have a heart-to-heart with Barbara. How many more lucid days would there be? How many more miracles like tonight?

"I hope you don't get the wrong idea about Barbara," Ellie added. "She's a good girl at heart. And I love her more than life itself. In fact, I always will—no matter what the future brings."

"Have you told her that?" Amy asked.

"I'm not sure." Ellie furrowed her brow. "I suppose I did." Her gray head dropped, and she gazed at the cat curled up in her lap.

Amy feared that Ellie might be drifting away again, back to the prison of her mind, but when she again looked up, emotion filled her eyes. "I have a few admissions to make, too. I pushed Barbie too hard at times. Yet even as a little girl, when she'd drag her feet when pressed to do something, she'd always do the right thing when I gave her time to think it through."

"Does that mean, given time, that she'll eventually be happy to meet me?"

"I think so. Her biggest fear is that Joseph will be upset when he finds out what she did. And with whom."

"I certainly won't make life difficult for her. I'd just like to meet her, to tell her about my mother. To thank her for giving her up for adoption. I can't imagine my life without Grandma and Grandpa Rossi in it."

"You have no idea how happy I am to hear that." Ellie stroked the cat's back, then gazed at Amy. "Family is very important."

She was right. And that's why Amy had been so unhappy with Brandon's inability to grasp that concept.

"You know," Ellie said, "I was pretty hard on Barbie at first. I found it difficult to believe that she'd do such a thing, especially when poor Joseph was overseas. But I don't think that was the right approach."

"What do you mean?"

"I should have been more supportive of her, more forgiving. I was all she had."

"It seems as though she was all that you had, too."

"Yes, that's true. But I have my faith and the church. I also have dear friends, like Maria and Captain."

Amy didn't dare tell her that Captain had died. Not yet. She didn't want to veer from the conversation they were having.

"I really should have married him when he asked," Ellie said.

"Married who? *Captain?*"

Ellie's gaze grew wistful. "He proposed a few years ago, but I'd been burned badly once before and feared a third marriage. Besides, I thought we were too old for that nonsense."

"He would have been good to you."

"I know." Ellie leaned forward, and while stroking Patches, added, "And then I wouldn't have had to grow old all by myself."

"I'll be here for you," Amy said, surprising herself at what she was promising.

"Thank you, honey. I appreciate that."

They sat like that for a moment, embraced by the silence, by the memories. Then Ellie asked, "How about you, dear? Are you happy? Is your husband good to you?"

"I'm divorced. Well, almost. It's not final yet, but it will be soon."

"I'm sorry. Did your husband treat you badly?"

Not in the sense that Ellie's second husband had treated her, and for a moment, Amy questioned her decision to move out and take Callie with her. But only for a moment. "He didn't have time for us, but I wouldn't say that he was mean."

"And you've made up your mind?" Ellie asked. "There's no chance that the two of you can work something out?"

"I'm afraid not." Yet the words rang hollow, especially since Brandon had been so determined to make things right. "My husband grew up in a dysfunctional home and doesn't have any idea what a real family is supposed to be like."

"Sounds like maybe he needs you to show him."

"I tried, but he was never at home."

A knock sounded at the door, followed by the bell. "That's probably Maria," Amy said, sorry for the interruption.

"I'll get it!" Callie scrambled to her feet and ran for the door.

Amy followed her daughter, who welcomed Maria, Eddie, and the kids inside.

"We came for Ellie," Maria said. "Thanks for watching her."

"The pleasure was all mine. She's having a good evening. I introduced myself, and she knew who I was. We've had the most wonderful conversation."

Maria brightened. "That's great. I can't remember the last time I was able to really communicate with her."

"It's been a real blessing," Amy said. "An answer to a prayer."

But when Amy turned toward Ellie, she was met by a blank stare. The light that had warmed her eyes just moments ago had died.

Chapter 19

Chuck had been fiddling with the TV remote and was just about to pitch it across the hospital room when a young man in an expensive suit walked through the door.

Tall, with dark hair, brown eyes, and a square-cut, no-nonsense jaw, he was impressive, to say the least, the kind of man a fellow took seriously. Yet that wasn't what caused Chuck to sit up straight and take note of him. It was recognition.

It might have been fifteen years since Chuck had last seen his lanky teenage son, but he would have known Brandon anywhere. At least, he liked to think that he would.

Brandon still favored his mother in a lot of ways, which had been both a blessing and a curse after her death.

Try as he might, Chuck had never been able to spot so much as a drop of the Masterson blood in the boy. But then again, that didn't necessarily mean anything. Did it?

Still, Chuck blinked a couple of times to make sure he wasn't seeing the chemo-cocktail version of a pink elephant.

"Hey," Brandon said as he made his way toward the hospital bed, walking with a bit of a limp, as if his shoes were a couple of sizes too small.

Chuck struggled to come up with something clever or welcoming to say. A couple of lame thoughts came to mind, such as, "Look what the cat dragged in," or "How 'bout them Padres." But he knew better than to let something like that roll off his tongue. Jabbering about the first thing that came to mind wasn't going to do him any good.

What did a man say to the son he

hadn't seen since he'd gone off to college and never looked back? *I love you? I've missed you something fierce? I'm sorry for failing you time after time?*

No, that wasn't any way to break the ice after ten lousy years together and another fifteen apart.

"You're a sight for sore eyes," Chuck finally said. And it was true. Brandon had filled out, matured. "You look good. *Real* good."

"So do you."

Chuck didn't buy that, but he suspected Brandon was also at a loss when it came to knowing what to say.

They remained like that—sheepish and awkward—for a couple of beats. Then Chuck forced himself to say, "Thanks for coming, Brandon. I've wanted to talk to you for a long time."

"Yeah, well, I've been busy."

"I'm sure you have. And things didn't end very well between us, so I understand—really." Chuck tried to manage a breezy smile, but he suspected it fell short. "I have an apology to make. Quite a few of them, actually."

"That was a long time ago," Brandon

said, as if time had eased the pain and made apologies unnecessary.

A very human side of Chuck wanted to take the easy way out, but he was a new man these days. A dying one, but new just the same, and it was important for him to come clean, to admit his mistakes, to make amends with the people he'd hurt or disappointed.

"I'm sorry for the crappy childhood you had, at least, after your mom died. I should have made life easier for you. Instead, I made things worse. I'm also sorry for not being the kind of dad you deserved. And for all the drinking I did, all the embarrassment I caused you. I also regret that I didn't enjoy the time we had together in a healthy, wholesome way. If I had it all to do over again, and, of course, I don't, I'd take you to ball games and movies, and we'd go to the park and fly kites. All the things we'll never get a chance to do again."

Brandon seemed to ponder Chuck's speech, although he didn't actually respond. But Chuck couldn't very well expect the kid to roll over and say, "I forgive you, Dad."

No way. A man couldn't make up for ten bad years with a couple of heartfelt sentences.

"So," Chuck said, steering away from all the touchy stuff, "tell me about you, about your life. You've obviously got a job. A good one, from the looks of that suit."

Brandon nodded. "I'm an attorney for a law firm in San Diego."

Chuck wanted to tell him that he was proud of him, but somehow, it seemed as though he'd lost that right, especially when he hadn't had a hand in any of it. He stole a glance at the nice-looking, successful man the boy had become, saw him looking at his feet as if he felt guilty about being here. Or maybe he was just uneasy.

"Is there something you want to tell me?" Chuck asked, thinking that a casual visit was too good to be true. "It seems like you got something weighing awfully heavy on your mind. And if you'd like to give me a piece of it, I wouldn't blame you."

"I . . . uh . . ." Brandon inhaled deeply, then blew it out. He seemed to be struggling with something, which didn't make sense. But then, he'd been pretty pensive and introspective when he was growing up, just like Marianne had been.

In fact, they'd been so much alike that each time Chuck had looked at Brandon, he'd been reminded of Marianne, of her deathbed confession, the air she'd wanted to clear.

"I guess this might sound weird," Brandon finally said, "but I was told that I'm having marital trouble because I've never dealt with my relationship with you."

"That's a surprise."

"Why?"

"Here I was prepared to take the blame for a lot of things, but I can't quite see how our relationship—what we have of one—has affected your marriage. Who told you that?"

"Some homeless guy named Jesse."

Chuck leaned back, and his head sank into his pillow. "Oh, yeah? Then I guess we'd better work on patching things up. I've come to believe that Jesse's able to leap tall buildings with a single bound."

"Personally, I think he's been living on the street too long." Brandon chuffed. "But my marriage is falling apart, and I'm getting desperate to save it."

Chuck supposed he had to be if he'd been willing to seek out the father who'd been one major disappointment for most of his growing-up years. But then again, maybe Jesse had given him a little nudge. Either way, Chuck was glad he'd come.

"Family's important," he said. "I'm afraid that I failed to grasp that in time to do you any good. I'm not trying to excuse my behavior by any means, but I sank so deep into depression, self-pity, and the bottle that I failed to value what I had—and that was a son any man would have been proud to have."

Brandon seemed to think on that some, but Chuck was uneasy with the silence, with the memories of a time in his life he'd just as soon forget. So he asked, "Do you and your wife have kids?"

"Yes. I've got a five-year-old daughter. Her name is Callie."

"Does she look like you?" Chuck asked, realizing that he might be projecting his own baggage onto Brandon. Or maybe he was just trying to see if the Masterson genes had come into play with the next generation.

"I think she looks like her mother." He reached into his back pocket and pulled out a wallet. Then he withdrew a picture and handed it over. "My wife gave me that last spring and insisted that all dads carry pictures of their kids."

Not all of them, Chuck supposed. But the good ones did.

Chuck took the photo and studied it carefully. A smile stretched across his face as he looked at the little girl. She was a cutie, that was for sure. And he could see Brandon in her, although she was blond and fair.

"She's beautiful," Chuck said, reluctant to return the photo to Brandon.

"Yes, she is, especially in person."

As Chuck handed him the picture anyway, Brandon shook his head. "No, you can keep it. I can get another one. Maybe I'll take her to a photographer the next time I have her."

"Do you see her often?"

He shrugged. "Actually, it seems as though I see her more now that her mom and I have split." He chuffed and frowned. "Sad, isn't it?"

"Yeah, I guess so. But at least you have

time on your hands, time to correct things. I let it get away from me."

Brandon again glanced down at the floor, and Chuck could see the wheels turning. He just wished he could do something, say something to help, to make things right again.

When Brandon finally glanced up, he said, "Maybe that's what I needed to hear."

What? That Chuck had made a lot of mistakes? That he was sorry, and that he couldn't correct a single one of them?

"Amy wanted more of my time," Brandon said. "She complained about all the hours I worked. That I had no idea what a real family was like."

"But you do," Chuck said. "Just try and think back to the time before your mom died. Things were normal then."

"All I can remember is how sick she was those last few weeks."

That was true. Marianne had really suffered once the diagnosis was made. Chuck supposed he had the same thing to look forward to.

"Cancer is nasty stuff," he said.

They pondered the awful truth until

Brandon said, "I heard you've got it, too."

Chuck nodded. "Yep. That's what they tell me."

"I'm sorry to hear that."

"Thanks, but I'm okay with it. I mean, I'd rather not have it, but I figure my days are numbered anyway. Besides, I've got a lot of faith now, and I'm certain that my future's secure."

Brandon arched a brow, thick and dark, like Marianne's father's had been before he turned gray. "I'm not sure I know what you mean, Dad."

"I'm sorry. I didn't mean to get all lofty on you. It's just that I've given my life to God, and I'm a lot happier now than ever before."

Too bad telling Brandon about how good things were now only served to remind Chuck of how bad they'd once been. And now all his old failures, which he'd tried to stack in a far corner of his mind, tumbled front and center.

He suspected that the same had happened to Brandon, although if they had, he didn't comment. Instead he took a seat beside the bed—a good sign, Chuck decided.

"I'm glad things are going well for you," Brandon finally said, "other than the cancer. That's tough. What's the prognosis? What treatment options have they given you?"

"They say I need a bone marrow transplant, but my health isn't all that good anyway. I guess you could say that I'm paying the consequences of my alcoholism."

"Have them test me," Brandon said. "I'm willing to help out."

"Thank you. I appreciate that." Chuck pondered coming out and telling him what he feared most. Would it help their relationship? Would it make it worse?

Yet he realized that if he was going to have any kind of meaningful relationship with his son, even for whatever time he had left, it ought to be based upon honesty.

"There's a chance you might not be a match," he said.

"I know that. It's never a sure thing."

"Yeah, but there's a possibility you won't even come close."

Brandon furrowed his brow. "What do you mean by that?"

"I started dating your mom before her divorce was final. And right before she died, she told me that her ex-husband might have been your father. Apparently, she was still seeing him sometimes. And while she'd always hoped that I was your father, she wasn't sure."

Brandon drew back his chest, as though slammed by the news. "Wow."

That's what Chuck had thought, although coming from Marianne at a time like that had packed a more brutal punch—like a wallop to the gut.

"That revelation might have made your mom feel better before she died, but it really messed me up. I loved you. Still do, of course. But I let her words drive me crazy. I never told you before, but I used to have a serious drinking problem when your mom and I met. With her love and support, I kept it under control. But after she died . . . Well, I let it consume me—not just the guilt from having caused that accident, by your mother's loss and her suffering. That had a monstrous effect, too. But

I was crushed to think that you might not be my son."

Brandon bent forward, resting his hands on his knees. "I had no idea."

"Yeah, well, I didn't deal very well with the news myself. But for whatever it's worth, even though I felt betrayed, I considered you my son. Still do, that is, if you don't mind me claiming you."

Brandon seemed to think about that for a long time before he looked up and their gazes locked.

"I'm still willing to donate bone marrow," he said, "if we're a match. So I'll tell your doctor that I'd like to be tested."

Chuck didn't know what to say, what to do. He'd convinced himself that an offer like that would never come, and the fact that it did shot him full of holes. So he offered the kid an easy way out. "Thanks. I appreciate that. But the procedure can be painful. It'll probably prevent you from working for a while, and it sounds as if your job is important."

"It isn't as important as family," Brandon said. "I think that's what I was supposed to come away with from all of this. I just hope I didn't come to that conclusion too late."

So did Chuck—for Brandon's sake, more than his own.

When Barbara first arrived at Maria's house, there hadn't been any lights on inside, which she'd thought was a little odd. But before she could ponder the situation, Maria's minivan pulled into the driveway with a man Barbara didn't recognize behind the wheel.

While they all piled out of the car, Barbara remained in her Jag, thinking that she'd allow them time to go into the house and get settled before she knocked at the door. Yet when she realized her mother wasn't with them, that the house was dark, a shudder of apprehension shivered through her. She reached for the door handle, ready to rush to the minivan and quiz Maria, when she saw that they were all heading toward Amy's house.

Was that where her mother was?

She watched until minutes later, when they returned with her mom, who walked between the man and Maria, her gray head bent, her shoulders slumped, her steps shuffled.

An agonizing ache spread through Barbara's chest as she realized her mother was failing more and more each day, and nothing, not even Joey's condition, took the edge off that heartbreaking fact.

Barbara wasn't entirely sure why she'd come here tonight, especially since a meaningful conversation with her mother was impossible. But at least she could bare her heart and apologize.

Her mom, of course, wouldn't be able to respond to any of it, but going through the motions might ease some of Barbra's guilt, some of her pain.

Why hadn't she done it sooner?

Pride and stubbornness, she supposed. But where had that gotten her?

Maria's front door opened and the lights went on. Everyone went inside, yet Barbara remained in her car.

It was getting late. Maybe she should go home and come back tomorrow. At that time, she could also pick up her mother's belongings and take them to storage. Ron Paige had left a voice-mail message earlier, telling her that Amy had everything boxed and ready to go.

She hadn't returned his call, but she could tell Amy she would send someone for the stuff tomorrow. So she climbed from the car and headed toward the house in which she'd grown up.

It was weird, yet she still felt as though she was coming home, even if someone else lived here now. But she rang the bell.

Amy, the tenant, answered, holding her purse. Her daughter stood beside her, a pink backpack dangling from her hand. Obviously, they were preparing to leave.

"I'm sorry," Barbara said. "I should have called first."

"That's okay. Is there something I can do for you?"

"Not really. I was in the neighborhood and thought we could set up a convenient time for me to send someone to pick up my mother's things."

"Oh. Yes, of course." Amy pointed to the boxes that had been stacked in the living room. "You'll probably need a truck, unless you want to make several trips."

"I'll keep that in mind."

Their gazes locked for a moment, and while Barbara wanted to break eye contact, she couldn't bring herself to be the first to look away. Something about the young woman caught her interest, although she couldn't put her finger on just what it was.

Maybe it was seeing her at this house, knowing she'd touched her mother's things. Or maybe it was just some crazy need to talk to a real human being tonight, when the people who'd always been her family were unavailable and might never be there for her again.

"Thank you for helping me out," Barbara finally said. "My son's been ill, and . . ." Her voice caught, and she feared she would start crying in front of a virtual stranger.

Amy placed a sympathetic hand on Barbara's upper arm, an intimate gesture that had caught her off guard, yet was comforting. "I'm sorry your son has been so ill. Isn't he doing any better?"

"No, and I've . . ." She blew out a wobbly sigh. For some reason, she felt like venting, like sharing private thoughts with her tenant, and she wouldn't do that; she *couldn't* do that. "Actually, what I'd really like to do is sit in my mother's kitchen with her and have a cup of tea, like we used to when Joey was little. But those days are gone. I'm afraid that I'll never be able to do that again, and it's bothering me more than I care to admit." She straightened, swiped at tears in her eyes, and forced a smile. "I'm sorry for being so weepy. I'll be okay. *Really.*"

"Please come in and have a cup of tea with me."

"Oh, no." Barbara shook her head and took a step back, suddenly wishing she hadn't come to Fairbrook at all that evening, that she'd fought the compulsion to see her mother and had stayed home where she belonged. "I didn't mean to imply . . ."

"Please come inside, Barbara. There's something I need to talk to you about, something you need to know." Amy stepped aside to allow her into the house, and she found herself complying.

"Callie," Amy said to her daughter, a cute little girl about the age of five, "turn on the television. We're not leaving yet."

The child clucked her tongue, but she

removed her backpack and made her way to the TV.

As Amy led Barbara to the kitchen, she said, "I had an interesting conversation with your mother tonight."

Barbara tried to tamp down a rising tide of jealousy. "You had an actual two-way conversation with her?"

"Yes, and your name came up."

She stiffened as she pondered how that happened, why they'd talked about her. "I don't understand."

Amy pulled out a chair at the kitchen table, indicating that Barbara should take it.

"Your mother told me that she loved you more than life itself," Amy said.

Barbara settled into the chair she'd always considered hers. She didn't doubt that her mother had adored her at one time, but how could she say that when things had been strained between them for years—decades, actually? The affair, the pregnancy, the adoption had always stood between them, even if the actual subject had rarely come up.

Amy went to the stove, removed the

teakettle, carried it to the sink, and filled it with water. "She said that she'd always love you, no matter what the future might bring."

"What do you think she meant by that?"

"That you're her only child, and that nothing can change the way she feels about you. Even though she can't say the words and respond to you in an appropriate manner, the emotion is still there, as strong as ever."

Until that moment, Barbara had no idea how badly she'd needed her mother's love, faith, and forgiveness. And Amy's conversation with her earlier might be the closest thing she would ever get to having it again.

"I suppose I'll have to be content with that."

Amy placed the teakettle on the stove and turned on the burner. "She also wanted to apologize to you about a few things."

Barbara couldn't understand why her mother would open up to a stranger like that, yet she hung on the words, grappled with the possibility that miracles happened—even to people like her.

"What did my mom want to apologize for?" she asked.

"For pushing you too hard at times, for not trusting you to do the right thing without her prodding."

Her mom *had* pushed, and Barbara had reacted by digging in her heels—a bad combination, it seemed, and one with lifelong repercussions.

"For what it's worth," Amy added, "she admitted to having a stubborn streak herself."

Amy removed two of Ellie's china cups and saucers from the cupboard, but instead of carrying the dishes to the table, she faced Barbara and leaned her hip against the kitchen counter. "I think God had a hand in it, and I'll tell you why. I'm not just a single mom who drove down Sugar Plum Lane and spotted a house for rent. I came here specifically to find you."

Barbara's heart rate spiked, then sputtered. Had Amy been sent by Susan Rossi? Or did she work for the long-haired PI who'd encountered her in the hospital parking lot?

"Why were you looking for me?" she

asked, trying to downplay her suspicion with normal curiosity.

"Because my mother was adopted as a baby, and I was looking for her birth family."

Had she not been seated, Barbara might have dropped to the floor. "You're Susan's daughter?"

Now Amy appeared stunned. "You know her name?"

"Yes. She found me about a year ago."

The confusion tightened across Amy's face. "But she never told me. And I'm sure she would have. Finding you was so important to her."

"It's not anymore?"

"My mother passed away six months ago."

"I'm sorry." Tears filled Barbara's eyes as a myriad of emotion—grief and shame, to name two—swept over her. "I had an opportunity to talk to her, but I refused."

"I'm not sure that she was actually looking to have a relationship with you. She told me that she couldn't explain it, but that she had an overwhelming compulsion to find you. Looking back, I think that's because of Ellie's prayers."

"What do you mean?"

"You may not know this, but your mom prayed for that baby—my mother—every day. She asked God to bless and watch over her and the family who adopted her. In her heart of hearts, Ellie truly believed God would someday bring them together again. And she was able to have that brief connection through me."

"And you think that's why my mother was able to carry on a conversation with you tonight?"

"That's exactly what I think."

The teakettle began to whistle, and Amy filled their cups with hot water. Then she carried them back to the table.

Barbara took a long, hard look at the young woman who was her granddaughter, realizing that shutting her out of her life was no longer an option.

She had a great-granddaughter, too. A darling little girl with platinum blond hair and big blue eyes.

How could she walk away from them now that they'd actually met?

Barbara had no idea what Joseph planned to do. He'd walked out of the house and had yet to call or contact her.

He might decide to hang in there, at least until Joey took a turn for the better. Or he might pack up and file for divorce while things were still up in the air.

It was hard to say.

At one time, she'd thought she would be crushed if Joseph left her, yet right now, a sense of peace had settled over her. Oddly enough, she felt as though she was right where she needed to be—seated at her mother's kitchen table, having a long-overdue conversation with a woman who no longer seemed to be a stranger.

"I suppose I ought to tell you what happened," she finally said, "and why I gave up your mother."

"If you'd like to."

For the first time, she did.

"I married Joseph Davila in nineteen sixty, and we bought a little house near the beach in Coronado. Two years later, we had Joey. Life was good, and my relationship with my mother was better than it had been in a long time, probably because I'd finally grown up and had a family of my own." Barbara opened a tea bag and dipped it into her cup, even though she wasn't particularly thirsty. The casual movement seemed to help her sort through her thoughts, her memories. "Joseph was a Navy pilot, and when he was sent to Vietnam, I was incredibly sad and lonely.

"Before I got married, I had a crush on Joseph's best friend, another Navy pilot. Darrel was handsome, an athlete, and a charmer. But he wasn't interested in me." Barbara took a sip of her tea, realizing she hadn't sweetened it. But it really didn't matter. The warm brew quenched her dry throat and made it easier to speak of the time in her life she'd so badly wanted to forget.

"One night," she continued, "a couple of friends invited me to a beach party. My mom babysat, thinking it would be good for me to get out. Darrel was there. And we had a couple of drinks and shared a few laughs. One thing led to another, and I did something I shouldn't have done." Barbara glanced at the young woman who sat across the scarred oak table from her, wondering if she was passing judgment and not blaming her if she did. "The affair didn't last long, but my mother soon put two and two together. Her disgust and her lectures only made me more defensive, more secretive. When I finally ended things with Darrel, I assumed that no one but my mother would be the wiser. But then I found out I was pregnant."

Amy, who didn't appear to be doing anything other than listening, filled in the blanks. "So you decided to give the baby up for adoption."

"I had no other choice, not if I wanted to save my marriage. And I did."

"For what it's worth," Amy said, "your mom eventually came to the conclusion that you'd done the right thing by giving up the baby. She might not have told you, but she wanted to."

"That's good to know. Back then, and for years afterward, she'd made me feel as though I'd not only given away my flesh and blood, but that I'd sacrificed a child that was a part of my dad."

"Did she tell you that?"

"She didn't have to. I could see it in her eyes, and in spite of trying my best to shut her out of my life, not a day went by that I didn't feel guilty about it all—the affair, the adoption, the rift between us. And each time it did, I tried my best to make up for everything, at least as far as my husband and son were concerned."

"Mommy," Callie called from the doorway, breaking the tension, shifting their focus. "Can I please have a cookie and some milk?"

"Sure, honey."

As Amy got up from the table, Barbara studied the little girl, her blond hair pulled back in pigtails, her eyes the color of a summer sky.

Callie was an adorable child, and from what she'd seen so far, Amy was a nice young woman. They already had loving grandparents in Mr. and Mrs. Rossi, but maybe Barbara could be a part of their lives, too. She hoped so, although she probably didn't deserve a relationship with them and wouldn't push for one.

The muffled ring of her cell sounded from inside her purse. At any other time, Barbara might have ignored it, but she didn't dare do that now.

"Excuse me, Amy. I need to check to see who's calling." She dug through her handbag, found the phone, and looked at the lighted display. "It's Cynthia, my daughter-in-law. I have to take this." She pushed Send and lifted it to her ear. "Hi, Cyn. What's going on?"

"I have some good news, Mom. They're going to move Joey out of ICU."

Relief, like the rays of the sun peering out from behind dark clouds, poured over Barbara, warming her from the inside out. "That's wonderful, honey. Have they scheduled the surgery?"

"No, not yet. But it finally looks more promising. The lab results show his blood sugar level is stabilizing. It seems that the new treatment is working."

"Thank God. That's the best news I've had in ages. Is there anything I can do? Anything you need?"

"No. I'm doing okay. But I have to go, Mom. I'll talk to you later."

When the call ended, Barbara looked at Amy and smiled. "I can't wait for you to meet my son and his wife. I'm sure the news will come as a complete surprise to them, but they've got big hearts. And they love children." Barbara caught herself and reeled in her enthusiasm. "I'm sorry. I don't mean to push myself on you. It's just that, if you don't mind, I'd like to get to know you better."

"I'd like that," Amy said, reaching out and placing her hand over the top of Barbara's. "I'd like it a lot."

Barbara's heart swelled to the point of breaking, and tears of joy welled in her eyes. She had no idea what tomorrow would bring, but for the first time in years, the future looked bright and promising.

Chapter 20

Barbara stayed with Amy until late that evening, talking, sharing, and getting to know her better. It was nearly ten when she decided to leave, and as Amy began to walk her to the door, they stopped near the sofa, where Callie had fallen asleep with Patches curled up beside her.

"Look at her," Barbara said. "She's precious, Amy."

"Thank you. I've always felt blessed, but I hadn't realized just how much or why that might be." Amy made a quick scan of the room in which Ellie had often sat and read her Bible, where she'd prayed for all of them time and again.

She supposed, in a way, she really should thank Ellie for that. God had certainly answered her prayers.

"You know," Barbara said, as she reached the front door. "I'm going to hire round-the-clock care and bring my mother home to live with me. I'd worried about how Joseph would handle the inconvenience, but I don't care anymore. He left after I confessed to the affair, and to tell you the truth, I'm not eager to have him come back. We never fought, but things were always tense. My life might be more peaceful without him there."

Barbara had mentioned that her marriage was strained, yet when she smiled at Amy, it was clear that she was happy with her decision, maybe even freed by it.

For the first time since Amy had met her grandmother, she began to see traces of her mom in the woman: a light in Barbara's eyes, the shape of her smile. Funny how she'd missed it at first.

"If you're free, will you and Callie have lunch with me on Sunday?" Barbara asked.

"Yes, I'd like that. Thanks."

After writing down her address, Barbara waited as Amy went to the sofa and carefully lifted the sleeping child into her arms.

Yet in spite of Amy's best efforts, Callie awoke and scrunched her eyes. "Where are we going, Mommy?"

"Home, baby."

"But what about Patches? Can she go with us?"

Amy looked at the cat, which had jumped to the floor and now peered up at her with soft brown eyes.

If it hadn't been a stray with street smarts, she might have considered taking it home with them, but what would they do with a cat?

"Patches lives outdoors, honey."

"But only because Ellie can't take care of her anymore. She needs a family, Mommy."

"But we already have a dog."

"Cookie won't care. He likes cats. They just don't like him very much. But I'll tell him that Patches is nice."

Amy needed both a dog and a cat like

she needed a hole in the head, but how could she tell her daughter no?

"Please," Callie pleaded again.

Amy relented, but not just because of her daughter's pleas. The poor stray did need a loving home. And she suspected that Ellie would have been pleased to know that it had found one with Callie.

"Okay, but I hope I'm not sorry for this later."

"Are you taking the cat home now?" Barbara asked.

"Maybe it would be best if she stayed in familiar surroundings for tonight. I'll pick up some supplies at the pet store tomorrow morning, then come back for her."

After making a bed for the cat in the bathroom and providing her with food and water, Amy locked the house, said good-bye to Barbara, and secured Callie in the backseat. Then she drove to Del Mar.

The next morning, she sat in the kitchen nook at the townhome, having her first cup of coffee and waiting for Callie to wake up so they could return for Patches. She'd let Cookie out in the small backyard to go potty and hoped Patches wasn't making a mess of that bathroom. Maybe she ought to wake Callie up and tell her it was time to go.

She'd just gotten to her feet when a car drove up and parked out front. Curious, she peered out the window and saw that Brandon had stopped by.

Her heart slipped into overdrive, and she lifted her hand, fingered her wet, stringy hair, which she'd washed earlier, and glanced at the worn robe she wore. If she'd known he was coming, she would have gotten dressed, would have dried her hair.

A little more uneasy with her appearance than she should have been, she met him at the door, opening it before he had a chance to knock.

"Hey," he said with a sheepish smile.

It wasn't often that she saw him dressed so casually—what was with the khaki cargo shorts and a surf T-shirt on a weekday morning? Yet he looked good and more relaxed than he had in ages.

"Aren't you working today?" she asked.

"No. I called one of the senior partners at home last night and told him I was taking some time off, starting immediately."

That was certainly out of character, and she wondered what had provoked him to do something like that.

"Would you like a cup of coffee?" she asked. "It's fresh."

"Sounds good."

She led him to the kitchen, and moments later, they were seated across the table from each other, drinking her favorite Starbucks blend out of white mugs. For some reason, it felt good. Right.

"So why are you taking time off?" she asked.

"For a lot of reasons. First of all, you said that I had my priorities confused, and I decided you were right. Secondly, I talked to my dad last night. His health isn't good, and I'd like to spend some time with him."

"Your dad?" Amy, who'd lifted her mug to her mouth, held it in mid-motion. Brandon hadn't talked much about his father, other than to say he was a loser, that they hadn't been close. "How'd you find him?"

"It's a long story, but I'm glad that I went to see him. He's not the same person he used to be." Brandon took a sip of coffee. "I'm not sure how much time he has left, and I'd like to take Callie to visit him."

"Is that why you're here?"

"Primarily."

She studied the man she no longer seemed to know, noting the changes in his demeanor, his appearance.

"What's the matter?" he asked, apparently picking up on her curiosity.

"Nothing. It's just a little surprising. That's all."

"I've had a lot of time to think the past couple of days, Amy. I've done some soul searching, and like my dad, I'm making some changes in my life, too."

Had he decided to start dating?

Her stomach stirred, and she set her coffee aside. The idea that Brandon might be seeing someone didn't sit very well with her.

"If you're dead set on this divorce," he said, "then I'll let you go, even though I don't want to. But either way, things are going to be a lot different from here on out."

Dead set? It made her sound so headstrong, so stubborn . . . so much like Barbara and Ellie.

"What kind of changes are you making?" she asked.

"If you don't have any objections, I'm going to put the house in La Jolla on the market."

He *loved* that house. It represented all he'd achieved in life. "I don't mind, but . . . ?"

"I don't need it, Amy. If you don't take me back, along with my promise to put our family first—and it appears that you're not going to do that—then I don't want to live in that big house alone. I'll buy something closer to you and Callie. I plan to be a major part of her life and will do whatever it takes to be there for her."

"Brandon, I don't know what to say."

"I guess I'm not asking you to say anything. I love you. And I love Callie. Nothing will change that. *Ever.*"

Her heart, once hardened toward him and their marriage, was thawing fast, and she wanted to believe him. Could she trust him to put their family first?

She searched his gaze, saw the love that burned from within, felt the spark she hadn't felt in a long, long time.

The man she'd fallen in love with was seated across from her, baring his heart and soul. And in that instant, she knew that she couldn't just throw it all away. Not after all she'd learned from Ellie.

"I love you, too, Brandon. And I haven't been a perfect wife. For one thing, I should have been more supportive and understanding. So if we're going to make changes, it'll be in Callie's best interests if we make them together, as a family."

He reached for her hand, and as their gazes locked, she realized that Ellie had been right, that children, either born from the womb or chosen by the heart's design, deserved to grow up in happy homes with parents who loved them.

And in their case, with God's help and a little counseling, she and Brandon would create the home and family they all deserved.

Two weeks after Captain was laid to rest, a celebration of life was held at Parkside Community Church, just as the elderly man had requested—without fanfare or tears.

The church had been packed since,

over the years, Captain had accrued many friends, including Chuck Masterson, who came with Brandon and Amy and Callie.

When the tribute was over, everyone crossed the street to Mulberry Park, where they released a colorful assortment of helium balloons—reds, yellows, greens, and blues.

The string of one of the yellow balloons had gotten stuck in the branches of the big mulberry tree that grew in the middle of the park. When Callie noticed it, she'd asked her daddy to get it down for her, but he'd said, "I'm sorry, Cal. It's too high for me to reach."

"But, Daddy," Callie said. "It won't go to Heaven with the other ones."

Brandon appeared stumped, and at that point, Chuck stepped in to distract the child. "Hey, Callie. Why don't you take me to the playground and show me around? It's been a long time since I've had a chance to play."

A grin splashed on the little girl's face, the lone balloon soon forgotten. "Okay, Grandpa. Do you want to play on the swings with me?"

"That sounds like fun." Chuck took Callie by the hand, then winked at Amy. "We'll be back when it's time to eat."

Earlier in the week, Maria had suggested the two families pack a picnic lunch so the kids could play after the memorial, and Amy had agreed.

What better way to spend a Sunday afternoon than at the park with family and friends?

Now, as she and Brandon held hands while seated on a bench overlooking the playground, Amy counted her many blessings, including Chuck, who was grinning ear to ear as he pushed his granddaughter in the swing.

He'd been released from the hospital early last week, and even though blood tests confirmed that he and Brandon were related, they hadn't been a match for a bone marrow transplant.

Brandon had been disappointed, but Chuck had brushed it off with a smile. "Being accepted as a part of your family is more than I'd hoped for. So I'm feeling pretty confident that they'll find a donor through the bone marrow registry. And if they don't? I'm convinced that things will work out the way they're supposed to."

So they'd all decided to take one day at a time—together.

"Hey, Grandpa Chuck!" Callie called as she swung high, her pigtails flying behind her. "Want to watch me go on the slide now?"

"You bet, sweetheart." Chuck slowed her to a stop, then waited for her to hop off the swing and dash across the sand to the slide.

"Your dad's really good with her," Amy said.

"Yes, he is. He meant what he said about wanting to enjoy every moment he has with his family."

Amy gave his hand a squeeze. "Who would have guessed just a month ago that we'd all be here right now?"

Brandon tossed her a grin. "Not me, that's for sure. But I'm glad we are."

True to his word, Brandon had placed the La Jolla house on the market and then moved back into the townhome with her and Callie. It was small, but so much cozier, even if Patches and Cookie didn't always appreciate each other's differences.

And speaking of differences, Amy couldn't believe the changes in her husband, in their marriage, and, more importantly, in herself.

Brandon had gone back to the office this week, and so far so good. He'd called her on Thursday, saying he'd be late. But instead of chuffing or clucking her tongue, Amy had told him she loved him and that she'd keep his dinner warm.

What a difference a new attitude made. When he'd gotten home, he'd treated her to a quiet, romantic evening.

A slow smile stretched across her lips. If they had many more nights like that, Callie just might get a baby brother or sister.

They'd need a bigger house, though. And just the right place came to mind: a certain old Victorian on Sugar Plum Lane. She and Brandon had discussed making an offer, and something told her that nothing would please Ellie more.

As Amy and Brandon continued to bask in the sunshine, in the happy voices of children at play, Eddie approached their bench. It was heartwarming to see how he'd taken to Maria, as well as her kids.

"Hey, Brandon," he called out. "Are you up for a little catch? Danny and I have an extra mitt."

"Sure." Brandon got to his feet and brushed a kiss on Amy's brow. "Call us when you ladies are ready to eat."

"It won't be long." Amy glanced toward the restrooms, where Maria had taken Sara and Wally to clean up just a few minutes ago.

No sign of them yet.

She returned her focus to the playground, spotting Callie seated at the top of the slide.

"Watch this," the little girl told her grandpa.

The elderly man beamed. "I'm right here, sweetie."

"Amy?" a woman called out.

When she turned and saw Barbara striding toward her, she smiled and waved. They'd missed seeing her at Captain's memorial, which she'd planned to attend. But she might have decided to stick around the house, since Joey had come home from the hospital last week.

Somehow, without a medical explanation,

his blood sugar levels had righted themselves, and the doctors had been able to schedule the bypass surgery he'd needed.

As Barbara drew closer, Amy noticed her red-rimmed eyes and feared the worst. So she stood and closed the gap between them.

Before Amy could ask what was wrong, Barbara craned her neck to the right, then lifted her hand to block the sun from her eyes. "What's that PI doing here?"

"What PI?" Amy glanced in the same direction, only to have the bright sunshine blind her to anything but a glare.

Barbara dropped her hand from her eyes and slowly turned back to Amy. "Didn't you have a long-haired, bushy-faced private investigator helping you find me? An average-size, middle-age man with blue eyes?"

"No. The investigator my mom had hired a year or two ago was young, Asian, and clean-shaven."

"That's odd." Barbara turned to the right again, then shook her head. "I could have sworn I saw him, but he's . . . not there now."

Amy scanned the area where Barbara had been looking, but didn't see anyone.

"He did that the first time I talked to him in the hospital parking lot," Barbara said. "He just showed up and then seemed to disappear. It was the strangest thing. He knew a lot about me, about my mom. And when he looked at me with those stunning blue eyes . . ."

"Did he appear to be homeless?" Amy asked.

"Yes, why?"

"Because Brandon mentioned meeting someone like that. His name was Jesse, and he . . . Well, Brandon seemed to think that he might have been an angel."

"Do you believe that?" Barbara asked.

"After everything that's happened, I don't know what to believe. But Jesse was instrumental in getting Brandon to reconcile with his father."

"He might have been the same man I spoke to." Barbara took a deep breath, clearly baffled by it all, then blew out a sigh. "I'm sorry for going off on a tangent. I came by to share some bad news. My mom has congestive heart failure, and the doctor called in a hospice. It could be days or, if we're lucky, a few more months. I thought that you might want to come by the house and see her when you have a chance."

"Yes, of course." The thought of losing Ellie was unsettling, although Amy knew the elderly woman hadn't wanted to live the way she was.

"Joey and Cynthia are with her now," Barbara said, "and they're staying for dinner. I thought you, Brandon, and Callie might want to join us. That way, you can have some time to talk with her before she becomes too ill. Or maybe tell her good-bye in your own way."

"I'd like that," Amy said.

"Mommy!" Callie cried, pointing to the mulberry tree. "Look! The balloon got away all by itself!"

Amy turned to the center of the park and spotted a single yellow balloon soaring off on its own.

"The doctor said there's always a chance Mother could pull out of it," Barbara added almost wistfully.

But she won't.

The words came to Amy as clearly as if

someone had commented while standing beside her.

Her time has come.

Amy watched the balloon soar behind a cloud and out of view. She wondered if somehow it was a sign that Ellie had just slipped away. It was certainly possible. Her journey was done, and all of her prayers had been answered. Maybe not as quickly nor in the way she'd hoped, but each of them had come to pass in God's perfect timing.

"I'm so glad that I took her home with me," Barbara said. "But saying good-bye and letting go is going to be difficult."

Under the circumstances, Amy thought, instead of good-bye, she planned to tell Ellie that she'd see her again.

She had no doubt of that.

All in God's time.

A READING GROUP GUIDE

THE HOUSE ON SUGAR PLUM LANE

Judy Duarte

ABOUT THIS GUIDE

The suggested questions are included to enhance your group's reading of Judy Duarte's *The House on Sugar Plum Lane*!

DISCUSSION QUESTIONS

1. Brandon was running from his past, and Amy was seeking hers. Is there any truth to the adage that one needs to make peace with the past before embracing the future? Why or why not?

2. Barbara kept a secret from her husband. Is it kinder to keep things to oneself that could cause heartbreak to a friend or loved one? Or is honesty always the best policy? Do you think this should apply to life in general? Do you feel differently when it comes to marriage?

3. Maria's ex-husband was incarcerated, and Eddie had a criminal past. Do you think everyone deserves a second chance? Do you feel differently toward Maria's ex than Eddie? Why or why not?

4. Ellie feared she would get dementia and prayed that she would be spared. Do you know someone who has faced or is facing dementia or Alzheimer's? Has either disease affected someone in your family? How do you think you would have handled Ellie's condition?

5. Amy saw Ellie's moment of clarity and lucidity as a miracle. Do you believe in miracles? Why or why not? Have you had any miracles in your own life?

6. Chuck faced his mortality with courage and acceptance. What do you think he learned from his lifetime that may have helped him at the end of his life? What part did faith play in his ability to accept his death?

7. What is the major theme in this book? Is it relevant in your life?

8. Barbara spent more than forty years trying to make up for wronging her

husband. Do you think a person can make up for past wrongs by living a better life in the present?

9. Do you consider Brandon's workaholic lifestyle a form of marital infidelity? Or was it a part of his coping mechanism to live a different life than his father's? Did Amy react to his perceived neglect in a way that you would agree with?

10. Maria's incarcerated husband wanted to maintain a relationship with his son, which was evident by the letters he wrote to him. Was Maria right or wrong to hide the letters from Danny? Do you agree with Captain's advice to Maria—that she should talk with Danny and ask how he felt about having a relationship with his father?

11. Was Ellie to blame for any of the rift between her and Barbara? If so, in what way?

